The Joyful Mysteries

Pam Jones

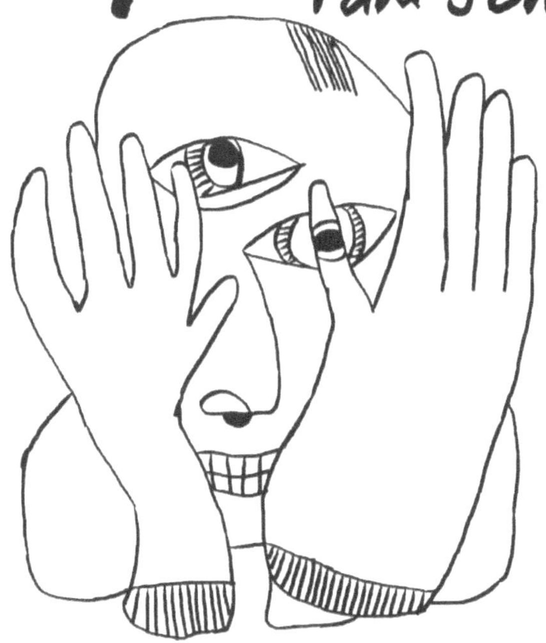

ATLATL

Atlatl Press
POB 521
Dayton, Ohio 45401
atlatlpress.com
info@atlatlpress.com

The Joyful Mysteries

To Andrew Hopkins

In an obscure night
Fevered with love's anxiety
(O hapless, happy plight)
I went, none seeing me
Forth from my house, where all things quiet be

> —St. John of the Cross,
> "The Dark Night of the Soul"

AJ, LC, AND ET left the hospital on the same day, at the same hour. AJ and ET, discharged, LC walking along to the gate and then away with them forever. They had all given their supervising doctors false addresses and phone numbers, knowing the hospital staff would never follow up. On their departure, they were given two changes of clothes, a kit bag each for their toiletries, lists of local shelters and food pantries that would provide meals. AJ had his copy of the King James Bible. LC had a little pillbox, cloisonné, a scarab on its lid in blue and green, small enough to fit in her pocket. ET had a wallet, containing a joke driver's license, bought in Roswell, New Mexico, and made out for a little green man called Al Eon. AJ and LC had given it to her on her birthday. At the time, it really had been a joke. "They said you have to have an ID," LC had said. "This ought to do until they take you down to the DPS for a new one."

ET had thrown hers away the day before.

AJ and LC had left theirs behind at the hospital.

AJ said it would be easier to travel this way. He said it because it was what ET had told them to do before they left. He was in the grip of it now, in it the thickest of the three of them. LC, to a lesser degree, but touched, nodded, believed. ET, who had been the most thickly in the grip of it two days ago and was now released and feeling empty, wanted to talk sense into the two of them. September was golden in the daylight, beginning to go stiff at night with the coming chill. They would need to get indoors. ET envied them. In the grip of it, you were warmed by a campfire you knew to always have been there. You did not hunger, not with the same awful appetite you had when you were emptied. You understood the need to be nimble, taking what was necessary so you were light on your feet and could hear what was coming long before its approach. Emptied, you might as well be deaf, blind, enfeebled. You were too greatly concerned with the little things, what you were going to eat and when, where you were going to lay your head. In the grip of it, you knew those things for what they were—silly, momentary, animal.

But ET was hungry. She wished she hadn't said anything and couldn't believe she had.

However.

HOWEVER, THAT WAS what you had to remember about being touched. It was given so it could be taken away so it could be missed and ached for and wanted until you had the capacity to hold it again.

Otherwise, none of what they did made sense.

For instance, tonight they had come upon a Girl Scout camp, deserted for the season, and were holed up in one of the cabins. It reminded ET of Tent Number 8 at Camp Scott, where those three little girls had been violated and beaten to death in their sleeping bags. She had listened to a thing about it, maybe saw a thing.

"We're not in Oklahoma," LC said, as though it made all the difference.

"No." ET felt something that was not quite inside of her slip and went on. "But Oklahoma's not that far." And that made sense. She breathed, and then it didn't anymore, and she felt emptied again. The Okie Girl Scout murders became, like certain colors and words, the Holocaust, the numbers five, seven, and forty-four, a fixture in her storage of necessaries. She might not think much of it now, though in time it would take on the same significance as detecting the odor of gas in a home, the symptoms of a stroke, things to know, to be ready for the coming pandemonium.

The cabin had a door that locked from the inside. There were space blankets enough to sleep under and a surplus to pin over the windows. In the attached water closet, the toilet did not flush, but there was paper. The sink was filled with water overlaid with scum, moss around the taps. Bug carcasses crisped underfoot and turned to black crumbs when they lifted their shoes. AJ set to work occluding the windows, for he had understood what ET had meant beneath what she had said. He said there was nothing to show that they ought to be anywhere else.

ET tried to remember that. It was easier to do as the night went on and, by morning, she was full again of secret things and knowledge of the halcyon days to come, so long as she kept the faith.

They planned to stay in the camp for a week. In the mess hall, there were canned goods, black beans, kidney beans, lentils, tomatoes, corn, chickpeas, chicken stock, vegetable stock, tuna fish, and jars of bread-and-butter pickles and peanut butter. The electricity had been shut off in the kitchen, as it had been shut off throughout the camp, but LC had been a Girl Scout herself, from Brownies to Cadettes, and taught ET and AJ to build a fire. Using what they could scrounge in the mess hall, pots and bowls and spoons, they made chilis, stews. AJ went to the back of the pantry and found a box of Nilla Wafers, dunked them into the peanut butter. To pass the time, LC taught them what she could recall of her Girl Scout days, halcyon days in themselves, and this calmed ET. She taught ET the Girl Scout Law, first the recitation, then in sign language.

On my honor, I will try:
To serve God and my country,
To help people at all times,
And to live by the Girl Scout Law.

The rec room had foosball and a ping-pong table. There was an upright piano, on which AJ would play his repertoire from his own halcyon days as a minor prodigy.

"I was at the Manhattan School of Music," he told them. No one at the hospital had quite believed him, for there, as here, he played the same songs on a loop, Debussy's "Children's Corner" suite segueing into Brubeck's "Take Five." But ET had done a bit of sleuthing and found articles lauding AJ's achievements. At ten, he had played at the White House. At fifteen, he had been accepted at Manhattan, had been there two years, but did not graduate. She asked him why he did not take any of his sheet music with him when he was discharged. He tapped his temple with one finger and said, "It's all up here in my noodle." In addition to Debussy and Brubeck, he'd had Rachmaninoff and Mozart, Saint-Saens and Chopin. He had been lauded for his performance of Sandor Veress's "Hommage a Paul Klee." Why didn't he play any of those? "I hear it all the time. I can't see it. This—" he was on Debussy's "Little Shepherd," "—this I can almost see. If I keep going, I can get something sometimes, at different speeds."

There came a time at the tail-end of September, jutting into the first week of October, wherein the temperature rose and it was almost like summer. They stripped layers from themselves and went around in their t-shirts and underwear. The camp was on a lake, and this was when they decided to really take advantage of their surroundings, swimming out to the buoys, diving from the lifeguard's platform to the muddy bottom where they found treasure. LC was petite and could hold her breath for close to five minutes. She said she had a memory of another life in which she had been a pearl diver off the Izu Peninsula. It must have been true, for she found the best things, change amounting to ten dollars and seventy cents; a charm bracelet with a mermaid tail, a letter A, and a crown, all in sterling silver ("One for each of us," AJ said, and took the A. ET got the crown, LC the mermaid tail.); a house key on a chain; an Honor Sign pin in blue and gold; a whistle still on its lanyard; and an earring inlaid with a real pearl. LC let out a gust of air in a long whistle when she brought it up, and in between one moment and the next, after the whistle began and before it ended, she was surfacing in the Pacific Ocean, salt in her eyes, an oyster in her hand, very old (though perhaps now she was very old already and did not know it).

She was the one in the grip of it now.

ET, in a middling place, knew there was something to the little crown she had and tried to remember. She put it with the rest of her treasure trove, in the most hidden pocket of her knapsack.

AJ was empty and jealous. He missed what he had.

He was the one who decided they move on before the weather turned again. Trying to look at the upside of his new (hopefully temporary) condition, he reasoned that, while the world was flat, while everything had the guise of being one thing going one way, dulled, mortal, at least he was able to make plans. He, like ET and LC when they were empty, knew when to get somewhere warm, when it was time to hunker down for the night, who to speak to outside of their trio, when to call attention, when to keep quiet. You were like an animal; you were not divine, but you were practical.

It made ET think of the difference between kiddom and growing up. She had her youthful memories, concrete things like school, kisses, people she talked to, going home to her parents' house at the end of the day, what her bedroom looked like. She had never been more cared for or better managed. She told this to AJ and LC and they nodded, anticipating more. And there was more. In spite of all that, she remembered wildness, that feral practicality that descended when she and the others were empty. Never had she been more aware of how she smelled. Never had she been more aware of how she and the people around her moved, talked. The people you sat with defined you more than you did; Kevin Arnold said something like that in *The Wonder Years*. You were groin-driven, constantly straining, bloodthirsty, everything had the power to arouse or kill you. LC nodded, vigorously, AJ too. Panties always wet, hard-ons manifesting in the middle of math tests. Everyone could see you and everyone could smell you and everyone was hungry. Dennis Cooper wrote about it. Kathy Acker wrote about it. Jamaica Kincaid wrote about looking at her teenaged self in a store window and, taking in her acne, her gnarled hair, the odd fit of her clothes, compared herself to fallen Lucifer.

AJ read the Apostle Paul's first Letter to the Corinthians, all of the thirteenth chapter. It was the part that talked about looking through a glass darkly, the tongues of men and angels. He got to the verse, *When I was a child, I spake as a child, I understood as a child, I thought as a child: but when I became a man, I put away childish things*. It was also the chapter people liked to quote at weddings, though here, instead of *love is patient*, it translated to *charity suffereth long*.

Were they suffering? They looked at each other.

Right now, AJ was slipping back, filling up.

Just before, he brought them to a community center, one of the last of its kind where you could stay the night, but only for the night. "Nowadays," he'd said, "it's getting more and more like any other private gym." And it was somewhat true. There were reduced rates and outreach programs, kids' sports, but gone were the days in which you could stay as long as you needed. You were let to sit long enough to have a cup of coffee. And if you weren't going to buy a membership, you had to leave. Even this place, a YMCA that had its top floor devoted to beds and showers, a kitchen, a laundry room, dinner at night and breakfast in the morning, was talking of ending its overnight policy and turning the top floor into classrooms. People complained. Tomorrow, they would have to find somewhere else to go.

ET didn't think they were suffering. And LC, who was now the empty one and who consulted the list of shelters provided by the hospital, didn't think so either. If I were, say, fifteen years old, she thought, I might have been scared out of my mind. Or so embarrassed at where I was. And when I'm not in the grip of it, I begin to feel that way. ET caught the thought and told her she shouldn't, You're more than how you smell. You are divine. I know that and AJ knows that and I'm certain a few others know that, too. LC listened and, though it was difficult, believed her.

They could talk this way, heart to heart, brain to brain, all eyes and no lips, when they were in the grip of it. If LC could do it, it meant her time as the empty, practical beast was ending. There was no telling who would wake up emptied the next morning.

Corn flakes for breakfast, with tea from packets.

LC had circled places on the list and handed it to ET across the table. ET studied it, AJ peering over her shoulder. She hunched into herself, uncomfortable, though she had showered and put on new clothes, provided and cleaned by the Y's staff, and wore deodorant. Her other clothes, and AJ's and LC's, were in the dryers. She would pack them all into knapsacks, instead of layering. "It's supposed to be eighty degrees today," she told them. They countered that it made more sense to layer because you had everything in one place and nothing could be stolen or fall out of anywhere. "It's supposed to be eighty degrees," she repeated. "You know what I mean? You'll get heatstroke. Just put it all in the backpack, keep it zipped up, and it won't be a problem."

It was like talking to kids. She had to remember the phenomenon, that in these moments she was the kid, the feral one, and they were the pundits shaking their heads at her from their holy mountaintop.

They had a pair of new shoes each, the old Reeboks hospitals throw away. By midday, they had reached a strip mall and, because they were washed and wore clean clothes, were able to sit inside a Starbucks without hassle. ET bought them iced teas and consulted the list again. "LC," she said. Did her voice sound as hard as that? Nevertheless, it was what came out and it didn't stop. "LC, honey. Can I ask you—why did you choose places that are so far away? You know what I mean? There's a Covenant House on Clare Street. Look here. Why did you mark the one on Francis Ave.? That's more walking than we need to be doing."

AJ, peeved at being pulled from his tea, the sunshine through the window, Sting on a radio outside, scowled at ET. "There's the bus," he reminded her. "We have money."

"Not enough. Not enough for all the way out there—" ET paused. LC's eyes were wide, watery. She had circled the shelters when she was empty. It ought to have made sense to her then, and ET told her so. "I mean. What makes the one on Francis any different than the one over here?"

LC swallowed, throat bobbing, face quivering. She was about

to cry, but its tenor was different, not the indignation of having done wrong and being scolded for it. She shook her head, the sage on the mountaintop, losing patience, the grievance of knowing much more than the kid savage at the bottom. She sniffed. AJ handed her a napkin. ET relented and they all took a moment to collect. They listened to the Four Tops, *Still waters run deep, still waters run deep.* Finally, LC murmured that they were much more likely to be poisoned at the Clare Street Covenant House. She had read an article the night before, hailing the shelter on Francis Avenue for its use of allergy sensitive cleaning and their pledge that their residents would sleep in a place that would not trigger any reactions to dust mites or to the chemicals commonly used to disinfect. "People get asthma attacks from Mr. Clean as bad as they do from the dust. We use organic anti-allergens only," the staff was quoted.

"Ammonia," LC whispered.

"I'll bet you anything the Y we were just at uses ammonia to clean," ET sighed. "And you made it through the night."

LC, head wobbling side to side. Charity suffereth long, indeed, on the cosmic axis. "I won't go there." She hid her face in AJ's shoulder and took comfort in his stink.

ET began, "It'll only be for one night—"

"No. No. I won't do it. I'll sleep outside."

"Honey, that's ridiculous. There's more crap outside than there would be in a place full of ammonia."

"I'LL SLEEP OUTSIDE."

And the barista hovered nearby, asking if all was well. "We're fine." ET waved her away. "She's just—she's okay, she's fine."

AJ eased LC from his shoulder and, glowering at ET, suggested they give the place a call, at least. "Just to verify. If they clean organically on Francis, maybe they do the same thing on Clare."

The city had taken out the payphone on the corner. The barista let them use the phone behind the counter, though it was for employees only. LC insisted she speak to the director of the Covenant House on Clare Street on a matter of great importance. She might have been filing a formal complaint or handing down an indictment. She got a Reverend Mother Seton on the other line. "I may be coming your way momentarily. I may be coming your way, regardless of what I want to do because I will be doing it against my will. My question to you is this—" And she gave a recap into the article she had read about Francis Avenue, about dust mites and ammonia. "What do you use to clean with at your location?"

The opposite end of the conversation led to Mother Seton, a six-minute walk away. She was sixty years old, had been married, been in the army and completed her last tour of duty in Serbia, gone to law school on the GI Bill, advocated for criminals, been widowed, and now this was where she was. In another life, she had lived in a brick house, two story, a pool in the backyard and a sign in front that read, SECURED BY ADT. A maid service came every other week. Her sister said she was nuts to leave it all behind, even more bewildered by her conversion at forty-nine. "You're an atheist. We were raised Methodist. We went to church on Easter, if that. What's the deal?" She did not wear a habit, for they were uncomfortable and the times and expectations of her consecration had changed; her order got blue jeans from St. Vinnie's and provided sweatshirts and t-shirts with the crest of her order on the breast pocket.

From her office on the ground floor, she could see the Starbucks from where the call was placed. The commotion was small from here, framing something that might have been huge if Mother Seton got closer. As it was, here was an episode about a girl (a grown woman?) living in fear, of ammonia today, aliens tomorrow. In these instances, Mother Seton imagined Rod Serling narrating the whole thing; it helped her empathize and to disengage. *You are about to enter another dimension, a dimension not only of sight and sound but of mind.* There was the action and here were the words reaching her ear in tinny consonants, like an old transmission from a lost cosmonaut.

She told the girl at the Starbucks, not wanting to lie to her, that at the moment, the Clare Street facility used whatever they could get in bulk and, yes, a lot of what they cleaned with contained ammonia. She pressed her forehead to the window. Down the way, the girl trembled, paced, catching her sweater in a potted areca palm until she could take no more of it and tore the leaves from the stalks. The barista flapped his hands, otherwise rooted behind the counter.

LC sobbed into the phone, "Then, that's it. That's it. I'll just die, then, because they won't let me sleep anywhere else." She wailed, her eyes small and red and wet. "Not even outside."

Mother Seton tapped on the glass. A volunteer watering the flowerbeds picked his head up, followed the Reverend Mother's beckon into her office, wherein he stood at attention. He nodded, big-eyed, as Mother Seton, in whispered intervals, explained the situation. She blocked the phone's mouthpiece with the ham of her palm, saying, "Call the police, I'll keep her talking. Thanks, Simon."

Down the way, the barista trembled, jumped when she felt her supervisor looming behind her. Palm leaves on the floor, the worst of the tantrum had outwardly passed, and LC had sunk to the floor, not quite sitting, not kneeling, holding all of her weight on her ankles in a painful squat. ET covered her face with her hand. AJ covered LC's face with his sweatshirt, and when they had shut out this much of the world, they were mildly pacified. LC, in fact, was beginning to sober up, go empty. She blinked and eyed the phone in her hand, even, yogic breaths coming as she watched everything clear. The barista turned. "I don't know what to do," she hissed.

The manager, though stern, was a kind woman. If Martha John had got on the phone herself, she might have been shocked to find that the person on the other end had been in her platoon in Kosovo. She might have wanted to ask how Elizabeth Seton was doing, laughed about her incarnation as Reverend Mother and would recant, telling her, "That's great, though. Wow, a nun." And then she might have got Mother Seton up to speed on her own doings. Well, she had divorced, amiably, and rented a little house over on Mountain Road. She had two grown boys, Phil and Paul, and a granddaughter, Phoebe, in nursery school. Before, for many years she'd run her own place, a bakery specializing in pies made to order, sweet and savory, and with a little sit-down area by the window where you could sip coffee and watch the world go by. But the economy crapped out, she got tired more than she used to. Life happened and now this was where she was.

Instead, she told her barista to keep an eye on the girl on the floor. "Just stay where you are, I'll go call the police. Thanks, Pete."

Simon did as he was told, as did Peter, for they were as dogs, loyal, watchful. They would take shifts on his days off, back-to-back, midway. Simon worked for nothing, save for volunteer credits. Peter worked for minimum wage. Both would record their experience on their college resumes, reluctantly summarizing it to the dates worked, their duties. Covenant House and Starbucks were not so different. And yet, if you were to compare them side by side, according to the boys' rundown of things, you might not have told who worked where. Opening and closing up. Restocking coffee, napkins, other supplies as needed. Answering the phone. Customer service. Here, they watched, Simon from Clare Street, Peter behind the counter. This, they reasoned, would fall under customer service. Peter considered writing about it for his application essay, but the thought dampened almost as soon as it rose. Simon would write about it in a journal, a hobby he would keep up for a year and then abandon, and when he dug it from a drawer, long after all of these events had passed, he would read it and wonder at why he could not remember it.

But it would return, in dreams, in daylight, blindsiding them both in the brightest afternoon, like a projection from a third, inner eye. Their obedience had made of them witnesses.

ET, AJ, AND LC would leave long before the police arrived. When an officer did appear, they had relocated across the street to a park, peering over the fence, looking just as curious as anyone else who might be wondering at all the hurly-burly. They were all three in the grip of it. Now that ET and AJ had returned to the fold, they were able to calm LC's storms and lift her and themselves into gentle euphoria. It was a lovely day. They moved through it without hunger or exhaustion, stopping to drink from their canteens, and once to look at the clouds. ET saw a canoe. AJ saw a horse. LC saw a beaver—maybe an otter.

The park had a walking trail that looped around the main roads and farther into the trees. It was not quite the wilderness, for they had entered the suburbs and their purlieus, the peaks of houses jutting now and then through the timber, the silence broken by a barking dog or a kid howling, "NOT IT." The path looped around the neighborhood, close enough for them to catch sight of a gap in the bushes that opened to a cul-de-sac. The houses were single story, frothy in front with mophead flowers.

ET said aloud that she might have lived here once, or somewhere like it. AJ asked if it was before the hospital. ET said she was unsure. She, like him and like LC, did not know how old she was when she was full. It was not a matter of forgetting so much as it was like looking through a prism, the facets, the refracted light and resulting colors distorting it until it took on the appearance of someone else's life, a gap in between the end of the old cycle and the reincarnation. You never remembered being anything else. And that, ET thought when she began to empty, was for the best.

She was the one who led them through the park, onto the path that came into view of the lake. They could still see the road through breaks in the trees and the pavement had turned to dirt. The houses were sturdier, taller, colored brown and green to blend with the pines. Here were the summer cottages, still peopled while the weather was warm. Here was the time of day when the grills were going, suppertime, hamburgers and steaks. When they were full, a notion entered each of them, forbidding them from eating any meat. AJ and LC did not hunger. ET had them all pause at a tennis court farther into the woods, within sight of its nearby house. It was closed, ET found when she crept up to peek through the windows. But going back, she was able to cut through the yard next door, spying a picnic table littered with barbecue remains, burger rinds, bags of potato chips, bottles of ketchup, mustard, mayo, tomato slices, onions in half-moons. There was no one else around, the party seemingly having moved indoors. ET worked quickly, nabbing the chips. The burger leftovers she swallowed on the run back to the tennis court.

AJ read the bag of chips. "Cheddar and sour cream," he pronounced.

They ate and moved on, taking a path that split at a sign which read, ALL DOGS MUST BE ON LEASHES. Somehow, LC and AJ understood the message to be for the three of them. LC held AJ's hand, and AJ tried to lace his fingers through ET's. But his palm was clammy, and she reattached him to the loose strap of her knapsack. And this was how they came upon the Girl Scout camp at afternoon's end, marching right into a firepit, the ashes cold and black, like the blind leading the blind.

Now, hunkered down in the cabin, ET had sunk to that middling place, between being in the grip and not, in which doubt could easily overwhelm. Panic set in, you were taken and shaken. Things that ought never to have troubled you in your life assumed new meaning. You were burdened by words in magazine articles, the colors of cars, the smell of a particular Dunkin' Donuts' restroom. You were never more aware of having eyes on you, and you wanted to ask what it meant, what did everyone want, what ought you to be looking for, worry without direction. The worst of it was the emptiness, the sharpness of it; it did not have the same tenor as it did when you really were empty. Here was the possibility of real finality, the gray desperation. Just as there are no atheists in foxholes, there were none in the middling place. You made demands, you bargained, and the bitterest part of it was that you never had a face to gnash your teeth at. It blindsided you, sending you into a tempest, making you cold, making you stiff, filling your bladder. It got hold of LC, and she came out of it like the survivor of a shipwreck, panting, perspiring, full again with great, radiant relief.

All shall be well, and all shall be well, and all manner of thing shall be well. Julian of Norwich said that, walled up as they were now.

John Nash thought anyone who wore a red tie was a Communist. When again on an even keel, he worked out new models in game theory and won the Nobel Prize.

Imagine what would come of their middlings.

SHE WONDERED AT what they must look like. Her own hair was matted, made a bit tidier for her use of a fork on the rats' nests. Normally, it was puffy when short, ringleted when it grew out. AJ kept his own hair knotted at the top of his head, giving him the look of a bodhisattva; his beard was long enough to braid, which he sometimes did, though he was talking about cutting it. Before she left the hospital, LC had scissored most of her hair away and what was left perked around her scalp in little cowlicks. They scrubbed their faces when they could, but in time, it might become difficult to see them as anything other than a homogenous grit-streaked trio—or, more likely, as one person, three headed.

The last movie she had seen was *Mulholland Drive*. In it, there was a scene in which a fellow describes a nightmare in which a horrible creature with a horrible face pounces at him from its lair behind a dumpster. He goes to the dumpster to conquer his fear, and lo, the creature is real and the creature is there, but it does not attack. It shows itself and slides back into its lair. And if you pause the film, you can just make out the human features underneath the horror, which was only grit. No sex, no color, no industry, no speech, no ambition.

And maybe, ET thought, filling up, that was for the best.

She watched them sleep. AJ did not dream, but LC did.

LC had given her name several times, all beginning with L. Loretta, Linda, Lucia, Lidwina, Lubaba. ET peered into her dream, tried to see what was true and what was not. When you were in the grip, you could do that. In the dream, LC lived in a desert with many other children, as many as thirty. No one looked a day over thirteen, all on bicycles, scooters, dragging the cherub-faced younger ones in wagons, kicking up dust. This was true. In the dream, her name was Lynn-Lee. This was not true. In the desert, they lived in trailers and ate canned food. There were seven mothers and three fathers. This, from what ET could tell, was true. Maybe there were more mothers, fathers, children. There was a comet, or the comet was coming. This was not true.

AJ remembered who he had been before and he said sometimes he wished he didn't.

ET remembered who she had been before in fragments. A smell, a sight, a sound would call her back, but only for a moment.

LC remembered who she was every day, and then the narrative would change, even in slumber. She had been a nun, a macrobiotic chef, a makeup artist. She was from New Mexico, Florida, Minnesota. "Before the hospital, you mean," AJ would prompt. And she would tell him, no, that she'd meant before that. Sometimes, the way her name changed, her personhood would, too, in the ether of dreams. She was River Phoenix, Sojourner Truth, Grand Duchess Anastasia Nikolaevna of Russia. She said she could recall pieces, not the life as a whole. And ET understood LC had not meant amnesia. ET was intrigued. Imagine the possibilities if you knew what you had been before. Had LC been a dog, too? Or a camel, or a lizard? She said she couldn't remember that.

When ET slept, she dreamed she was in a movie theater that was also a temple. There was no spectacle, no picture, no sermon, just hundreds of people filling the seats and answering the trivia on the screen in the manner of game show contestants. WHO WAS EDWARD JENNER? WHAT IS IPSO FACTO? WHAT IS SOMA? Not WHAT IS THE BRAT PACK or WHO IS HALLE BERRY? Nothing to do with movies. She was not sure if it was because the questions came and went too quickly from the screen or if there had been a momentary lapse in her ability to read, but she heard herself shouting the answer a moment too late. The fellow next to her would turn, he would shake his head in grossest disappointment and tell her, "No, it's WHAT IS THE WATERBUCK? It's WHAT WAS THE DIET OF WORMS? Keep up." She could not have said how, though it was understood that she, as they, were here as captives, their release dependent upon the most questions answered. WHAT IS THE FLEHMEN RESPONSE? WHAT IS UFOLOGY? WHO WAS CALIGULA? WHO WAS ROBERT BADEN-POWELL? WHAT WAS THE KAZOKU? She was not bound to her chair and she could not move. She was growing leaden, sinking into the cushions. WHAT WAS THE BATTLE OF MONS? WHO WAS MAX YASGUR? And at last, time slowed, or her eyes had sharpened. For there on the screen was one she could answer, putting her forward, if only by an inch. THIS VOLUME IS THE SECOND INSTALLMENT OF POET JAMES MERRILL'S EPIC WORK, *THE CHANGING LIGHT AT SANDOVER*. It was the last book she had read before leaving the hospital, half-finished, faceside down, spine broken, abandoned on her bed. She saw it as she drew breath for the answer.

"MIRABEL."

She opened her eyes. And she hoped she got partial credit for giving only part of the title. And she was not freed, but held fast to the floor as if by a great and pulsating weight. In their corners, LC slept and AJ slept and saw nothing. And ET saw nothing. She tried to recall this kind of burden elsewhere, and thought of electric blankets. She might have chosen to stay this way forever, cocooned, never slumbering, never waking. Was this what we return to, when there are no more lives to live? And that terrified her, and air came in sips. In this state it was dark. She wrenched her head to one side, where all of her, down to her fingertips, seemed heavy as bricks, and it was morning.

It was the fullest she, or any of them, had ever been, and LC and AJ could see it. She told them they would not leave until the right clues had presented themselves. But what was coming was great and golden.

(In the hospital, they were told a thing was what it was. They were told not to read so much into it. A nurse liked to say, "Let a rose just be a rose." But didn't she know? Didn't anyone know a rose could mean a whole lot of things, depending on its color, as the Victorians knew, depending on when you saw it, where it grew, whether it was in bloom or withering? It might be the signal for a charge, or a warning, or good luck. They were everywhere, if you had the eyes to look.)

She chose not to say any more about it, for she wanted to see if it would happen again the next night, and then the next, which it did, the same theater as a temple, the same Trivial Pursuit across the screen. There was much mumbling. WHAT IS APACHE KAFKA? WHAT IS THE SUMMER SOLSTICE? WHAT IS BELGRANODEUTSCH? WHAT IS DIM SUM?

This time, she saw a face above her. She was held fast, not yet out of the theater, and she felt it all falling away, save for that face, a round rosebud face.

THIS PLUM IS A DELICACY FROM THE FRENCH LORRAINE.

"MIRABEL." She woke to LC to her left, AJ to her right. She sat up between them. "I'm hungry."

AJ said, "We're out."

ET asked, "What about all that canned stuff? All the rest."

"It's pretty old, as it turns out. I guess the campers wolf down everything before it has the chance to carry botulism. If you look at the dates on the cans, you wouldn't trust them either.'

"And the cookies? The stuff in the pantry?"

LC told her, "The cookies were the only good thing. Everything else is full of rat turds. This place might have been shut for longer than we thought. Years, maybe."

ET slumped back onto her elbows. "All right."

LC blinked. "All right."

AJ sniffed. "All right."

They had not as yet received any signal to do anything different. None of them had fallen out of the grip, save for ET's exceptional hunger. They lived this way for five days, marking their passing on the rec room wall with a blue pen. They boiled water from the lake and drank their fill. LC went diving and brought back sunfish, which they ate roasted. Too, she found a pair of glasses, a mood ring, giving them to ET. "You can add them to the treasure trove," she said.

ET nodded and pocketed them. LC mentioned that anything that went into the trove never seemed to come out again.

"Unless it's money," AJ put in.

And this was true. Somehow, when they were low, when there was nothing that could be traded, when they had to follow the secular rules of empty days, there was just enough. A bus ride, a bottle of water, a phone call, a sandwich from Jimmy John's and, once on a particularly bad day, three movie tickets that got them out of the rain. Change appeared when it looked like the end of the line and the empty days were here forever. That was when things looked the most hopeless, no patterns, no egg hunt and games, even if it led you to knowing things you wished you didn't, like LC and ammonia. Now and then, items from the trove would vanish. ET remembered a diamond ring among them, something that was there and now she didn't have it anymore; but the next day, three quarters, eight dimes, and nine nickels appeared, enough to finish a load at the laundromat, just when they all thought they'd finally had it.

"It's like alchemy," AJ said. "Put in an old bottlecap, and you get gold."

"Or three dollars ten," LC added, because she had been the one to find the bottlecap.

While they waited, they read to each other aloud from AJ's King James Bible, or pored through the books in the rec room, the *Ramona Quimby* series in its entirety, *James and the Giant Peach*, *The Secret Garden* and *The Hobbit*. LC had liked the Judy Blume books she'd found, but stopped when she got to *Blubber*. "She just couldn't win," LC said of the title character. "No friends at the beginning, none at the end." She swallowed, and uttered Blubber's real name. "Poor Linda."

The others made do with water. ET, hungrier than ever, felt called to the leaves from the trees. They did not disagree with her and, after a while, she thought they might make a very nice salad if paired with a good vinaigrette, maybe a few croutons. Meantime, they tried to divine their answer. AJ found a Bananagrams set wedged in between Monopoly and Jenga. It was like Scrabble, but you played without a board. They noticed they all had words like RISE, DAWN, and DEBUT. ET munched a leaf. She also found FEAST.

AJ had taken down his knotted hair, which had grown very stringy. LC had taken to holding her hands over ET's belly as though she were warming them before a fire, and shortly thereafter, AJ did the same. ET wondered. There was nothing there, nothing to suggest another life. And why should there be?

"Mary wasn't intimate with a man, either," AJ noted.

In the empty days, before ET understood just how empty they were, she had imagined pregnancy as little more than two organisms sharing a body. It swung between tapeworm and demonic possession, if she had to compare it to anything. And, if she were honest even now, tapeworm was her knee-jerk to it. If you had something inside you, you had to get rid of it. You were the only occupant of your flesh. Why ought you to share it?

In another life, LC had been with child. She had lost it.

"Did you retrace your steps?" AJ asked. "Did you think of where the last place you left it might be? Maybe asked around, if anyone saw it?" He was quite serious.

LC wasn't angry. In that other life, it was there with her and then not, washed out in a day's worth of gushing and stink. A little like ET's bag, turning one thing into another. Or something being there, and then gone.

When they were all of them empty, which happened rarely, they understood, very reluctantly, the things that occurred to them when full were what some called "spells," some called "fantasies," some called "notions," or, worst of all, "whims." Recalling the nurse with her Gertrude Stein maxim, it was not a case for imagination, turning it on and turning it off, letting a rose be a rose. Imagination suggested play, and this was not. The three of them made it play, yes, when looking for signals, because it lightened the load. But the signals were there, always had been, appearing when called for when the hour came for them to be seen, if you had the eyes for them. Sometimes, the things occurring to them were not so subtle. Sometimes, like now, they leapt out at you, no warning, no color or sound. You had a dream and this is what it meant.

"It's hot as an oven," LC breathed, laying her hands.

ET looked down at herself. Something did pooch out, just a bit. AJ, emptying, said it was gas from eating nothing but leaves. He'd been saying they ought to pick up and go, there was no point in staying. He studied the list of shelters, tapping one, sighing that he didn't care anymore if they used ammonia to clean there or not, he'd take the risk. Then he lay down and turned on his side. He'd been like that for almost two days, and was having trouble keeping down water. LC twirled a tuft of hair around her finger; it came out, dropping to the floor like down.

ET, meanwhile, looking in the mirror, was pink. She was swollen where she ought to be and had already eaten most of what she could reach from the elms and oaks. If a platter of barbecue were to appear, she'd lick it clean and ask for more. It had been some time since her last period, not having thought much of its absence before, thinking of it as a side-effect of irregular meals, and a convenience while they were on the move. She went to the counselors' office, found a tear-off-the pages calendar for the current year, illustrating three hundred and sixty-five days of corgis. She counted and tore, coming to today, a corgi in a pumpkin patch. Three months. No reason, as yet, to believe either way.

She was the strongest of them now, and still the fullest. AJ, when awake, begged to leave. LC, even LC, was emptying, saying she would try the shelter on Clare Street, just for one night. But they couldn't move now, not when ET had had the dream again, a fourth, fifth, sixth time. THIS SUBURB OF MONTREAL. THIS CALIFORNIA MINING SETTLEMENT. THIS SPECIES OF MOTH FOUND IN THE RUSSIAN FAR EAST. MIRABEL, the same answer every time. Some nights she woke shouting it, others mumbling it in her sleep. Gilgamesh dreamt of Enkidu coming to him from the wilderness. Jacob dreamt of the ladder to heaven, with angels ascending and descending. Had Gabriel visited Mary in a dream? Or had it been Joseph?

"Joseph," AJ murmured from the floor. "*For that which is conceived of her is of the Holy Ghost.*"

Was that what it was? It certainly would be convenient for ET, seeing as she had never been very good at intimacy, before or aft. It was something to have found herself linked to LC and AJ. Good things come in threes, that nurse had also liked to say. Here it was, six-fold, twice as good. At the hospital, before being discharged, she could not imagine a life apart from them. And they could not imagine a life apart from her.

Minus one, the structure was unsound. You could go from empty to full and back again in a matter of a few hours, and it made the trade-off uneven. The depths of the empty days and the glory of the halcyon days rendered you useless, in either state. You plunged too soon from the height to get up, look at anything and, alternately, you took off too quickly to see what you were leaving behind, in the clouds, impractical. Either way, you forgot to eat and sleep was brittle.

People died in such extremities. There had been two at the hospital, a man and a woman. The fellow had plunged and no longer saw the point to anything, just hid his face under his pillow and did not sleep, did not speak, did not eat, did not move even to use the toilet. Nurses had to give him sponge baths and his sheets were changed by the hour. One day, he stirred enough to bite his tongue, and he emptied out completely. The woman, on the other hand, bounced from one room to another, never still, full to the brim of love for one and all, delight in absolute. She could do anything, she said, and, watching her, you believed it. She could speak to animals, from the squirrels in the garden to the therapy Labrador. She had received the stigmata, or picked at her palms until they bled. She did have dermatitis. She predicted a hailstorm one summer day and, after reading a biography of Padre Pio, she climbed to the roof of the administration building, intending to fly, and jumped.

There had to be one stalwart.

"I might die," AJ croaked.

"No, you won't," ET countered.

LC nodded, a little timidly.

When it looked as though he might, wouldn't you know, that was when a hand came knocking, one-two-three, on the rec room window. ET looked out and went to open the door, calling "Hallo?" She was getting peaky by now herself, though still pink. The creature inside (she had not yet resigned herself to call it a baby) had begun to stir, much sooner than she would have liked and, despite her diet of leaves, kicked and rolled and did not stop even when she told it to.

The woman who met her outside on the step saw her belly first. Just the same, ET saw the creature the woman carried, not inside but on her back in a sort of kangaroo pouch. But her legs dangled out on either side of her mother; if standing she would have been the taller of the two. Her eyes were large and unfocused, her head wavering up and down, side to side, slowly, as if to compensate. She opened her mouth and puffed a word, "HA," into her mother's hair.

"How long have you been in there?" Both mother and daughter's breath rose in pale fog.

ET didn't know, guessing a month now. Mornings were cooler and they did not swim in the lake anymore. Only LC, who never seemed to feel the chill, bringing up marbles, a Swiss army knife, a plastic brush, two tiny trolls with orange hair, a pink retainer. They had plenty to trade now, if there was any need. She went into her bag, rooted around until she found something good, the retainer, and showed it.

"You don't have to do that," the woman said, shaking her head. "Just follow me. We're not far from here."

"HA," the girl on her back huffed. Her hand, its fingers long and deliberate and elegant, pawed at the air until ET gave her the retainer. Her mother asked her if she liked it, a little sweeter than you might if talking to a grown person, but not like a baby either. The girl repeated, "HA."

The woman reached around and squeezed the girl's foot. "That's Holly." With her other hand, she gestured to herself, then held it out to ET, contact, a close encounter. "Rosemary. Or just Rose."

A rose is a rose is a Rosemary. Let the heathen nurse look here.

AJ, too weak to walk, had to be piggy-backed. ET, still the strongest and fullest, took him, waved LC and Rosemary away. "Not in your condition," they cooed, but they relented when ET bent and swung AJ over her shoulder amidst everything.

In their way, they linked. AJ reached for LC with one hand and gripped ET's hair with the other. Ahead, Holly, who had been clapping to herself, looked behind and grabbed a hank of hair from ET's bent head. ET reattached her to the knapsack's strap, patting it there. And as Rosemary said, it was not far through the woods to her house. Over ET's shoulder, AJ watched the camp vanish through the leaves, green and gold now, like Magh Meall receding into mist and myth. They had to blink when they got to the road. LC let out a little cry when a tow truck growled past, dragging a Jeep. She kept her eyes shut for much of the trek back into town and loosened when they were off the main road again, on one winding limb of a residential back street.

Rosemary's house was on a corner, where town and neighborhood met. You could hear commotion, though only mildly, giving the illusion they were at the edge of a small village in the country. The house reminded AJ of the kind you read about in ghost stories, which was not to say that it inspired horror. A ghost story was as much about a life passed and what lingered; reading the Acts of the Apostles, you could see where M.R. James got his ghouls. Here, the house was old, very lived-in by years and many, still white with green trim. Unlocking the door, Rosemary told them it was built by her grandfather in 1890. "Or was it 1870? One of those." Its foundation would withstand the end of days. Holly said "HA" to that.

They went in.

TO BE FULL up was to be in love, with everything. To be in love with everything was to know God. Dostoyevsky had said something like that, though the three of them agreed there was not a God. How could there be? God was what you called circumstances you did not like and, in order to have something to blame, you put on it a face and a name. How could there be when it was you all along? You, who understood the pattern in this wilderness and built up from it, for beauty, for blood?

AJ caught these moments of absolute fullness so rarely he became crystallized in its grip, frozen with the stupidest grin, blushed pink at the flattery of being one piece of this great mechanism. In these moments, he wanted to tell everyone, I LOVE YOU. And he did, and if they did not turn away, they felt what he felt and knew they must deliver the same message, whispering in ears like a wonderful game of Pass It On.

And what do you feel when you're in love? AJ basked in it. His eyes, heavy, feeling the turning and turning, the widening of his pupils to let in all the light they could. He blinked often, tears unshed, stuck in his throat, which made his voice a little husky, a little out of breath from having to sigh. Romance was longing, the beautiful ache of knowing what was there and wanting more, the greed of discovery.

In Holly's and Rosemary's house there were not many rooms, but they were wide. They came in through the kitchen, which smelled of bananas, and into a sitting room, what had likely once been a dining room in its Victorian days. There were cushions about the floor, plants hanging in baskets, fronds in corners, flowers dried and live, strawflowers, salvia, amaranth, larkspur, hydrangeas, and roses and sprigs of holly. There was a stereo and stacks of albums.

AJ recognized his face on the cover of one of them, *Duets for Keys and Strings*. He was sixteen then. He had red hair and sat opposite Edin Karamazov. Rosemary gawked when she caught the resemblance and then his name. "Stop it," she breathed. "I don't believe it. That's you?" He confirmed it was, looked to ET and LC, who nodded. LC was adamant, for she had seen him perform, another life, a stage, plush seats, tickets please, house lights, syrupy Shirley Temples, New York, empty days before she knew them to be empty. There was no piano in Rosemary's house, but she piped up that she did have a guitar. LC said he played that, too, but not with the same expertise. "But he's very good, I think," she added.

Holly, who had been positioned onto the biggest pile of cushions, slim legs crossed, hands poised apart, puffed. "HA." And she clapped when AJ played, picking up where he left off with a hesitant "Golliwog's Cakewalk." He stood and bowed when he was through, formal. Was there anyone he ought to thank? ET? LC?

He did not remember his mother. What remained of his father was ghostly, a wraith never quite visible, looming over him during his lessons until he got them right. Not a bad man, but not a very nice one, having come to see him once in the hospital and turning away weeping, more like a mother than a father, "My baby, my boy," as though AJ were dead. Thinking fast, he held his hands out to Holly.

Holly gripped his forefinger, mouth open. Her smile yielded a mouth of large teeth, crookedly set. Her hair was threaded with gray and her eyes round and wide and green, like those of a fish. She giggled when AJ leaned over to kiss her crown.

The light changed and evening came. Rosemary put music on, Joni Mitchell this time, *Song to a Seagull*, skipping the tracks until she found what she claimed was Holly's favorite song, "Sisotowbell Lane." "Did you know it's supposed to be an acronym?" Rosemary said. "*Somehow, In Spite Of Trouble, Ours Will Be Ever Lasting Love*." She set to work getting dinner, bringing out large pots and large pans. She asked LC to go into the laundry room, that she would find a broom closet in there, and get her three butternut squashes and four turnips. While LC peeled, AJ cut, wiping his eyes on his sleeve when he came to the onions. ET sat at the little table, for Rosemary had said she ought to rest. She had lifted Holly from the cushions and set her on the floor, all fours, to creep about the house. "Here's what you can do. Keep Holl company for a little bit. She'd like a buddy."

The smell of bananas gave way to sesame oil and garlic, rice thumping as Rosemary dumped it into the pan. ET asked why she was making so much, seeing as there were only five of them. Rosemary brought out dishes from the cupboards, stacked them by the stove. She looked to be preparing a banquet. Rosemary tasted from a pot of beans and said, "It's for whoever turns up. They usually start showing up around this time." From the oven, she removed a pan of acorn squash halves, buttered and filled with maple syrup.

"Dinnertime?" ET asked.

"Oh, they don't come here to eat. Mostly, it's to see her."

Rosemary pointed her spoon at Holly, blew her a kiss. "But it's a nice gesture. You know, just a bite of something good."

ET wanted to ask, "Why would they come to see Holly? What was she to them?" She was coming out of it now, emptying for the first time in days and the sinking was horrible. She looked at her belly and swollen breasts with contempt, at the creature inside. From where had it come? Emptied, she had to assess, as they had told her to do in the hospital. *How shall this be, seeing I know not a man?* Weren't they saying nowadays that Jesus' real father had been a Roman soldier called Pantera?

What men did she know, just socially? AJ was not a man, not as she remembered men to be. He was not a eunuch, though something from him was missing. LC said that in another life he had been a great believer who had condemned all intimacy in favor of simplicity. "Who?" ET had asked, and listed mystics. Mother Ann Lee of the Shakers, Tuccia of the Vestal Virgins, Leo Tolstoy?

"No," LC had said, and leaned in to reveal. "John Kellogg."

"Who's that?"

"The corn flakes guy. The guy who invented corn flakes."

"HA," Holly declared.

Here was Holly at ET's knees, hands coming together and springing apart. To ET, she had the look of one of those mechanical monkeys that bang a pair of cymbals when wound up. Rosemary turned from the stove and nodded to her. "She wants you to play."

How old was Holly? How old Rosemary? You get to a certain point in life and you could easily pass for forty as sixty, if blessed with good genes. Earlier, in the sitting room, Rosemary had mentioned she'd birthed Holly at thirty-four. Didn't give the year of the birth or her age now. ET assessed and put Rosemary at around sixty, which would make Holly twenty-six. Think of it. What kind of life was that, for mother and for daughter? Twenty-six, an infant. Sixty, the mother of an infant. The whole business seemed to her too fantastic, like something out of science fiction, too wild to happen in real life—at least, happen to her.

Looking up as though ET had said it aloud, LC said, "They're saying now that the word *virgin* in the Holy Land just meant a woman who couldn't conceive."

Pubescent. Menopausal. ET didn't remember how old she was, she wasn't that empty.

Diabetic. Venereal. ET didn't remember what she was sick with, only that she had been in a hospital.

"She wants to play with you." Rosemary looked as though she'd said it more than twice. "She has a game where you clap with her. Watch." She knelt to Holly. She waited, and Holly brought her hands together, once. Rosemary imitated, then Holly. Then, Rosemary clapped, one, then, two, three. And Holly clapped, one, two, three, four, five.

"Fibonacci," AJ murmured.

"I wouldn't know about that," said Rosemary, "but Holl loves it." She nodded at ET. "Give it a try. Folks'll be here soon. They'll be lining up to play with her."

In *Peter Pan*, you clapped if you believed in fairies. In Javanese gamelan, clapping was part of the music used to call God down from the mountains. And then there were the evangelical happy-clappers, the Zen riddle of the sound of one hand clapping. ET tried to remember the games she played at recess, the rhyming songs that became a permanent earworm long after you'd out-grown them. "Miss Mary Mack," "Miss Susie," "Miss Lucy Had a Baby." Were there any clap games that weren't about a Miss?

Rosemary called over her shoulder, "Try 'Pat-a-cake' "

ET did try it, a simpler version, just she and Holly slapping their hands together until ET had to take the other girl through "roll it, bake it, and mark it with a B/And put it in the oven for Baby and me." Holly grinned when it was over and did not let go of ET's hands, not even when the first of her guests began to arrive.

The evening went on like that into the small hours. ET watched them come in between games of "Pat-a-cake." They were folks of every walk, though you could tell those desperate from the ones who were merely curious.

The former were shabby, though they had a pinkness to them that suggested having scrubbed down themselves completely, eyes wide, they wiped their feet and shook Rosemary's hand when she let them in through the back door, into the laundry room and kitchen, out to the sitting room where they paused, swallowed, blinked, looked to Rosemary as if for permission before entering to sit before Holly. Some took off their shoes before going in. Then they began the clapping game, the same one Rosemary showed ET earlier that evening. Though now the simplicity was gone and play no longer the object. If there was a pattern here, a language, a code, ET could not find it. She was as empty as she had ever been, though now she knew fully the agony of it, the swollen cognizance of what she was missing.

LC said she thought she caught something of what was happening. It was hard to believe her because it changed as the night went on, though her certainty was always intact. "She's predicting the future. She's delivering aphorisms, an answer for every question. It's like the chimes before the Eucharist. It's like the gong in the morning and the drum in the evening."

The curious ones filtered in, the same gestures but without the fervor. They peered in the fogged kitchen window, the way you do looking through the bars at a zoo. They wiped their feet but left dirt. They were tidy only because it was a part of their secular routine, maybe having just come from work, running a comb through their hair, chewing a mint before going in. Like ET, they did not see the pattern. And they did not seem to know there was one. They might have said it aloud: "What's all the fuss about?" Yes, wasn't it all very nice, wasn't the poor thing sweet as could be. They did not touch her, save to pat her fingers away, like warding off the advances of a too-friendly dog. They did not eat the food Rosemary had laid out in the kitchen, waving her away, too, saying, "Oh, I couldn't. I just came from dinner. Very nice, very nice, but no thank you." And, shamefaced, they left her bills, folded and new, tucked by the sugar jar on the counter. AJ broke free from things and sat to count it. "Almost a thousand," he said. "They didn't even play with her."

Rosemary thought, wrapping a bit of gray hair around her finger. "I don't think they're sad for her. Or me, really. But I think they want to be. It'd feel better than being sad for themselves, which is what I think is going on. But I wouldn't know. It's just what I think. It's groceries for the next six or so months, and the electric. The house is all mine, paid for and everything. We live pretty simply. I won't argue with it. Put it in the sugar jar. I never put sugar in there, anyway. I keep it in the bag."

AJ opened the jar and looked in. He didn't need to count it. "Suppose someone takes it?"

"They wouldn't dare. Not on Holly's watch. Her hearing's out of this world. And anyway, it'd be going back to the same place. I don't see why anyone would bother."

The others left pretty things, much like what ET had in her trove. Chess pieces and the little silver top hat from a Monopoly set, multisided dice in different colors, the bell from a cat's collar, a plastic frog on a keychain. Rosemary took them with delight, for she knew their worth. Holly clapped for the dice, which were translucent and cast greens and pinks across the wall when you held them up to the light.

"You think of a name for your babe yet, darlin?" An old woman came to warm her hands at ET's belly.

ET squirmed. "Not yet." She thought her last name was something like Smith or Jones. Most names paired well with those. Abscess Smith, Rejectamenta Jones. Those things developed without your knowledge, why should an infant be any different?

Maybe I dreamed you.

LC piped up that in another life she had thirty-two brothers and sisters, not counting her. This was in the trailer compound, out in the desert. She listed their names. "Dovie, Helena, Alana— And you." Maybe now ET would learn LC's real name.

But she wouldn't, not today. LC nodded. "And me."

The old woman snickered. "Imagine calling everyone in for dinner. Or saying all that five times fast."

Thinking she meant it, LC took a breath. "Dovie, Helena—"

In Spanish, to give birth was to give a child to the light. ET thought about that and filled, if only by an inch. When you were full, or when you were in love, or when you were ecstatic, the logic of things went out the window. ET could hear Reason, squatting in the corner of her brain that told her true things, even when she was empty, that fire burned, water was wet, two and two made four, to drink when thirsty, eat when hungry, the sky was blue and the Nile was the world's longest river.

Reason said, "You have not been intimate with a man."

And this was true. Weren't there women who had phantom pregnancies, the way amputees had phantom limbs? You knew it wasn't there, but you did what you would normally do if it were, don't drink, take a step.

Reason said, "Just relax. Some things are impossible."

It was difficult to hear Reason when she was filling. Holly noticed it, too, and cooed, no louder than she had before, though to ET, hers rose from the other voices in the room, so much so she might have shouted. Reason rolled its eyes and went to do a crossword. "All right. Blessed art thou among women, if that's what you want to hear."

ET didn't know if she said it aloud or not, but she said to Reason, "It's not about what I want to hear. Or what I want. It just is."

"Assess things. Really look at it and say, does this make sense?" Reason sounded very like the nurse who told her she should let a rose be a rose. The nurse had liked crosswords, too. She wasn't a mean person, quite a jolly woman, actually, who played Scrabble with the patients and had a tattoo of a rosebud on the inside of her wrist. Once ET asked her what the tattoo meant. The nurse had said it was for her birth month, which was June, adding that in the language of flowers it meant a return to happiness.

ET sniffed at Reason. "So much for letting a rose just be a rose."

She looked to her belly, which, with her t-shirt lifted, was red and rounded. Like the hymn: *Lo, how a rose e'er blooming* . . . Might she learn to like it, after all?

Holly's visitors shuffled in and out of the kitchen, filling plates, taking empty ones, getting more for those who wanted more, nap-kins, cups of tea, boxes of Nilla wafers Rosemary forgot she'd had. "When did I get those? They're not even past the best-before date." They took turns kneeling to spoon-feed Holly, wipe her lips, her chin. She seemed to know how to chew, but had to think out each separate mechanism before going to work on the food. The understanding was that food was necessary, if possibly dangerous. You had to know how to get around its tricks. ET knew that, LC knew it, too. AJ, not as much, though he did avoid all Subway items after finding a shard of glass in his sandwich. But that wasn't it. It was how food curdled once it went past your lips, breaking into bits that were never as small, never as soft as you thought they were. A child's windpipe is said to be the size of a straw. An adult's, not much bigger. ET had seen more people die of choking than anything else. It was how LC had died, in another life. "Do you know what I choked on? Guess. On a bottlecap, like Tennessee Williams."

"What were you doing with a bottlecap in your mouth?" AJ had asked.

"Likely the same thing you do when you chew on your nails." And for a while, AJ did kick that habit.

Holly's visitors closed the evening with a blessing. One by one, they linked hands from wherever they were in the house. They did not form a circle, but a long, winding loop that went from the sitting room to the landing on the stairs. LC recalled having done something like this before, though all was said and done before the meal, as well as aft; hers was a singsong that went, "Hallu-hallu-hallu-hallelujah, praise Ye the Lord!" all around rows of long tables, kids divvied up by age, the oldest boy seated with the two fathers and seven mothers. Here in Rosemary's house, there was no hymn. Instead, they sang a collection of Holly's favorite songs, though ET wanted to know how any of them knew they were Holly's favorites. A lot of Joni Mitchell, "Both Sides Now," "The Circle Game," "Big Yellow Taxi." Some Raffi, too, "Baby Beluga," "Oats and Beans and Barley." Holly liked it well enough, waving her hands until they let her go to clap.

The only one who didn't know any of the songs was AJ, for he'd been groomed for the orchestra. Now and then, he would hear a snippet of something, an arpeggio, a swell, that he'd been trained on, put on repeat and spliced into something modern. He never knew Pet Shop Boys, but he did know Pachelbel's Canon. And it was rare, but it happened: in an idle moment, even when he thought he had emptied for a day or even for good, he would catch a chord, very faint, as though it were being played in another room and he had to press his ear to the wall to hear it. It was the only time a thought had ever become a thing, and ET and LC both admired and envied him for it.

Some folks at the hospital heard voices, muffled congregations that narrated their days, or critiqued them, just over their heads, over their shoulders, never quite descending. "Have they told you to do anything?" the nurse might ask, also, parenthetically, *Are you a danger to yourself and others?* One patient said they were never frightening, but could be a bother when he was trying to watch TV. "I sit down to catch *That '70s Show*, and they tell me when I can expect the laugh track. You tell me let a rose be a rose. I want to tell them let a joke be a joke. Sometimes you just want to veg out." Another liked the company; she was a woman who had previously lived alone, but was rather shy. "It's like going to a restaurant and having all the chitchat around you. You can interact or not."

About AJ, though, the nurse was curious. She knew who he had been, and asked if he had ever tried to make compositions out of what he heard. That was the thing. The music was never persistent. It never interrupted. It might be years between two chords. He wondered at what it might sound like if he were to take them all and transcribe them and play them. The hospital had had a piano and a guitar; everywhere you went, it seemed, there was a piano and a guitar. He had his suspicions that, come together, it would play out like the warped banging a kid would make if left alone with any instrument. That alone ought to have discouraged him, but it didn't. He was forever chasing it, ears open for the swell from that next room.

Holly looked at him and laughed. "HA."

ONCE, WHEN ET was a kid, a stranger came into the house. It was not a break-in; how could it be, if the fellow had come up the walk and through the door as though by invitation? Her mother was at home, but in the backyard. ET had been the one to greet him, as it were. He might have been a vagrant. He did not smell fresh and he wore his clothes in layers. She tried to recollect clues as to what else he was, for no one was ever just a vagrant. Was he tattooed? Did he wear any decorative pins with slogans, *I Love Jesus But I Cuss a Little*, *I'm So Poor I Can't Pay Attention?* He did have one, she remembered, on his collar that said, *Your design here.*

She watched from the stairs as he let himself in, following him a few feet behind as he poked around, went into the kitchen to help himself to a banana, a snack bag of Doritos, other things from the pantry, slipping them into his knapsack. But then he went into his coat pockets, coming out with things that shone. In place of the missing banana, the chips, and everything else, he left treasures: a gold ring set with an opal, a seashell, a blue cigarette lighter, a rosary with turquoise beads.

He must have sensed she was there because he did not turn around to address her. "The lighter belonged to Blind Owl Wilson. That'll buy you a week's groceries."

She remembered asking, "Who's Blind Owl Wilson?"

The fellow turned then. He had a gap between his front tooth and canine on top. "You mean, *Who-ooo's* Blind Owl Wilson?" he hooted.

Her mother came in as he was going out, her through the back, him through the front. She saw his coattails as the door swung shut. She asked ET if she had let him in. ET told her she had not. She asked ET if he had tried to do anything. "To you," she added. ET told her he had not.

"He took a banana."

ET's mother nodded. "Was that all?"

"Some chips, some cans of soup—"

"So, nothing of value?"

"—some cookies, some peanuts. He paid us for them."

Her mother shook her head, following ET's finger to the counter and finding, not cash, but things that shone. ET told her mother about the lighter. "He said it would buy a week's groceries."

Her mother fingered the rosary, brought the opal close to squint at it like a real jeweler. She claimed they were distant relations of Charles Lewis Tiffany. "*That* Tiffany," she would add. "To know quality when you see it is in our blood." And ET did have an aunt who worked at the jewelry counter at JC Penney's. The light fell to set the colored streaks ablaze, pink, green, blue, gold. It almost didn't look real, like an artifact from a fairytale. ET's mother went on, "So, he just left it here? I wouldn't wonder where he got it from. Likely doing the same thing he did here, helping himself to other people's bananas and family heirlooms. Still. Still, we wouldn't know where to take it back to if we don't know where he got it. It might be interesting to see what it's worth, don't you think? What say we take it somewhere? Get it evaluated."

ET thought of her aunt. "To JC Penney's?"

Her mother scoffed and put the ring in a plastic sandwich bag for safekeeping.

In the end, they brought it to an appraiser, who determined the ring's value to be somewhere between two and three thousand dollars. "Fourteen karat white gold," the appraiser said of the band. "And a solid Boulder opal, floral pattern. From Queensland, Australia, I'm sure. Three-millimeter thickness. I think this'll get you more than groceries. Down payment on a car, if you want."

ET kept the lighter until its fluid ran out and her mother threw it away. The seashell they kept in the bathroom where it anchored the stack of washcloths. The rosary her mother added to her own jewels, wearing it once to a holiday party before it made her break out in a horrible rash. She had been ready to throw that away, too, but it disappeared. "Just as well," she sighed. "Let the angel get an allergic reaction." It was what she called the fellow who had let himself in, following the ring's fortuitous appraisal.

This was also an era in which angels were a big thing. Victoria's Secret introduced its show of angels, Tyra Banks and Stephanie

Seymour in wings and lacy negligees. *Touched by an Angel* and *Wings of Desire*. Those cherubic crystals you could buy in New Age shops. Everyone ET knew at the time seemed to have a plaque or an embroidery sample or framed watercolor of the Psalm, "The angel of the Lord encampeth round them that fear him, and delivereth them."

Encampeth smacked to ET of tents, campfires, clothes worn in layers, footsore, crooked smiles with gaps between front teeth and canines, scruff, odors, vagrancy. Like the hoboes of the Great Depression who followed their own code written by the railroad tracks to warn their brethren of unfriendly policemen, or to point them in the direction of work and a meal. A cross meant "angel food," wherein ministers fed transients after Sunday services.

Where were your wings?

Where were you now?

Maybe it was a week or a month following the opal's appraisal that a neighbor called the police. A man had come into the house. He had not taken anything, nor did that seem to be his mission. As at ET's, he had let himself in, but he did not poke around. He had not even gone as far as the kitchen. The police speculate that he sat and waited, either in the living room or, more likely, on the staircase's bottom step, taking his patience in sips, maddening calm, the way a feral cat stilled itself before pouncing. No one was around but him. The neighbor, come back from an afternoon of shopping, might have been hindered going in, arms full of frozen food and a package of paper towels. But the door had glass insets, intricate, pretty, if not entirely functional, clear enough to catch a dark shape on the other side. She could see its pulsing, raising and lowering a little with each breath, so she knew it was alive and unwelcome. Looking airy, unconcerned, trying not to run, she made it to ET's mother's house, asked to use the phone.

The police said he'd had a knife.

ET never did learn if it was the same man.

IN MY HOUSE, she thought, I should be able to let anyone in, even my enemies. I should forgive. I should foster. I should feed.

My door should be unlocked, closed to the elements, cracked for admittance. My pantry should be well-stocked, my dishes plenty. I should have enough to feed an army of a thousand or just one. I should have space enough for beds, my linens fresh, extras of toothpaste, brushes, soap, Band-Aids, Q-Tips, clippers for hair and nails. Everything should be viewer-ready, as realtors like to say.

I should be passive, as Meister Eckhart said. I should lower gingerbread in a basket from my window for the neighborhood kids, as Emily Dickinson did. I should play the acts of protection and stewardship as I would a game, as Krishna was said to do.

It should be as easy as it sounds.

Very likely, it's why I don't have a house.

IN THE FIRST light, everyone looked blue. LC was the first to wake and the first to rise. Many of Rosemary's guests had left after the meal, but about ten or so remained and spent the night on the floor. LC had slept between ET and AJ, as was their custom. In another life, she had slept this way in a large bed, herself flanked by mother and father, all of them bundled under a single blanket. When she rose in that life to stand at the edge of the mattress and look down at them as if from a great height, they were like bread loaves or burrowed animals, not Brother Sun and Sister Moon. With them asleep, the house was hers.

She stepped over bodies, blue and breathing, then tried to wade through them in between after she stepped on someone's fingers. It was a little like playing I'm Not Touching You or Cross the Lava, inching toward the safety zone. She let out a bellow of air when she reached the hallway.

Rosemary's bedroom was on the bottom floor, shared with Holly. "Most everything upstairs we don't really use. I don't think I've changed the beds up there in—oh, well over a year. At least. It's kind of creepy up there. It's why I told everyone to just camp out down here. No ghosties." Theirs might have been an office at one time, the way the living room had once been a dining room. She hadn't noticed it before, but the library across the hall had been repurposed, too, the shelves for books now filled with canned food and preserves. Now in this small first floor room there were two beds, gauzy curtains on the big bay window. Both asleep, both blue and breathing.

Holly's bed was the closest to the door. LC crept to the edge and knelt. Her eyes shuddered behind their lids, lips twitched, quickened in that other world by the suspension of her earthly limitations. People often dreamt the opposite, horrors that handicapped, teeth falling out, biting off your own tongue, trying to scream and finding your voice had gone, trying to run and finding you are rooted to the ground like a tree. Once, AJ dreamt his leg had detached itself and inched away, bending and straightening like a worm. It was horrible to watch and LC couldn't sleep for the rest of that night, though it was not her dream.

Holly's were glorious, LC was sure, the kind of dreams in which you flew: you grew wings, levitated, or swam through the air as you would through water. LC put her head on the pillow, but did not climb into bed. Would it be like living a memory? Or would it be something new and fantastic?

The result was disappointing. And if another pair of eyes were looking, those of a watcher emptied of light and full of all the wrong things, it would have been truly insulting. Here was everyone Holly knew, everyone who came to see her daily, monthly, some she had seen only once ten years ago. Here was ET and AJ and LC, and she felt very humbled to be included. Everyone looked so silly. There was no other word for it, but there it was. And LC became infected with the humor of it, though it was without bitterness: Did they all really think pretty things could get them the future? Or that a laugh meant anything other than what it was? A laugh at you, instead of for you? You with your goggling eyes and your pawing hands. I am playing a game, not playing the messenger. I am imitating YOU. I haven't decided what parts of people I like best. Maybe one day, I will have gathered this gait, this intonation, this smile, this laugh and I will become what you call a real person, and you might not want to see me anymore. You'd rather baby me and tell me what you think I think. And I don't think I mind it much. How often do you get to live what are truly the best years of your life, over and over, without responsibility, without force, without asperity, without wish?

LC pulled away as Holly was waking. Her big eyes squeezed against the light and then opened, deep green and heavily lashed. She showed LC her teeth. "HA."

Her mother stirred, moaned, raised her head. She looked at LC with neither anger nor surprise. Was it the custom for people to watch her daughter sleep? She asked LC, "Is she wet?"

LC blinked. "How's that?"

Rosemary righted herself, then brought her arms above her head, hands lacing and breaking, reaching for the peak. "Is she wet? Did you check? She might need a new diaper." She craned her head to one shoulder, the other, grunting as she stretched.

LC was a child. She, like ET and AJ, did not know how old she was. Unlike them, she never shifted from that bright space, no matter how full or empty she felt. She did not know how to lie for she could not separate the untruths from the narrative that went, years long, in her head, ever extended and populated with angels and flowers, sylphs and salamanders, dreams that never quite dissipated upon waking. She was Ariel, a cherub, Ondine, Joan of Arc. *When I was a child, I spake as a child, I understood as a child, I thought as a child.* It was feral, yes, but it did not have the kill-or-be-killed sensibility ET claimed it had. Not to LC, anyway. If you believed in something hard enough, for long enough, it came true—only to you, if no one else, and that was enough. Why would you want to put away childish things when sylphs and salamanders protected you from that which you did not want to know or touch or recall?

That's not my job. I'm too little.

LC heard herself say, "I'll get my mom," meaning ET. She did not remember her own mother.

She tripped over bodies until she found ET, who twitched awake and growled. ET liked to sleep in when they weren't out of doors.

"I don't know how to do that," ET snapped to LC's request. "What makes you think I know how to do that?"

LC reminded her it was something she ought to know, soon. "You're getting bigger every minute." And it was true. LC laid a hand on ET's belly, where it was rubbery and warm as a hard-cooked egg. Yesterday, ET looked to be only a few months along. This morning, she looked midway into her second trimester. The "honeymoon phase," they called it; you weren't sick in the mornings, something ET noted gratefully. You have accepted your passenger. The resentment had gone and in its place was your sense of duty, if not love. The creature took form, and yet you might still think it a creature. It had a face and could make faces. It had fingers, it could paw and paddle. But, ET thought, an imp can do those things, too.

It hadn't even kicked yet.

"It will," LC soothed. And her eyes were so big and lovely, her voice so eager, that ET had to believe her, if for a minute. Maybe if the child is like LC, ET thought, it won't be so bad. It might be quite a lot of fun. And she kissed LC's crown.

She felt herself filling and things looked brighter. She took LC's hand to be helped up and led across the hall.

Meanwhile, AJ stirred, yawned. "What is it?" He had slept with half his face mashed into the pillow and he peered at them through red eyes, one shut and the other squinting, like a goblin. ET told him and, like a father to her mother, he nodded, gruff, pushing his blankets aside. LC half expected him to say, "A little less noise, there, a little less noise." If he had slippers, he'd put them on. If there were coffee in Rosemary's house, he'd make it. And if there was a newspaper, he'd settle into a chair to read it. LC giggled.

Instead, he followed the two to Holly's bedside, where Rosemary was already at work. Holly lay upon a towel, long legs lifted and paddling, feet puffy in woolen socks. Her clothes for the day were laid out on a chair, her night shirt and leggings stripped and thrown into a hamper basket. Her old diaper, which was damp, had been removed as well and the new one was not quite out of its package, high on a shelf, forgotten amidst powder and lotion.

Holly's hair was gray there, too.

Rosemary looked up. "Well, there you are," she addressed ET, pulling her forward. "You can give me a hand. I changed her once already, at about four a.m." She pointed to the box of diapers. "Grab one of those."

AJ and LC watched ET for a while, wondering if she would be doing her job the way she did if there had been more of a mess. She was not as stubborn about it as they thought she might be, and, perhaps despite herself, she fell into step behind Rosemary, how much powder, how much lotion, which socks. Through it all, Holly laughed and clapped; ET let her grip her fingers, pretended to bite them, to Holly's delight.

At both ends of life, you are an infant. But Holly was not as old as that. Was it grotesque to need diapers at thirty? At twenty?

AJ remembered reading about the old asylums in Britain, shortly before he came to the hospital. They threw everyone in Bedlam, it seemed, from epileptics to loose women. You could pay a small fee to watch the patients, as you might for a ticket to the circus. The object, like the bearded lady or the pinheads at freak shows, was comedy, and beneath that, gratitude. On the surface, you laughed. These were people who shat themselves and used it for finger paint. They chuckled inappropriately. They drooled. They exposed themselves, played with themselves. They claimed to be Jesus Christ, Krishna, Buddha, Jimmy Hoffa. These were people from the moon, belonging there, not here. The visitors, it was important to note, were not too far from Bedlam themselves, for they threw the poor into these places, too, and it was the poor who came the most, bleeding ten shillings for an afternoon. Beneath the laughter, gauze thin, they gasped, "At least I'm not you."

Would they have thrown Rosemary in, too? The book had quoted William Gregory, Lord Mayor of London, when its medieval transition from place of refuge to place of refuse began: "A Church of Our Lady that is named Bedlam. And in that place be many men that be fallen out of their wit." Of Holly's kind, there had been many, locked in cages, chained to benches, doused with cold water if they made noise, sterilized on civilized soil as well and as often as they would be in Nazi Germany.

AJ peered into their sitting room. He was emptying now,

knowing gray light and chilled air. Snores drifted up from the floor, where Holly's visitors either slept or lay cocooned in their waking before getting up. The kitchen, so bright yesternight, was full of brown shadows, the plates stacked on the counters, the little table, piled with food and bringing flies. From where he stood in the hall, AJ spied a cockroach, shuddered as it crept out from between the bottom row of cabinets, crossed the linoleum floor to wrest a crumb from another, smaller insect, and disappeared into a crack in the wall. He could hear them, beyond the drywall and nibbling through the pink, cotton candy layer of fiberglass, tens, maybe hundreds more, an army of cockroaches marching up and down the frame of this house, scuttling out when plates were left and bread abandoned.

And then for AJ, everything fell into sharp, gray proportion. The place was filled with crazy people. There was no other word for it. Where did any of them get the idea that here, in this old, high, and lonely house, there was something magical to be found? The girl Holly ought to be put somewhere, a hospital, a school, whatever euphemisms they had for the word "institution" these days, a place where she could be looked after. Her mother ought to be jailed. No, no, maybe not that. Her mother, at least, ought to know better. Rather, she ought to HAVE KNOWN better, for under the eye of today's technology, how could she not have known what her daughter would be, once light and air graced her? What were the options? Obliteration or no money and a ghoulish house.

Perhaps it was as simple as this: Holly was the ghoul her mother needed to make their house a haunted one. People visited Notre Dame for both Our Lady and for Quasimodo in his bell tower.

One of the folks on the floor stirred. It was an old man. There were a lot of old people, AJ noted, in hospitals and in churches. In both places, they often looked footsore, having come such a long way, seventy, eighty, ninety years, maybe more, just to come here. "Now," they seemed to say, "I can get some rest before I keep going."

AJ wondered if this old man was one of the ones from his hospital. Here were knotty hands, yellow in his eyes that had been blue, whiskers like hoarfrost. What had the fellow's name been? The nurse had addressed him often enough (using a diminutive of his first name, Bobby, Randy, Ray, or calling him, with goofy, Bobby Vinton affectations, Mis-ter Lone-lee) but, as clothing and toothbrushes and medicines were labeled with patients' initials, AJ could recall nothing but the two stark letters: RL. He stood over the old fellow and said his name.

The fellow rubbed his eyes, opened them. "Well, hey there. Look who it is." And he reached out a hand to shake AJ's. "Birdman." It was his nickname for AJ. RL gave everyone a nickname. LC was Pinky. ET was Milady. The nurse who called him Mister Lonely he called Missus Jones, crooning, *Me and Missus Jones, we got a thing goin on.* "When did they kick you out?"

"I called my father."

AJ was never too proud to use his influence where he could. And his father, a judge, was himself too proud to look anyone in the eye and tell them where his son had been. Now that AJ was out, his father did not want to know where his son had gone. Upon his discharge, he and AJ agreed he would go to his Aunt Dorothy's. AJ did not have an Aunt Dorothy.

RL nodded, chuckled. "Imagine that. I had to wait until they were overcrowding. I bunked with two other boys, did you know that? One of them was picked up in the park, talking to a tree. The other one—this you won't believe—the other one had a real adventure. He broke into his mother's house and with his bare hands—no he didn't kill her, just her parakeets—he killed her parakeets, five of them, he strangled them with his bare hands. Then he stole her car. Then he broke into a pizza place, through the basement, and was living down there for close to a month. The guy who owned the pizza place said they probably wouldn't have known he was there if they hadn't noticed their desserts running low in the coolers. They always seemed to be out of cheesecake, the pizza guy said. And I don't blame our boy. Who doesn't love a good cheesecake? He'd be in jail right now, if it weren't for his mother, who knows people." He whistled, then made a trumpet sound with his lips, three brassy *brrrp-brrrp-brrrps*. "Everybody's got a story. It's like going to camp." He paused, looked sidelong at AJ. "But you got to miss out on all that excitement."

At the hospital, AJ had had a private room, courtesy again of his father. And, save for the empty Girl Scout cabin, he had never been to camp, either.

From across the hall, fanfare and cheer and a small procession. At the head, LC playing the court jester, wearing a winter cap snatched from the hat stand with a long tail and a bell at the end. Next, Rosemary, the queen regent, bearing dead flowers from the bedroom. And bringing up the rear, the queen herself, Holly on all fours, carrying herself with slow grace, attended by her handmaiden. ET walked behind, taking careful steps, but speeding up enough and pretending to catch Holly between her legs. "I got you. I GOT you."

RL played the adoring serf, all simper and submission, questions to the queen about her comfort: Had she had any pleasant dreams? Was she up and at em, ready for breakfast? Her mother confirmed Holly was hungry and led her into the kitchen with ET. Some of the others on the floor were now waking and followed, looking to help. LC, staying behind, confirmed Holly had had pleasant dreams and wanted to tell AJ about them.

She blinked at RL, trying to remember where she had seen that nose or those eyes, in this life or in another, when he called her by his pet name, little Pinky, Pinky Rose, Rosy Pink, Pink Floyd, Pinky and the Brain. When he called her the last one, he bopped her forehead with one finger, intoning, "Pinky and the Brain-Brain-Brain-Brain-Brain." She delighted and cooed, rubbing her face into his hoarfrost as though he were a long-lost granddad.

AJ thought there really ought to be a way for folks from the old ward to greet one another when they met on the outside. A secret handshake? A code word? Mendicants had insignias or differed the cut of their robes so as to distinguish one order from another, Francis from Dominic, Barefoot Carmelite from Barefoot Mercedarian and so on. Gay men of the last century would ask a fellow if he was a friend of Dorothy. And AJ had always liked the sound of that one, the idea of a group, no matter how far flung across the globe, having one friend in common, if only an imaginary one. L. Frank Baum had written in his *Oz* books of Dorothy Gale being questioned about her "queer friends," and her response was something to the effect of, "So long as they're a friend, that's all that matters." And thus, a real-world camaraderie was built.

Maybe, following a similar train of thought, crazy people (being open and malleable to anything until one particular thing hits them, grabs them, and burrows in them like a parasite) do not respond to slogans or symbols as most people know them to. AJ took up the guitar and sat in the middle of the floor, the room now empty. Maybe, he went on (and he did not know if he was talking or thinking), it was that one particular thing in whatever form it showed itself. RL's nicknames felt right and they would feel right if AJ were pronounced well and competent by a full board of doctors, and he was sure he could speak for ET and LC, even the nurse also known as Mrs. Jones. He felt himself filling. He toyed with the strings, remembering tones but none of the notations.

"Take Five." "Dr. Gradus ad Parnassum."

The cycle started; he could hear ET moan "Not again" from the kitchen. But it kept him keen. He could see the pattern. There was a point to this, the nicknames, wandering, looseness and absorption and disconnect.

Was LC Pinky because she was like the rosy-fingered dawn, as Homer described Eos? Because she saw the world through rose-colored glasses? Was ET Milady because her birthday was March the twenty-fifth (how RL knew that was a mystery, but he'd conjured up a bunch of balloons and a package of Hostess cupcakes on the day), also known as the Feast of the Annunciation, also known as Lady Day? AJ thought he heard RL singing somewhere, "Lady day could use some dreams, some flowers . . ." and catching the thought. And what was AJ, also known (to RL, anyway) as Birdman? A thunderbird? An angel? LC had had a dream in which she saw a pair of wings growing out of his back.

He started when he felt the tips of rosy fingers tap at his back.

LC, at once a baby and a crone, traced the outline of two pinions, round at the top, over his shoulder blades, and jagged at the bottom, zig-zagging toward the base of his spine. He put the old guitar aside and kept still. Anyone else (anyone not in the grip, not touched) would be annoyed by her. There were no personal bubbles or sensible space. If LC wanted to hug you, she did. If she wanted to braid your hair, she would. It was best to let her do it; she would be very hurt, otherwise. RL came in from the kitchen, munching toast with jam, raspberry in his beard. LC had already put his mane into plaited ropes, giving him the look of an old wizard. He sat with LC behind AJ and, whispering to her, then bet AJ he could not guess what he and LC were playing.

"I probably couldn't," he said, wondering who he was humoring more.

Emptying, Reason whispered in his ear, reminding him it had been awhile since he'd played anything save for his cycle. Reason added, "Crazy is doing the same thing over and over and expecting different results."

LC stretched her fingers and shook her head. "Don't listen." Reason had long since given up on her, but still she feared, like one who has been exorcised, that the demon might come back.

Then on AJ's back she tapped. He tried to find the rhythm, hear the melody. LC said in another life she had played this game a lot, with her sister in their shared bed in a cabin in the mountains. Emptying, AJ wanted to ask if today she was Laura Ingalls Wilder or Heidi. He wanted to ask, "What about this life? The one you're in right now?" But he did not want to make her cry. Instead, he guessed. The code was an easy one, "Oh My Darling, Clementine." The next one also easy, "Yellow Submarine."

You were lost and gone forever.

We all live in a yellow submarine.

The next was more of a flurry, almost more tickling than tapping. "I'll give you a hint," LC said. "Shakespeare." Tap-tap-tap-taptap-tap-tap-tap. Then she sang, "With a hey and a ho and a nonny no." Then, "In the springtime, the only pretty ringtime," lingering on the last word.

He shook his head. "I don't know that one." He had an idea he'd heard it somewhere, in an old movie with a scene in an asylum, a lunatic cracking his skull against a wall and falling back onto his straw mattress. The next line came to him, "When birds do sing, hey ding-a-ding-ding . . ." AJ did not remember his father's name, but he did remember how his father had sorrowed "My baby, my boy" as though AJ was dead.

I did not ask to be filled.

On the day of his committal, AJ pointed to a passage in his King James, *Know ye not that ye are the temple of God, and that the Spirit of God dwelleth in you?* To that, his father said he wished he'd never put a Bible in AJ's hands if he'd known his son's mind would twist the way it had. If he'd given AJ a copy of L. Ron Hubbard's *Dianetics*, it would be no different, he would be sitting there talking about being filled up with aliens. He countered AJ with another verse, *Believe not every spirit.* "So, think about that," he added, and left.

The Apostle Paul had said we see through a glass darkly. Everyone knew that verse and knew what it meant, but no one knew what to make of it when they saw someone do it.

It differed from being full, which was really just another way of talking about euphoria, that crystalline certainty of joining your happiness with him and her and them. *Somehow, in spite of trouble, ours will be ever lasting love.* You felt it in evangelism. You felt it in a cult. You felt it when you watched *Titanic* in a crowded theater, or at Woodstock. Out in the world, you couldn't deny it looked a little strange; your eyes were dilated and huge, you loitered, you wanted the fellow next to you to have a portion of what you had and so you stared at him and then you touched him. Many a mystic has had the cops called on them. "I don't think she's dangerous," the 7-11 clerk breathes into the phone, "just—not all there. And she won't leave." Maybe there had to be a flock of you for it to work.

It differed from being full, in that it was something you could see, momentary, a blink and you might miss it, which you never did because how could you? It was too bright and clear, like refracted light through a prism, a flash of violet. LC, who never doubted, told AJ once that she had seen what he had seen. Not believing, he said, very blunt, "All right, what did I see?" He had no reason to speak to her so, for she was not cunning. If ET was a mother at heart, LC was a baby, absorbing all. She had seen AJ's mouth drop, had seen him blink. And had, against everything, seen what he had seen. It hadn't been much, a flash, not of violet alone but of every color lined with gold. It was bright, not clear. "Playing tricks with your eyes," people liked to say. (Had anyone said that to him?) A stoplight, a safety blinker on a cyclist, the glow of a city at night from far away. Let your mind wander and your eyes fog and they could be a demon's eye, a flaming chariot, the aurora.

But even that wasn't right. Not for AJ, at least. He envied LC. Where he saw smear, she saw shape.

She told him, "I saw wings. You have them on your back." Now he knew why RL called him Birdman. LC went on, "You probably saw my tail." Maybe that was why RL called her Pinky:

They're Pinky and the Brain
Yes, Pinky and the Brain
One is a genius
The other's insane

To know there was something about you that was extraordinary, beyond anything mortal—that was what AJ wanted to believe. LC believed it, and he wondered if that made all the difference. More than that, he wondered if she knew it to be true, and if her mind was, in fact, the clearest of anyone's, seeing what others couldn't, frankly and not in glimpses.

RL came in then, whistling through his teeth, his arm linked with ET's like a royal escort to a queen. There you had it, AJ thought. ET's belly was rounded and full (not with a food baby, as the nurse had liked to call her own gut following a big lunch), drum tight. When you held your hands to it, as LC had, you were warmed. Still, like Doubting Thomas, it was not enough. He asked ET if he could feel the baby kick.

And suddenly, it was as though he had asked to reach inside her so he may rip the child from her. ET swallowed, saw red and then watched it fade. Mother Bear vigilance (or general, though fierce, possession) led her hands over her belly, lacing the fingers. "No."

AJ, taken aback. "No?"

ET, stone. "NO."

AJ, like Peter. "Then, how do I know it's there? That she's there?" This last was for ET's glare. "How do I know it's not your gut?"

ET, like Magdalene. "You don't get fat on canned tuna and then brown rice and squash. Not overnight. What else would it be?"

What else would it be, if not a baby? The question echoed and completed and AJ heard it, and so did LC. And so did RL, who said, "It happens, you know." He brought up stories from tabloids, for he could not always distinguish between sensation and substance. A woman in Florida (always in Florida), after taking too many fertility treatments, had only to share the bed with her husband before conceiving. "She had triplets," RL pronounced. And another woman (also in Florida) gave birth to a healthy baby boy years after her last coupling with her late husband. Stomach pains brought her to the hospital, where they were ready to diagnose an ovarian cyst. But an ultrasound caught a heartbeat. "And," RL emphasized, "she was sixty-eight years old."

THERE WAS A ruckus in the flowerbeds that no one heard. There were peeping eyes through the window that no one saw. A stranger had made camp outside Rosemary's house and no one knew it.

He was not a man and would never be tall. He would never be a man either, but no one knew that. He was four-foot-two, thirteen years old, though he looked closer to nine. Like those inside, he wore his clothes in layers, the extras in a knapsack on his shoulder. His hair would be ringleted when it grew; it was easier, meanwhile, to keep it sheared. His name was Enda Michael Martindale, but he hated it, first, middle, and last. He hated it because his father used his first, middle, and last names when he was in hot water.

His brothers and two of his sisters had ugly names for when they were in hot water, *You creature* or *You reprobate*. They ought to have considered themselves lucky, Enda thought, for their given names were all for themselves.

When he left home, he waited until he was a good distance from the Martindale property before shouting into gauzy morning, "ENDA, the BEGINNING. MICHAEL, the MIDDLE. MARTINDALE, the FUCKING END." His father was also Enda Michael Martindale. Maybe the senior Enda would rename one of the other boys in the house. Or have a new baby and christen him thusly.

Since leaving, he'd been thinking of what he ought to call himself now.

His father had had a vast library on nearly every subject, from plague to the rise and fall of the House of Plantagenet. There was poetry, too, Hopkins, Blake, Wordsworth, Keats. For all its leaves, the library left Enda the Younger somewhat stupid. He'd been told to apply what he'd read to what he saw in the world, to know society was a vicious cycle, ever winding, all consuming, an ouroboros that would hunger for its own tail and choke on it. Only a few, the poets and mystics, could see their way through the muck, the sun that fell upon them and cast a shadow, and they remembered themselves. To Enda the Younger, it sounded no different than the ouroboros. Beautiful words, yes, but weren't they all just talking to themselves?

The Martindale family lived on three hundred acres of land, wound all around in a fence and shrouded by cedars. It was a hike from the main road to the front door if you made it past the gate. Enda's older brothers guarded the front when they weren't working the land. They had men come in from town to bring supplies and to take their wool and beef and eggs and vegetables to be sold. There was no need to leave and no one did.

Enda had only seen two cars in his life. His house had electricity, though he had never seen a stoplight or streetlamps or the blue glow from the inside of the houses along the road. He stopped and, drawn to it, he moved toward a picture window to get a good look.

Evil, the new pagan shrine. "Just as there is cancer of the brain as an organ, there is cancer of intellect," his father had declared. At last, here it was: Television.

And it did have a place of honor, in the living room, mounted over the fireplace. A man and a woman watched as they ate from plates in their laps. Enda started when the dog, a huffy old basset, spotted him and barked. But no one looked up. Enda began to wonder if the people were dead, when the man grunted, presumably at the basset, "Higby, go lie down." And like that, the dog did, looking to the screen with master and mistress. Outside, Enda came close enough to see what everyone was watching and, lured, made himself comfortable in the grass, propped against his knapsack. Funnily enough, it was a program about a dog. It was supposed to be a bloodthirsty mongrel, though Enda thought it looked a bit like the basset Higby, drooping eyes and wet jowls, more a teddy bear than a monster. As a remedy, the movie closed in a lot on its teeth. It spent most of the time circling a woman in a car, charging at her when she tried to crack open the door.

Enda felt he must have been watching it wrong because he found himself rooting for the dog. He was upset the people in the movie won in the end, shooting the dog, though it was mad. The woman, he thought, deserved to be the one shot, though the movie did not show any evidence for it. Who could hurt a dog?

Inside the house, the people wedged deeper into their chairs and channel surfed for a while. They set their empty plates on the floor for Higby, who lapped them clean, fixing his paw to the plate's edge so it wouldn't slip. Enda watched them watch other programs in fragmentation. Because he was still a kid, he could put together which show was which very quickly. *South Park*, Kenny gets killed. *That '70s Show*, the gang gets high. *Jane the Virgin*, Jane gets pregnant. *The Golden Girls*, the girls get cheesecake. Now and then, the people huffed, didn't quite laugh. Higby, full and flatulent, was banished ("Jee-zus, Higby. Nasty old thing. King, call him, put him in the bedroom.") and the overhead fan turned on. It wasn't much longer before the man and the woman succumbed, sinking deeper into their places on the couch and recliner until they were more or less absorbed, one arm or foot to suggest the furniture's new, twitching extensions. The recliner grunted, the couch snored. The TV went on. *Law & Order*, the squad gets the bad guy.

Enda thought it so loudly he might have said it. I WONDER WHAT THEY WOULD DO IF I—

A life lived under a great and awesome eye had not prepared him for everything freedom had to offer. Enda the Elder believed in one God whose facets peeled off into smaller, lesser gods that regulated the water, the storms, the sun, the land, the hearth. They were Jove, Juno, Neptune, Vesta, Diana, Minerva, Bacchus, from the epics his father believed never quite died with the Resurrection and the Life. His father's God, Enda thought, must be an orange. He didn't know how else the Commandment of having no other gods jived with his father's vision. But now he had left his father's garden and was out in the world and was beginning to understand the meaning of having a kingdom within. This was not the kingdom of God, where nothing was yours and everything fixed, a cold manor house where you lived like a guest who had overstayed his welcome. But this was the interior castle. This was Summerland; Enda had been good in his old life and he had come to a place in which he could do anything he wanted.

I WONDER WHAT THEY WOULD DO IF I—

He could make chaos.

He found a rock in the front flowerbeds, tearing petals, and hurled it through the picture window. He did not stay to watch the aftermath (people waking, Higby braying, the planes of the dream world and this one merging, then snapping). He stopped to breathe, having run far enough to hide in the dark, but not so far he could not still see the glass, fragmented, diamondlike, gathering toward the center, a bit of begonia sunburst dripping from the hole. He was at the top of a small hill, but its slope gave him the view of a great mountaineer, taking the summit. He saw a light in the dark, the beam of a flashlight flickering across the yard below.

The man from the house was prowling, trying to think how he thought a vandal ought to think, padding on the softest feet, one-two-three, and FOUR, leaping forward and throwing the light into the woods, at the birdfeeder, at Our Lady, Untier of Knots, sweet and concrete, looking at the man as though she had been the one to throw the light on him. The cord in her hands might have been yarn, her fingers defter than knitting needles. Imagine her as someone's mother, Jesus an errant teenager, sneaking in after a night of toking in the woods with John the Baptist, blinking as the kitchen lights turn on, Mary at the table, making a scarf. *And where the hell have YOU been?*

Enda didn't know who his mother was. It seemed as though he had never needed to know. His father had had many wives, dead or dismissed. The current wife was twenty-one. His father was nearly sixty. She would have another baby, another boy, and call him Enda, to replace the one who was on the top of a hill.

He ducked into the grass, throwing his knapsack in front in case he needed a shield. Below, the man went around the yard twice more, then plodded back to inside. He stood, peering out, and there was a moment in which he turned in the direction of the hill, just beyond the property line. He might have seen Enda, for the line between their pairs of eyes was straight and narrow. Enda froze, tormented now by the urge to pee. The man moved to close the door, but not before shouting, "I'M CALLING THE COPS."

Enda, too afraid, did not move. He thought of the things his father liked to say, and it seemed now they might have been coined with him in mind, scribes waiting for a miscreant with green eyes and curling hair who was small and smelly and belonged under a rock. *Fools' names and fools' faces always appear in public places. The dog always returns to his vomit. If you piss in the wind, it'll surely come back at you.* He knew nothing of the police. He knew of prison, of penance, of punishment. If caught (when caught), he would be the smallest of any man condemned. From the men who came in from town, he'd heard about prison bitches, how the bigger fellows would find new places in him to violate. He'd rather get Old Sparky. But he would go quietly. Better to face it like a man than to go kicking and screaming. He did not believe in hell, though he would not have objected if the ground were to open from under him. Weren't we all walking above Gehenna as though it were below a rotten covering, as Jonathan Edwards had said?

Enda waited an hour, then two. The lights in the house went off, one by one. Higby went quiet. No cars on the road, no paddy wagons up the driveway. Boldened, he rose and stood to pee and went down the hill. He crept to the front door. He turned the knob, laughing, breathless. In spite of everything, the house was unlocked.

It was cool, nearly more so than the outdoors, which was dewy. He stepped in, guiding the door into place and fixing it without a sound. The dimensions of the house, now that it was dark, were made larger by the coolness, like the rising vaults and naves in a cathedral. Enda had never been inside a cathedral, just as he had never been inside another person's house. His own, the old one, the one he left, did not have air conditioning. Here, it was the flat chill of fall, though it was late summer. It had not occurred to him how hot he'd been, how much he'd sweated, for his layered clothes grew heavy with old perspiration and stuck to him in patches. He picked at his first layer, a sweatshirt, just enough to pull the soggy cotton away from his navel, his underarm. He smelled of meat and urine.

He had not thought of Higby, had forgotten him entirely, and was as surprised as the dog himself when they came to face each other. No terrible shock, no readying to pounce. There they were, unexpected, but not out of place, as the act of taking flight in a dream can be. In point of fact, Higby had just woken. He smelled Enda before his eyes opened; in his dream, he'd been eating from the carcass of a great elk. He looked at the boy in his house and wondered where the elk had gone. Then, sobering, he remembered his duties and growled.

Enda knew what to do. The domesticated dog, his father claimed, was mankind's best invention, next to soap. And Enda knew this to be true. When you'd bred all the wild out of them, all that was left was the greatest devotion. Where else were you going to find a being that would love you in spite of dry food twice a day and being made to sleep out of doors? All they wanted in return was a pat on the rump. Enda wasn't about to do that, not right away, for Higby was not his dog. Higby had fealty, and Enda knew about that, too. Instead, he held out his hand and the basset sniffed and all was well, no enemies here.

Higby was loyal, if a bit too trusting. His master and mistress did not know this was hardly the first intruder the house had seen after dark. A fellow crept in, paused to whisper "Good boy" to Higby, and went into the bathroom, making off into the two a.m. chill with a tube of toothpaste and a bag of the mistress's disposable razors. He'd fed Higby well from his sack, half a Whopper, and was gone. No one seemed bothered about the missing toothpaste. The mistress seemed pleased at what had been left in its place, a pair of pearl earrings glinting like bright teeth. The mistress seemed to think the master had bought them for her and hadn't wanted to make a fuss about it, and she respected that, though she put extra bacon on his plate and petted him a lot. Higby felt a little sly and a little proud knowing the truth, and if he could have told them, he wouldn't have, for the mistress put bacon on his plate, too, when he'd done with his dry food. He liked it when the house had visitors. He felt as though the place were truly his own, and fell into a comfort at playing host, admitting whom he chose. The master and mistress were abed. Higby was lord of the manor.

He followed Enda as the boy explored, both moving quietly from hallway to kitchen, sometimes leading him onward to show him the refrigerator, the pantry, the fruit bowl on the counter. Enda was thankful to his host and knew to wait until Higby had begun to eat before he did. He brought the basset all manner of things from the fridge, portions of leftover meat, wedges of cheese, and tuna fish from the cupboards. He knew also to serve his host when needed and held the tuna cans to Higby's snout so the basset would not have to stoop.

Higby then led him into the big room, where the television was kept, and the two watched until Enda noted the graying light on the horizon. It was a modest house, Enda guessed, though its cushioned chairs, its stocked pantry, its TV that offered panoramic views of places he had never been suggested great luxury. Before, he had never seen a movie. Now he had watched *The Wizard of Oz* all the way through, and *Back to the Future*, *Independence Day*, and *Goodfellas* in fragments.

On one of the channels that seemed to wait for midnight, there was a Divine marathon. Divine, he found, did not at all mean what he thought it would. He gleaned, through the fiendish eye makeup and grapefruit bosom, that Divine was the stage name of Harris Glenn Milstead, an actor and comedian who specialized in female characters, all of whom written for him, all of whom also called Divine. Out of costume, Milstead was paunchy, balding, a pout and a wince, not much to look at. The marathon segued into three films from early in his career, and a great blossoming had occurred. A blonde wig, a ghastly red gown, gold lipstick and life in a battered pink trailer amongst the Filthiest People Alive. They ate dog shit and mothers blew their sons and they convicted their enemies of Assholeism and declared, "I AM God!" Of course, these were movies. But he had seen enough of them by now to know you have to get the idea from somewhere.

He mimicked her, trying for brassiness in a whisper. "*This is a direct attack on my divinity! Filth is my politics; filth is my life!*" He was uncertain about the getup, the gown, the wigs, the padding, and quickly decided these were not things he wanted for himself. But how he adored the brass, this brave new world that had such people in it. If only you were my mother and my father, Lady Divine. I would honor you until my last breath, my last sigh. Then would my mouth be filled with laughter. "*It was you that I burn for, and it is you that I will die for. Please remember, I love every fucking one of you.*"

In between films, he caught snippets of shows, some he had seen earlier through the picture window and some new ones. He liked *Aqua Teen Hunger Force* best, though it came on at two in the morning and he had to force himself awake for all of it. He buried his face into Higby's ear, inhaled. "Smelly old thing," he murmured.

It was a Saturday. Enda counted on his fingers from the day he left: Wednesday, Thursday, Friday, Saturday. Higby listened for the master and mistress, though he knew they would not stir until the sky had fully brightened. Outside, it was pink, still shadowy in the west. Enda determined, as did the basset, that now was the best time to go. The boy fiddled with the remotes until he hit upon the one that turned the television off. Saturday morning cartoons were beginning their first cycle. He would have liked to stay for it. Nevertheless, he was resolute and began to fill his knapsack with provisions from the kitchen. Higby watched, drooping eyes belying sharpness. He would not let the boy leave until he had paid.

"I don't have anything," Enda said. He'd given Higby ham from the fridge, leftover steak. Higby did not want it, pawing and huffing at his bag.

Before leaving, Enda had gone into his father's study, where a safe as big as two or three of him was kept. The code to it was his own birthday, May the first, five turns to the right and stop at five, one turn to the left and stop at one. He and Enda the Elder were the only ones in the house who knew it. (He did not know what Enda the Elder's birthday was; he assumed it was also May the first, when it was really spring and the world began.) He'd expected to find treasure; he'd assumed, the way he'd assumed he and his father shared a birthday, that the Martindale family was vastly rich, and that even a bank would not be able (or trustworthy enough) to contain it. Instead, he found boxes of bullets, enough rounds for every gun in the house to last at least five years; he found medicines, dark bottles that read, *Secobarbital*, *Amobarbital*, *Percocet*, *Vicodin*, 100 mg, 80 mg, 325 mg. He'd had to dig to find anything of value, and at last, he did: a small box, marble carved, its lid shaped like a sphinx. He'd seen the box before, only once, when his father told him that on the lid it was not a sphinx at all. "It is a daemon." Not the wicked spirit, his father specified, which was the kakodaemon. This was an agathodaemon. "Socrates had one. It looks after its host in all things."

"Like an angel?" asked Enda the Younger.

"They are one and the same," said Enda the Elder.

"Like a genie?" asked Enda the Younger.

"They are one and the same," said Enda the Elder.

"Where did it come from?" asked Enda the Younger.

"Traded, passed from hand to hand until it came to me," said Enda the Elder.

At the time of that conversation, Enda had been very small. It was not until now he'd begun to think a lot of what his father said had been horse hockey. And, having only been in the world for a few days, Enda could see that a lot of it was. He had not been plagued or molested or struck by lightning. But, in spite of the curtain being pulled away, the fog clearing and the sun coming out, he wanted some measure of the dream to persist.

Everyone, he felt, ought to have a daemon.

And so, he went into his knapsack, found the secretmost interior pocket that zipped and buttoned over securely. And he brought out the daemon box. Higby huffed and tapped his forepaws, which were so large and flat that to Enda they looked webbed. The sphinx creature on the lid did almost have the look of a basset hound, long of body, attentive and imperious. All that Higby was missing were his wings.

Enda smiled, lifted the lid, and clapped a hand over his mouth. So, the Martindales had been rich. Enda had never seen money before and could not have said how much there was. But there was enough to pay his host, more than enough.

He took two, then four coins. He did not know a silver dollar from a dime. He showed them to Higby, who yawned and seemed pleased, and placed them where he thought the master and mistress of the house would easily find them, in between the television's remotes. Higby saw him to the door and would go no farther. The basset owed fealty to his house; another stranger may come and may not be admissible.

Sun to the east, and Enda walked toward it.

He would still need to think of what he wanted to be called now. He walked along the lip of the highway, running up into the brush when cars slowed, then, when he knew all that had been in offer were rides, he waved them away. He began to feel his old imperiousness; he was the youngest boy, his father's favorite, for all it meant. He liked being alone, he found, for he could hear himself think. Previously, his mind had been crowded by too much else and it was a rich thing to hear his own voice. He thought he might like to be called Divine. Trying it out on his lips, buzzing consonants, rhyming it. "Divine malign assign bovine feline—" Shouting it into the air, as he had his old names, to see if it would come back to him and stick. It did not; if anyone were to call his name, he was sure, he would pick up his head and run to the sound, like a dog to his master. He consoled himself the old name would wear away, if gradually, letter by letter, dead epidermis, until ENDA had disintegrated and made room for DIVINE.

When he hungered, he found clear places in the brush and ate from his provisions. He shared now and then with swallows and doves that came close enough, feeling like a dryad when they ate from his hand. *Fade far away, dissolve, and quite forget/What thou among the leaves has never known/The weariness, the fever, and the fret*, Keats had said. "Ode to a Nightingale," from his father's library, and Enda the Younger felt a twinge of melancholy.

At home, they had also called him Babe, because he was the youngest boy.

The melancholy crested, then rolled away.

Zeal renewed and he picked himself up and for the next day or two or three, he repeated what he'd done in Higby's house, whether there was a dog to admit him or not. Admittedly, he felt more at ease entering a house if he had a dog's permission. He broke and entered a total of four times.

On the first two occasions, he was patient. He knew to wait, hiding himself in the woods and behind a car across the road until he was sure the people inside were gone. He watched an old woman close the front door behind her and strut two houses down, knock, go in. He watched a couple shepherd their two little girls into the family van, back out, drive away. He saw himself through the egress, unlocked; he was let through by an Airedale. He jimmied a back window, unfastened; he was let through by a mastiff. The dogs followed him, protective of the home, of course, but also a guide, a companion in a dark corridor. The Airedale barked when she saw her mistress coming up the walk, a warning to the stranger, not a homecoming. The mastiff was sad to see him go, watched Enda from the window as the boy faded into the ether.

The third time there was no dog and the men who lived there (four of them, scruffy, all about twenty years of age) were asleep in various parts of the house, one on a couch, another on the floor, as though their journeys to find beds had been too tiring. Stink in the air, green, civetlike, and Enda took it in sips and found himself liking it. It was something of a veil for the boy, too, for when the man on the floor stirred, opened his eyes, he saw Enda and he did not. He turned on his side, moaning, "Don't touch the peanut butter. Don't. Don't do that." Enda took it, among other things from the kitchen. From the daemon box, he left four coins, one for each. It ought to be enough, he determined, for peanut butter.

He wondered if it was true about the daemon box. Enda the Elder had told him the daemon who watched it would replenish its contents when needed. Enda the Younger counted. He had three coins left; his father had also said the holder of the box could determine the value of the coins. He peered into the box and he saw that the coins did not look any different. They might have been worth a man's life each, like fare for the ferryman. They might have been Monopoly money.

He squeezed his eyes shut. The stink from the last house made the edges of things shimmer with unwanted light. It was another morning, and now that the sun was rising, his eyes hurt and his skin twitched. He had not slept much since leaving the old home. When he did, it was where he could, under trees, tucked into bushes, in dozing intervals, in half-hours the way dogs sleep, awake and on guard at a snapping twig.

But it boldened him. It was like this: Here was Enda (Divine wasn't sticking yet, but it would), behind the veil. And on the other side was everything else. So long as Enda remained behind the veil, he could do anything he pleased. Imagine the realization of a life lived without consequence. It was delicious. Now the world shimmered, outlining open doors and windows, casting haloes around things that could be picked from pantries. In time, he might not even need the daemon box. Perhaps he would become a daemon himself, not the kind that could be trapped and

summoned at a magician's whim. But he didn't know of any daemon like that. He could be the first, maybe, and command his own
hoard of daemons.

Enda shivered. He sometimes scared himself with daydreams.

Perhaps that was what gave flesh to things like God and like
daemons. *If you think about things enough*, Enda murmured but not
aloud, *and if enough people listen, they become real. At least to them.*

He yawned. Here was the fourth house, old and white and
green-trimmed. The White Lady might live in a place like that, or
some other ghost. The idea of dropping down and going to sleep
on the curb was tempting, but not an option. Enda had come to
love the risk, the run, the rush; he was absolved each time, he
knew, so long as the daemon box could pay. And this was perhaps
his last excursion. He'd considered meting the coins out, one per
house, so he could potentially try this again thrice more. Too
much, he decided in the end. And this was to be his big haul until
the daemon box refilled itself. His knees creaked, for his sack
bulged with food. He would soon need a wagon. It might be ages
before he'd go hungry again.

He wished he had some sort of virtue to carry with him when
he did these things, even if he was behind a veil, even if there was
no one to see him do anything.

Inside the house were people, on the floor, on big pillows, much
like the third house, though here there was no stink. It smelled of
potpourri, which his father's last wife had liked to make from orris
root and cinnamon and cloves. It smelled of roses here, too, adding a heaviness to the perfume. His eyelids, purpled, weighed eons.
In *The Wizard of Oz* the Wicked Witch of the West cast her spell
over a field of flowers and, cackling, intoned, *"Sleeeeep. Now they'll
sleeeep."* He woke before falling into the windowpane. He envied
those in the house on the floor because they were all asleep. Exhaustion incensed him. He brought his hands to his eyes and
peeled the lids back with his fingers. Moving around to the other
side of the house, he looked in the window of a bedroom, where a
woman lay cooing like a baby in the first gray light.

He had never seen a person who looked as she did and because she was, to him, a freak, he stared. It did not matter if she saw him, too; she was made of putty, pulled into a clownish grin over her birdy bones. What she saw was not real to her, not in the way it was to him. She caught him out of the corner of her eye and made a shuddering, huffing sound, like a chuckle. Was she laughing at him? He pulled a face, tongue out. He might have made an ugly gesture with his fingers, but he didn't when he saw that she was smiling at him for real, mouth springy and curious, and was not all the time frozen in lunacy. She laughed when he touched his tongue to his nose and again, so hard she made no sound at all, when he brought his front teeth out like a gopher's and crossed his eyes.

He had been a baby once, too. It was hard to remember, growing impossible as the years went by. Imagine the rest of you growing, but not the stuff inside. Every day to the freak in the bed must not be days at all; it must be one eternity, sunup, sundown, hours as moments, the way time must be to a god. Enda Martindale did not know a day in which he did not walk, talk, see to his own toilet, read to himself (sometimes aloud, sometimes not), name things and people and places and have an authority in knowing this was a dog, that was his father, and there was his house.

The worst of knowing all that was knowing that once you'd left the dog, father, and house, you could not go back to them.

He knew that some houses, if any were like his own, had storm cellars. Higby's houses had had one and Dorothy Gale had had one in *The Wizard of Oz*. He went around to the backyard, which was not much more than a little eighth-acre patch between this yard and the next, with not even a fence to separate. He looked out at it, feeling a little proud. His old home had been a true homestead, the nearest neighbor two miles away, a winding path that led the Martindales to the kitchen garden, the smokehouse, the above-ground root cellar, the half-acre vineyard from which they made their own vintage from black muscadine, the barn and its stables, horses and mules and a bobcat they had domesticated and called Furfur and who caught and killed the mice that ate the feed, the patch of nubby cacti the children and the wives were never to touch because his father grew them and could see the gods in all their multitudes when he ate from them. By comparison, this yard was a crumb. It was barely enough for the cellar door that stood out against the house like a hump. The grass was knee-high and Enda waded through to pull it open.

He had a flashlight and shone it into the mildew. A bare dirt floor like the one at the old home—but nothing else. Again, the old pride for the old home, where the cellar was stocked with MREs and batteries and packaged foods he was otherwise never allowed to eat and jars of preserved beans, tomatoes, carrots, beets, squash and jams from their own berries. Enda the Elder had been right, at least in one thing: No one else would be as prepared as they for End Times. But no one else seemed to worry about End Times the way they did. Not in this house, nor in the others. In this house, the cellar had no shelves, no blankets, no extras. Did these people live from day-to-day? Enda the Younger thought at how freeing that must be, if a little too lax. This cellar door hadn't even been locked. The one at the old home had a chain and a padlock and his father kept the keys at his waist like a lord. They added new supplies at the end of each week.

Enda sighed and saw his breath, steam rising and smelling musty. Day-to-day stuck to his brain, growing warm and easy until he had the idea it must be like absolution: A day ends, so another begins, the old erased. His father believed the gods' memory was collective and long. His father believed in gods, as above so below, the virtues, the vices, the sacrificial meat, never knowing whom he had angered, whom he had pleased. In his father's house, there was no absolution. You kept the gods' temper at bay, just as you kept Enda the Elder's, until the day it all became too much and the earth was consumed by fire and the ones who were left (the smart ones, the ones who knew to prepare) would begin a world anew and the gods would reveal themselves at last and all would be right.

It made Enda tired. He hated the idea of a new world because it didn't sound any different from the one he lived in. There was always a catch. Asking his father about the new world one day, when his brothers and sisters worked outdoors and he was studying, Enda the Elder said, "You'll watch your step as you always did. Now more so, for the gods can see you and you them." Enda the Younger sighed, must rising. Living in a world of tattletales, walking the straight and narrow, keeping your head down, only now it was Pan who set him up for trouble and Jove who came to slap his wrist. Too much horse hockey and the whole heavenly body would gang up on him and eliminate all trace of this incarnation of Enda the Younger, not a footprint left, and Enda the Elder would have to make a new prodigy.

One day, Enda's brother took him aside and whispered, "Dad's batshit. You know that, don't you?"

Upstairs in the bedroom came cooing from one baby. Downstairs in the cellar came weeping from another. Enda, the Younger, the Babe, wept without noise, holding his breath, letting it out like steam, licking tears and runners. No noise, but he could hear his heart and see the pulse, a rhythm that went, *I want to go home I want to go home I want to go home.*

LC WAS NOT allowed to be around children. This was the key term of her discharge.

Upon her release, she could not live within one thousand feet of a school, playground, a public park, or any kind of community center. She could not obtain employment that would bring her into a private residence, such as that of a delivery person. She could not consume alcohol. She could not travel unaccompanied after nine o'clock in the evening. She could not have contact with any minor under the age of sixteen.

Upon her release, she would register her whereabouts with the local authorities. She would take a periodic polygraph under the supervision of said local authorities. (The hospital argued the latter was unnecessary, as LC had been declared incompetent, but this was overruled.) She would disclose to her future employers and roommates of her status. And she would keep regular appointments with her doctor.

"I think I can do all that," she said and gave the hospital the address of her Aunt Dorothy. LC did not have an Aunt Dorothy.

To be clear, the hospital prefaced, LC was not a predator. She was not a deviant, nor a pervert. She was not cunning, nor was she malicious. It was on these grounds that, for the murder of her children, a court of law assigned her care to a state-run institution for the insane.

She remembered there were seven children, five girls and two boys. There were other children, too, older ones, with some her own age. They did not call her Mother because she was not their mother. Only the seven youngest did, chirping from her brooding nest.

She had lived with them in a little house in the country. She had been married. Recently, she had gotten to a point at which she thought she knew the names of her children, but not her husband. She had gotten to a point at which she thought she knew the names of her children, but it would unravel and she would have to start again. Liesl, Friedrich, Louisa, Kurt, Brigitta, Marta, Gretl—no. Grumpy, Happy, Sleepy, Sneezy, Dopey, Bashful, Doc—no. She did not fret, for in time, it would come. All of them came from her in quick succession, one-two-three-four-five-six-seven, each eleven months apart. They called kids born like that Irish twins.

LC had been not much more than a kid herself when she married. It seemed to her that everything, from the long-sequestered virginity and its vanishing to the life in a little house in the country, had been ensured to keep her small and young and imaginative. She had never been tall and charmed people with her antics, which were like those of a nymph. She was a good mother because she was the oldest child in a gang of children. Her husband had doted on her, she remembered that; he had liked to call her his fairy queen. The children followed in tow, her pages and hand-maids. *Over hill, over dale/Thorough brush, thorough brier/Over park, over pale/Thorough flood, thorough fire.* She planned picnics and made games of chores. She celebrated birthdays with flowers, many-tiered cakes, fireworks bought at roadside huts and set off in the pre-dawn black to mark the day. She sewed their Halloween costumes, a robin red breast, a frog, a parrot, a tiger, a deer, a salamander, a fox. She taught her seven children at home, reading to them from the Psalms and the Proverbs and the Parables. She staged performances of Shakespeare, casting her children as Puck, Caliban, Falstaff.

LC built their empire from fragile stuff. It wouldn't take much to make it fall.

They lived in the country where snakes and lizards and things that crawled on their bellies were common enough. They crept in from holes in rocks and into her garden. The ones she could not pick off herself her husband dealt with. He had an arsenal in their bedroom, under lock and key, in a cabinet with a glass door, a .22, a .38, a .45. He used the .22 more often than not, telling her as he told all of his children, "Turn away, don't look." He was also the one who disposed of the snakes (LC never knew what he did with them), and so it was as though nothing had ever breached their kingdom and all was safe.

But what did you do when you were outsmarted? What did you do when things that crawled knew all your safeguards and had foiled them? It is known the serpent is more subtle than any beast of the field.

Outsmarted, soon outnumbered.

She had used the .22 herself now and then, telling the children just as her husband did, "Turn away, don't look." She supposed her husband took the snakes out to a field for the birds to peck at. But didn't he know about snakes? Didn't he know that snakes, like cats, could resurrect themselves and, remembering the final moments of the life before, come back to settle the score? A snake began as it meant to go on, birthing more and more of them until it had built an army. When LC got a snake, she took a knife and cut off its head, then, if it had one, its rattling tail. When that didn't work, she placed it whole in the firepit and the garden smelled of fouled meat. Soon, she claimed her post, mornings on the back porch, evenings at the front, watching the grass, barely breathing.

She knew secret things now and she meditated on them. Even now they were still not clear to her. There were lives, past and future, that were hers. There were dreams from others she could see, and sometimes these frightened her, others made her laugh. Her husband would ask if she was all right and would try to take her back indoors.

When she did not watch the grass, she watched the sky. She understood, without anyone having to tell her, the name of the god of this world. His name was God Death in the Cloud. She was almost proud at having come to that knowledge all on her own. Before, she'd been educated by someone else, someone who had only ever gotten their certainty from books. Her husband used to read to them all from the Scriptures; the Apostle Paul talked about seeing through a glass darkly. He had also said, *Though I speak with the tongues of men and of angels, but have not love, I have become sounding brass or a clanging cymbal*. LC knew words sometimes meant different things. LOVE did not have to mean romance or even affection. It could mean RECOGNITION and UNDERSTANDING. And if you listened and did not understand, you may as well hear not words, but a big, noisy Sousa march. LC saw God Death in the Cloud in his winding form, chameleonic, just blended in with the blue and gray and white and yellow above, changing to pink and red in time with the sun's pattern. But she could see the green of him because she had the eyes for it. He saw her see him and he cackled (masked as summer thunder) and he sent forth something horrible so quickly down to the earth and through the grass that even LC with her prophet's eyes could not see where it had gone. But because she was possessed of RECOGNITION and UN-DERSTANDING, she knew God Death in the Cloud had sent something dreadful, worse than the snakes, into the house, where she thought they had all been safe.

Now her husband would ask what was the matter and try to take her back outdoors. "You can't stay cooped up all the time. It's not healthy."

She could never quite convey to him it was not the same as the snakes, for you could *see* the snakes, any fool could. It was a matter of KNOWING and having to wait until the thing that had come into the house had relaxed enough to show itself. She thought it

66

might be in the walls. She heard a scattering and a creaking ("Mice," her husband said. "They make nests. You know that.") but then there would be a lull in between her husband's talking or the children's playing and she would hear it—a gliding, slow, steady, wet between the walls. And then, because it knew she knew, silence, until the noise could start up again.

The children listened, too, for it was to them a game, no different than seeing who could wash the dishes the fastest. They had listened to the house's innards before, when a family of raccoons made its home in their chimney, and when an armadillo wedged itself under the porch. These were moments of excitement to the children, who rarely had the chance to see an animal up close before it knew they were there and darted away. "They're more afraid of you than you are of them," their father would say. Unlike the snakes, he did not shoot the raccoons, the armadillo. Instead, the children would pile into the truck with him, on the way out to a meadow or a creek bed where they would loose the animal from its makeshift cage (usually a laundry basket covered with a board over top) and, waving and watching, call, "Bon voyage! Don't hurry back!"

In the evenings, when LC's husband read from the Scriptures, he would end the assembly in prayer, short words before bed: "Bless these children." And LC felt herself included, the oldest child in a gang of children.

But she could not tell him gods died. The God of the Scriptures had gone, she knew, withered and small, eaten long ago and replaced by something stronger and far craftier. It was not the devil; she had always understood the devil to be a necessity, there to tempt and to test, not really evil, but a bugger, nonetheless. If God of the Scriptures had gone, then the devil had, too.

She understood God Death in the Cloud was what they were now faced with, but she did not understand his ways. One minute he was small, barely there, a smear of green out of the corner of her eye. The next, he had swollen tenfold and kept growing. In a night, as the family slept, he had encircled the house and wrapped himself around it and its environs and squeezed, choking all of them. LC had feigned sleep, sipping air while she could, wrapped in green and frightened wet. Hours as eons, the world in pandemonium. Everything vibrated, disguised as summer lightning. LC chanted and panted and waited for the end, when she opened her eyes and saw gray light, dampness in the trees, sourness in the air like bestial markings. They had survived it, the children chirping around their toast and eggs and bathing in the gold of a new day, never knowing they might not have lived to see it.

"Father will be back soon."

"Father went out.

"Father said for us to keep the roof on the house while he's gone."

"Father's in the city."

"Father said to tell you."

"Father said not to worry."

"Father said he'll be back before lunch."

She had not asked anyone where her husband had gone. It was when the thought had come into her head. She had not as yet looked around for him. She wanted to ask the children how they knew to speak to her about Father in particular. Who told you to tell me?

And, like that, God Death in the Cloud sat at her table. He was a superimposition, laid upon this world like gauze. Her children, green and winnowing and bulging under scales that dripped and scales that flaked and scales that looked ready to drop to the floor in crumbs, cooed behind him.

"Will we take lunch to the creek?"

"Will we play *The Tempest?*"

"Will we race to pick beans?"

"Will we have to do arithmetic?"

"Will we make a rhubarb pie?"

"Will we do *Twelfth Night* instead?"

"Will we put the clothes on the line before we take lunch to the creek?"

They dripped and flaked and crumbled. Pieces of them fell to the floor. LC did not recall their names or how old they were, even then. Perhaps that was what made it so easy? Or so necessary? She told her children to think of chores as games; she told herself to think of horrors as chores. In another life, when creatures like God Death in the Cloud were as part of the world as any pestilence, as the wild boar that trampled their sorghum or the snakes that lurked in their garden, LC had killed a demon with seven heads. This was in the time of Herodotus, when people used bows and arrows. The demon had wept high and sweet, an infant's wail, made all the more horrid because there were seven heads to wail from, seven heads pierced with an arrow for each. But its seven horrible heads remained, dripping, flaking, scabrous, and this was the thing that made LC, THAT LC, take up her bow and aim for its heart.

Her children were still her children. Though they were not demons, they were sweet and plump. She knew God Death in the Cloud had his appetites. His belly growled, masked as summer thunder.

"We will play that it is Halloween."

And the children did not care that it was summertime and not the fall because it meant they could wear their costumes. They still had the ones from last year, kept in garment bags and good as the day they were sewn. The older ones complained at first that this part no longer fit, for since October they had all grown. But they made do of the situation and kept masks and wings and paws and tails, which could all be detached, and added bits from their own wardrobes, a bright plaid shirt for the robin, a dress of brown and white for the deer. Girls in shirts, boys in skirts. They assembled in the kitchen, a robin red breast, a frog, a parrot, a tiger, a deer, a salamander, a fox. "Will we play?"

> *The next thing then she waking looks upon*
> *(Be it on lion, bear, or wolf, or bull,*
> *On meddling monkey, or on busy ape)*
> *She shall pursue it with the soul of love.*

Oberon said it of Titania. *She shall pursue it with the soul of love.*

LC's husband said it of his wife, whom he called his fairy queen. The hunt, the chase, beasts in the grass and not her children, though she would sooner see them dead than eaten.

She imagined how horrible it would be to have a tail like God Death in the Cloud's because it was so scaly and wet and everyone (who had the right eyes) could see it. She imagined it, and then she had one. It dripped down her leg like thin urine and wrapped its end around her ankle.

A .45 was not a bow and arrow. It was heavy. But it could be maneuvered. The children faced her and it was behind her back; the children turned away and it was steadied. Her palms were dry, the barrel dangling between her legs like a fig leaf. God Death in the Cloud laughed through tears, a poor disguise this time, for everyone knew (LC knew) that it was not summer rain.

It was the brightest day and the children saw color through the mist and the light. "Will we play?" When gods died it was what you did. You played while you could until the next one was born.

She had five months until the next child came, her first in a hospital, where she would serve a quarter of a fifty-year sentence.

She opened the back door and told them to RUN.

AJ THOUGHT THAT a saint was someone who could have done anything with his life. And yet, he chose to give it all up to live on a single, divine crumb. And that was what made him admirable. But what did you do if the divine crumb was all that you had ever been fed on? What did you do in the absence of any other nourishment?

ET tried to fill him again. She found that her hands were as large as his and wrapping his in hers calmed him the way some people might take to sinking into a hot bath. Now, because there was ET and her babe, her passenger, it made him warmer and filled him quickly. She still would not let him touch her belly and most of the time that was all right. It was still her body; the baby, growing by the minute, was big enough that you had to call it a baby. He asked himself how he might feel if someone came and tried to touch him.

70

But ET never asked to touch him; she waited until she knew when. And this made him cold and it was a struggle to stay full up.

These days, he watched LC play the clapping game with Holly. LC, never serious before, took to it with gravity, and the patterns grew more varied and when AJ began to see the code, the game would stop. Holly could not speak and LC, when she played with Holly, would not speak, and so he could never tell which rhyme the pattern was meant to be. He thought the last one might have been "The House That Jack Built." *This is the house that Jack built/This is the malt that lay in the house that Jack built/This is the rat that ate the malt.* This is the cat. This is the dog. This is the cow. This is the maiden. This is the man. And on and on, like "The Old Lady Who Swallowed a Fly." He muttered what he remembered of it, eyes on hands that flew too fast now for him to catch. Something in the pattern was always off.

I once played Chopin's *Four Ballades* to a crowd that included the Queen.

"I think it's 'The Hearse Song'." Rosemary came to sit beside him. "You know. *The worms crawl in, the worms crawl out, they eat your guts and spit them out.*"

AJ shook his head. "I don't think I heard that one." He asked if it was true that Holly told the future through the games.

"I wouldn't know." There was no preface, *to tell you the truth, to be honest.* Rosemary shrugged. "I always like to think I see the most there is to see in her. But then someone comes along and sees something else. I don't know if I ought to be jealous or love her all the more." She looked at him through the corner of her eye where there were crow's feet. "I'm jealous, mostly. It only took one little lady I invited in for tea to say that there was something about Holly. I thought she was a kook; she was a New Agey kind of person, I saw her at the bus stop and she looked very lonely. She talked a lot about auras and things like that. She said she could read the seeds in bird crap. She did. And tea leaves. She read mine and said it looked like a zebra. I don't know how she came up with that one. It was all streaks at the bottom of the cup. It's supposed to mean *travel and adventure in foreign lands.* I ought to have asked her where she thought I might find the time or the cash to do that. Up and fly to Bali, why not?"

"Well, why not?" AJ wasn't being polite. He wanted to know if it wasn't too late to up and fly to Bali.

"Right. That's what I say to myself. Why not?" Rosemary sighed. "But they all mean that. A horse means the same thing, and a bear, and a rabbit. I could understand the horse. I don't know why I'm going on about it, anyway. It's just Constant Comment." She looked to ET, administering to LC, who had been playing too roughly with Holly, who was now making noises of protest. "But she said there was something about Holly. Everybody eats it up if you tell them their kid is special. I did. I do. I always will. I'll never say different. Otherwise, what's the point? Holly almost died being born. I almost died birthing her. She could die any day, you know. If that's all there is to it, what's the point?" She paused, eyes flinty, arms folded, head erect. "The lady who saw said it and I thought, Finally. Someone sees what I see. The lady said she had a way of calming, not just you, but—do you know what I mean? Not just you, but everything around you. I mean, a big part of the reason why people have the issues they do is because they don't know. They don't know what'll happen the next day, the next minute."

AJ nodded. He had never wanted to know about the next day, the next minute. He had always wanted someone to know it for him.

Rosemary went on, "I don't think it even matters to most people whether or not the next day is good or bad. If it's good, great. If it's bad, at least they can prepare for it and it'll be over with at some point, anyway. Something is set, you know? Anyway, Holly clapped when this lady talked to her. And they started a game. Holly will play all day long if you let her, but this was something else. It was game after game after game. And usually I can tell which game it is, but this time I couldn't. I thought it was 'Oranges and Lemons'—you know that one? *Oranges and lemons, say the bells of St. Clement's.* But that's a slow one for a clap game and it was like there was an extra beat to it. This must've gone on for hours; I invited this lady in at teatime and it was suppertime and they were still playing. All the good manners in me said that this lady had overstayed her welcome, I should tell her it was getting late. I didn't want to. And it was about that time that the game stopped. I came into the room when they stopped, and I said something hokey, *Well, is this a private party or can anybody join?* And the lady put her hands down, laced them together. And she told me—that Holly told her—the day and the hour of her death. As well as the day and the hour of her greatest happiness."

Here comes a candle to light you to bed

Here comes a chopper to chop off your head

Across the room, Holly babbled witchy words, not quite language. LC babbled in turn, Holly following after, heads jutting up and down, cocked right and then left, parrots in a parrot house. It might have been a game of Telephone, though here there was no need to whisper from ear to ear; the objective was to find the word through the gobbledygoo. ET sat between them, her belly the mediator, and murmured her guesses, looking from one to the other. "Vacuum? Thank you? Baboon? Bassoon?" And now and then, she would hit on something. And now and then, Holly would repeat the word with nearly crisp enunciation, as though she were not crippled. You could see her for what she was then, as in other moments that were few and far between, her crookedness and her infancy and her gray hair coming into focus to make an image of the sage beyond time, casting riddles and embedding codes that could so easily be dismissed, even mocked, if you hadn't the eyes to see. And that was what made you the anointed one, in turn, the one who had answered the sixty-four-dollar question when no one else could.

Then you blinked, and everything fell apart, leaving a sad tableau: a cripple and two fools. Goya would have titled it, *Charlatans*, to mean, *Blatherers* or *Quacks*.

AJ wanted to know if that woman was still living. He hoped she was not and was pleased to learn she had died not long after Holly's prediction: the cough that turned into a fever that was pneumonia.

"Don't you want to know what her greatest happiness was?" Rosemary asked.

AJ told her he did not. He did not want to know because he would not have understood it. There were things everyone told you to be happy about, that if you had them it would solve everything. And then you got them and it wasn't enough. The greatest happiness ought to be like being full. You knew what it was and how it felt and how you ached when you were emptied; the trouble was it had no shape. Your happiness was your happiness, for you and you alone, for now and then gone.

Instead he asked, "Just if she got it, is all."

Rosemary nodded. "Yeah. Yeah, she got it."

MIRABEL WAS GOING to be a girl and that was that. It was how ET wanted it. This was one of the few scraps of bastardized information from her mother she still believed to be true, that women were the ones who decided what their baby was going to be. Now that she lived in a world in which people announced years later that they were really a boy and not a girl, or vice versa, or neither, she didn't know how this was all going to pan out.

How did you bring a god into the world at all?

ET wished things would remain the same. In their places, their names, the time of day beginning and ending when it should. She had never liked change, though she moved with it when she had to. The fullness helped. Mirabel helped.

ET was not old—that is to say, she did not feel old. Her mother, from when she was about four on, had delighted in singing that awful Beach Boys song at ET, whenever she passed with her brow furrowed and her shoulders a little stooped, *Everybody's sayin' that there's nobody meaner/Than the little old lady from Pasadena.* And ET would say to her stonily that they did not live in Pasadena. And her mother would tell her to lighten up, "And goddammit, straighten up." As though ET came to her from a place in which things moved with graduality. ET thought she could sometimes remember it: A sky large enough to see the increments in which the colors bled together and began to change; a horizon wide
74

enough to catch what was coming from many leagues away, so you had time to get used to it. You knew what the weather would be a decade in advance and what food you would eat and what clothes you would wear. When she was a girl, ET had liked to wear the same clothes every day until they could not be worn anymore. To combat this, her mother bought her three identical dresses, four identical pairs of pants, four identical shirts. "You dress like a cartoon," she'd once told ET, who took the word "cartoon" to mean silly and loudly colored. What her mother had meant was that cartoon characters are never seen changing their clothes and appear the same way in every episode, Bart Simpson's red t-shirt or Doug Funnie's green vest. She liked routine was all. When you were a child, it was nice to know that a day was going to be like the one before.

Her mother had liked parties, giving them and going to them. She had come to earth from a planet of bossa nova, dewy air and clicking palms, rivers of sangria you had only to dip your glass into. ET thought of her mother and pictured a grand entrance, a big star, Cher or Diana Ross. She wore mules with kitten heels. Where her mother came from, the national anthem was "Midnight at the Oasis." She had named her daughter something glitzy, like Evelyn or Estelle.

ET had never wanted to be called by her real name; she was glad when the hospital put her initials on all her things and before she knew it, that was what everyone called her.

She placed her hands on either side of her belly. When nothing moved, she laced her hands over the top. Her navel, normally deeply inverted, was beginning to turn outward, and she let LC push it back in, watch it pop out again. It was strange, she thought, how little she'd appreciated what her body could do. Just think if Mother could see me now. Even Mother had needed a Father to make me. All I had to do was dream it. Like she always said, "If you can dream it, you can be it." Well, I bet she never thought I could do it—all on my own, too. What would she say if she could see me, which of her pronouncements? *Fancy that? Who'd've thunk it? I thought they'd find Hoffa before I saw you in the family way?*

Was Mirabel too glitzy? ET had never truly, deliberately chosen the name. And it wasn't as though a name determined character. She herself was Evelyn or Estelle or whatever it was, and you would never catch her wearing mules.

She was an Aquarius, her mother a Taurus. She didn't know what Mirabel would be, seeing as she already looked to be in her second, maybe even third trimester. ET glanced outside: leaves aflame, a little bite in the air. Mirabel, then, would be a Scorpio. She asked Rosemary to read to her from that day's horoscopes, not the predictions, but the little summaries of all the signs. Occupying both hands, Rosemary used one to clap with Holly, the other to flatten the newspaper on her knee. Aquarians, she read, as air signs, were mutable and enjoyed change and challenge without the hindrance of emotional attachment. Scorpios, as water signs, preferred to invest themselves fully in the changes and challenges they met.

From the corner, a fellow muttered, "That's some shit." He was a new one, come the night before and who actually had a very sweet disposition. He had an odd inability to put his sweetness into words. He called Rosemary a cunt and patted her hand in gratitude. He looked reverently to Holly and told her to go and fuck herself. With regards to the newspaper horoscope, he might have agreed wholeheartedly. ET wondered what sign he was.

She wondered if Mirabel was real. She was emptying now, slowly, as though the stuff that bonded her to the rest of the world was leaking out through her toes. She wondered if Mirabel was a game, gone on too long and now it had become real. It used to happen quite a lot when she was a girl, playing on her own in her bedroom or with the neighborhood kids in the woods. The closet in her bedroom led to a great kingdom, under an enchantment only she could break. There were ghosts in the swamp beyond the first layer of trees, and you had to prove your bravery by running and sticking one toe into the murky water. She did not recall much in the way of her grammar school years, not in the way of facts.

She did not know how old she was, or how much time had passed between one thing and another, but she thought she might die if Mirabel turned out to be a game.

At that point, LC piped up, "Are we going to live here forever?"

ENDA SLEPT FOR two days, and on the third he ventured upstairs. The people in this house operated like animals, in that, when the sun went down, they bedded down for the night and fell asleep quickly and deeply. He felt safe enough to leave his knapsack in the cellar and he felt warm enough to strip two layers of clothes from his person. He wandered the first floor in a long t-shirt and a pair of thermal pants. He left his shoes, too, and paused on the cellar stairs to feel the bottoms of his feet. The skin was spongy from confinement and bore the grid of his socks. He picked with his nail; callused bits crumbed between his fingers.

He was confused upon emergence, for the only way up from the cellar seemed to be directly to the house's second floor. Looking around, here was a storage room, packed full like an attic. Linoleum under his feet, tape on the windows. The streetlight outside threw itself into corners where boxes were stacked. Enda approached one, jumped when it fell, mashed his lips together should someone stir. No one did. And he let his breath come again, righting the boxes, reading their labels, inked in red. WINTER THINGS. SUMMER THINGS. Smelling of wool and mothballs, very like how it was at the old home, putting up linens when the cold set in, taking out sweaters and flannels. The equinox and the solstice; his father's home, like this one, faced east, filling with sun from March through September. His father had built his house that way and he wondered if the people who lived here had built theirs that way, too.

He reasoned there was so much here already that no one would miss one or two sweaters. There were enough boxes, all plumped with clothes and barely contained by the packing tape, to have dressed a large family.

Enda had been out in the world and knew, even before, that not everyone lived with as many children or went through as many wives. "One wife at a time," his father had said when Enda had asked, "never at once. We're not heathens." Wives dead or dismissed. The dead ones had markers on the property, along with the children who had been born, had lived, had died long before Enda's coming. He knew his mother was one of the dead ones. "Her life for yours," his father said. Her name was Emma, to mean industrious and whole; that was how her stone was marked, anyway. He wondered what happened to the wives who had been dismissed. "I could not keep them," his father said. "And it's not my place to make them stay." This last was said with grave finality, pity for flighty doves.

His name was Enda, to mean birdlike.

He wondered if anyone from the old home was looking for him.

He took from the box marked WINTER THINGS a very festive-looking sweatshirt, red and white, made to look as though its message was cross-stitched, but it wasn't. He shook it out, draped it against his chest. It read, MERRY CHRISTMAS, YA FILTHY ANIMAL. And it made him laugh because it sounded like the kind of thing you would hear in a movie (which, unbeknownst to him, it was). It wasn't too scratchy and he put it on. He had to dig for the next find, overpowered by Fair Isle and mothballs. He found himself coming up for air twice and having to pull his treasure from the very bottom, jammed as it was under wooly flotsam. This he put on right away. It was a hat, one that covered his curls and his ears; it was ruby and blue and had tassels, two braided ones that lay over his shoulders, and one tufty one at the top.

First from outside help at the old home, then from television, Enda understood the trappings of Christmas and, though this house was not his and these things were not his, tearing through the boxes had all the gaiety of a holiday. They did not celebrate Christmas at the old home. His father had said the veil between the worlds was thin on that day, and that song and story were liable to resurrect the dead or to summon wicked creatures. All Hallows' Eve was the advent of an orgiastic season, in which otherwise mild-mannered people took leave of their senses; men dressed in ladies' gowns, women in men's suits, children in the skins of animals. Eating your fill and then eating more, gluttony and waste guests at the same table, greed in its wake, the insatiable yearning for things you only wanted because your neighbor had them, all of it culminating in misdirected lust. "Playing God, from October to December," his father said. "Then the real winter sets in. And what do they have left?"

At the old home, Enda could see the lights, pink and green, gold and red, from the other houses down the valley. His older brothers and sisters remembered a time in which they did have a Christmas, but it wasn't much different than it was now. No lights, no gifts. "We had a tree and a feast," one brother recalled. "A little feast. We left most of the food for Pan." A sister grunted, "The buzzards got to it before Pan could." A few people from town, the ones from the churches and the lighted houses, took pity on the Martindale children and came to the gate Christmas Eve with parcels, mostly old clothes, and bags from HEB, rotisserie chickens from the deli counter, pies from the bakery aisle. "Dad chased them off," a brother sighed; this was the brother, Enda remembered, as the one who had asked him if he knew their father was batshit. Enda the Elder had come with a .45, aimed for back tires as the do-gooders peeled away, taking with them their gifts.

Enda the Younger decided that from now on, every day would be a holiday. In point of fact, every day would be his birthday. And if that was so, did it mean he would have to pay for the things he took?

He'd left his knapsack in the cellar, but he'd remembered to bring the daemon box with him. There was one coin left, would more be sure to come? He felt it rattle from one end of the box to the other, a penny or a fortune. In the two days he'd slept, he dreamt of his daemon. And he knew the importance of dreams. It was one of the things his father taught him that he'd decided to keep. He knew what it looked like, too. As Socrates' daemon had wings, so had Enda's, but it was neither grand nor glorious. It looked rather like Higby from the first house, humble and stumpy and a little short of breath, and his wings were not true wings, made instead of tinsel and turkey feathers. He had the look of a dog in a calendar: costumed in green for St. Patrick's Day, in angel's wings for Christmas.

But Enda recalled what was said of Socrates' daemon, that it only spoke if his host did wrong. And in the dream, Enda's daemon had been silent.

The same brother who had told Enda their father was batshit had said also their father had once been different. It was also the day Enda the Younger had decided to run. "I can't say how," the brother went on. "It's like he was here, all of him. All of him here and not there. I was too little, so I didn't know." He was quiet, speaking blasphemies, but he did not stop. "None of this is real. There is no god or anything like it. He's gone and switched it all up. You weren't born yet; back before you there was one god, now there's one god with a thousand faces, along with whatever little things he's fixed on in his moldy, goddamned library. Pan and Puck and God Death in the Cloud. I don't know what the hell. He keeps saying we let wicked things in, we can't leave, we can't leave until we've snuffed them all out. I'll tell you right now, he's liable to kill us all." And it was true the Elder had forbade the older sons from going into town anymore, and that his eye had taken more and more to the sky in the passing days. His newest wife was not let to leave his sight, her hand gripped in his and tripping in his long strides, standing where he could see her, holding his shirt sleeve when he had to have his back turned; she was younger than the oldest sister, who was about seventeen. The Elder's ambition had been to make his home a Paradise. The older brother said, "Look at it out here. It's batshit."

Enda, beyond the gate and birdlike, told him to come with him. "We'll send for the others, too." And the newest wife.

The brother bent over the fence, as far as he was able. "He'd be on his own. I can't do that. Leave him here by himself, I can't do that."

And Enda conjured a new image of his father, and he did not see a great man of the ages. Here in his place was Caligula, Richard II, Henry VIII, holed up in grand quarters, babbling, salivating, decoding whispers, deciphering shadows, a plot to oust, to poison his food, wrapped in his own divinity, talking to the moon.

He didn't know what to do now, now that he was in a house

that was not his. Now that there were footfalls on the stairs, commotion from below, a knock on the door, too much at once from out of a stillness he thought ought to last the night long. What time was it? Earliest morning or darkest night? He did not want to be found.

ROSEMARY TOLD EVERYONE to hide and answered the door. It was six o'clock, dark. The neighborhood where she lived was once grand, with houses built by the prosperous, industrialists first, and then, as the town began to grow, doctors, lawyers, men of business. Now it was hollowed of all that, and the Queen Anne homes with turrets and lace-edged verandas were divvied up into first duplexes, then apartments, some condemned, some demolished with only the chimney to mark its place. The doctors and lawyers had metamorphosed into college students and cat ladies, then devolved into crackheads and vagrants and squatters and schizos. And Rosemary and Holly.

When she was not preoccupied by the need to feed and house the others, to wash and love Holly, she worried about the State. More than once, the State sent one of their number in a compact car, soft-spoken and cunning, perfumed or cologned, just to ask a few questions, just to have a little look around. They bore titles that semaphored goodwill, they posed as messengers, they had names like Diane or David. They wanted to know about the electricity and asked to see where the fuse box was. They wanted to know about the plumbing and asked to use the bathroom. Rosemary maneuvered them through a long-devised path that did not go beyond the first three rooms of the ground floor. She plied them with tea, begrudgingly, from her best cups and showed them a bastardized version of Holly's clap game. She gritted her teeth when they cooed, for they were frightened of Holly and did not want to touch her.

This time, they wanted to know if there was anyone else living in the house. A minute before they stepped over the threshold, Holly's flock had scattered up the stairs, into the unused rooms, and peered over the balustrade like hunky punks. ET put her hand on AJ's head and pinched LC when she giggled.

"If you can't be quiet here, then you will have to go somewhere else." ET whispered, but was firm.

LC pressed her face into Mirabel. She heard blood, pawing feet. She wondered if Mirabel had a tail or wings. "No."

ET whispered again, "If you can't be quiet here, you will have to go somewhere else."

"I want to see."

AJ shook his head. "No, you don't."

"Why?"

Someone else spoke, a woman who had been coming here and then living here for over a year. "They're from the State." And the other hunky punks echoed her, growling around the words like a curse, "The State, the State, the State." One gleaned horrors from this. Here was a wonderful game that could be played at all hours, at any time and with anyone, and the State came in with its big boots and, with one footfall, could put a stop to everything. No more fortunes, no more music, time to grow up. The Apostle Paul said, *When I was a child, I spake as a child*, yes. But he said also, *Be ye therefore followers of God, as dear children*. It would be blasphemous to put everything away, compartmentalized into the right building and put into the right words for paperwork and pontiffs.

When you smote the fun, what was the point? What was left? Did the State think none of this was real? If that was so, why did they say there were rules, when, in the first place, they had never really played the game?

"Pollyanna had the Glad Game," LC agreed.

"And Sara Crewe had the Magic," ET added.

"And Dorothy Gale had the slippers," AJ amended.

The woman who spoke first told them all to shush. "No one else is supposed to be here, but for her and the girl." She gestured downstairs, where Rosemary had her company snared, barring any peek beyond the living room. The person from the State was very upright, seeming to catch everything in their periphery without turning their head. Those upstairs could not have told whether it was a man or a woman, for their suit was sharp, their legs long, their voice never above an even tenor. They touched the dried bouquets in the sitting room indelicately and the blooms disintegrated. Holly grabbed for a pantleg and they stepped away. Someone upstairs speculated it was really two people, one standing on the other's legs, knitted together by the long coat to form a single colossus.

"Gogmagog," the cussing fellow hissed.

"It's a vampire," said another.

"Gogmagog."

"It's a man," ET murmured. "Look how he walks. Bow-legged."

"It's a woman," AJ countered. "Look how she moves, in general. Hips first."

"Gogmagog."

And LC parroted the cussing man, whispering "Gogmagog" because it tasted as funny as it sounded.

The woman who first spoke told them you weren't supposed to know, so you wouldn't know how to play them when the State sent them into your house. "Not both like a normal person," she specified. "They're tricky. They're not people at all, that's the thing."

ET said it looked like nothing to her other than a person, and if that were true, what could it be?

The woman asked, "You know lizard people?"

"Yes."

"Well, I don't believe in those. That stuff's nonsense. But what we've got here is not so far off the mark from them. You know Betty and Barney Hill?"

"Yes."

"This is like that. But taller."

Men in black. Close encounters of a third kind. LC had a tail, AJ wings. And she with child. ET was sometimes the clearest of the three of them, of anyone in Rosemary's house, even at the fullest, and never once had she thought of herself as mad. Sometimes, she thought it was everyone else who was mad. She had to remind herself that her thoughts were not so far and away from theirs; this was what it meant to be full. Nonetheless, she had never expected to have to work for fullness. It was one thing to be clear and another to have doubts. She blinked and the glimmer was gone and her stomach was a balloon, her breasts beanbags, her endocrine winking midway lights, her baby a plastic prize bought with tokens. (She remembered playing a carnival game just like that when she was nine or ten; you had to hit a lady dummy with darts in all the curvy places under her dress, balloon boobs and a whoopie cushion rump.) She caught AJ's eye, and did not feel him as she did when she was full, but she understood. It hurt having to see things for the way they were. What did it mean when she had to try? Was she going to lose what she had and go back to the way she was?

Mirabel will be gone if that happens.

If Mirabel isn't anything, I won't be anything. I will be as Holly. I will be an idiot.

I have committed blasphemy, but I've said it. There it is. Holly is an idiot. No one will forgive me.

AJ, fortunately, was filling, enough to remember the way it was, and that it did not have to be. He put a hand to her cheek, bowed his head to rest on her shoulder. His other hand he held above her belly, but he did not quite touch it. He whispered, "Mom, I'm afraid." It was the first time he'd called her Mom.

ET kissed his hair. "No one's going to get you. It looks like the State's going soon, anyway."

And they all sighed. Soon the State would go and Rosemary would receive her assistance, her allowance and her food stamps that were really largess for the faithful—though on paper, it fed only herself and Holly.

It was a flip from the usual scam. In the rest of the neighborhood, people packed other people onto the paperwork, declaring households of ten or more. RL asked Rosemary once why she couldn't do the same here. "They'll give you more money if you can pull it off." She told him that the State would want a full background check on every last one of them. She said, "If they find out who you are and what you did, you'll go right back. And then no one gets anything."

LC had asked, "What did he do?"

ET told LC it wasn't any worse than what she'd done, and she seemed all right with that.

Downstairs, the person from the State poked at the radiator.

"Gogmagog," the cussing man grunted.

"Gogmagog," LC echoed.

AJ hissed at them both, finger to his lips, spitting between his teeth. His teeth, as it happened, were large in the front and there was a gap in between his upper left tooth and dogtooth. With his red hair and large teeth and beady blue eyes and his spit, he had the look of a dragon. It made LC yelp, and then, when she remembered who it was, laugh, a sudden, squawking sound that shook the hands along the bannister, making everyone jump, and making the person from the State take a solid step toward the hall. The shadow advanced, sniffing.

"A mouse," said Rosemary. "In the walls. We're getting people in to take a look. Shall I put on some music?"

And the State moved back into the sitting room, asking about the mice, how long they'd been a problem. The shadow looked right, left, retreated. Joni Mitchell drifted into the hall, ". . . *it's an old romance, the Boho dance . . .*"

In the gods, the blessed fools went "WHEW" and mopped their brows.

Then, ET rounded on LC. "Since you can't be quiet, you can just go somewhere else."

AJ murmured, "I'll take her," and got up to lead her away.

"Wait." LC grappled in the dark with her free hand. "I want DD to come, too."

ET looked at the rest of them along the balustrade, flitting from face to face to face. "Who's DD?" There wasn't anyone here she recalled by that name. But then, LC sometimes saw things no one else did. ET remembered everyone on *Sesame Street* called Mr. Snuffleupagus Big Bird's imaginary friend only because they never happened to be in the same place at the same time as he. And then in Season 17, they saw him and they believed.

From over her shoulder, a croak. "Gogmagog." LC held his

hand. The cussing man, DD, bowed his head to ET, primly, princely, and murmured, "I'll shit in your shoes." This might have been to mean, "I will look after the young lady, madam. No harm will come to her." He reminded ET a little of Arthur Treacher in one of his butler roles. It was impossible to believe him doing harm to any living thing.

She thought, watching them link hands and mount the stairs, how silly that was, for anyone is capable of anything. Think of the pleas: at the wrong place at the wrong time, not in his right mind, the devil made him do it, hadn't the wherewithal, hadn't the capacity, he didn't understand what he did. How could all of that be true when, in the moment of madness, nothing had seemed clearer, the place and time more orchestrated, just for you?

It was funny because the thing that kept slipping was time. Months were as days, and it did not matter where you were. It was her first sign of fullness, when the ruckus of the world dropped away and the eye of the world turned to her, and it did not frighten her, as she thought it should. She could be in one place, looking at one thing, a beam of refracted light along a brick wall, an anthill, her own pulse, and an hour would pass. Something might have happened in that time, whether it was wonderful or terrible, she would never quite know, in between seeing the anthill and departing from it. Perhaps an atom bomb had detonated. She would remain, skin hanging in ribbons from the blast, half-roasted, turning only when she knew she ought to move on. She would only know it had happened when it happened, not the hour or the date.

An hour could be an era.

She felt herself emptying again, and it hit her, as it sometimes did, strong and as though from a great distance, but really it had been creeping just over her shoulder and she had been shooing it away. Nothing gripped her and she turned to jelly. Everything gray, silly. And terrible contrition, undefined, though buoyed by the certainty of her wickedness. These were the worst of the empty times. The devil of it was that there was no devil, no deity, but she had made her peace with that. Worse, that there was no bond. A moment before, she could immerse herself in the electricity of everyone in the room, in the world; it was a comfort as simple as sinking into a hot bath, and it was easy to imagine it would last forever. It was not telepathy because it did not come as words, nor as images. Your thoughts were your thoughts, and their thoughts were theirs; there were colors you recognized in their composition, sounds you had heard once a thousand years ago, and there were sounds and colors they recognized in you, even the ones who did not have the right kind of eyes.

When you were empty, you were alone. It echoed because a chasm had opened, leaving her peering out from her own cliffside. Others she knew were worse off when this happened; at the hospital, some did not have a cliff to peer out from, wailing instead from the bottoms of craters where they would stay for days, and often it was there they would succumb. The word was big with distance: ALONE.

Mirabel did not stir. A doll under her dress, a dream.

ET ALONE.

She wondered what it was that she had done.

ENDA HID WHEN he heard footfalls. He found a door in the attic leading down a short flight of steps to a bathroom. Everything in place, like the room before, like the rest of the upstairs, nothing moved by a fraction of an inch, as made evident by the dust. There was a tub with a glass door, which he slid to one side, ducking in, squeezing himself into the far end where no one would see him, squatting so he did not have to sit on the drain.

Once when he lived at the old home, his father came to the door after a rapid tattoo, a small fist that bounced off the frame and vanished with its owner when Enda the Elder appeared. The Elder had not seen anyone, nor had his sisters, nor had his father's new wife. They were not expecting supplies from town, nor visitors. The Elder glanced the horizon, then looked down to the place between his feet where a scrap of notebook paper, shaped into a football, sat secured by a rock. He unfolded it, held it to the light. Enda the Younger came around the house in time to ask what the fuss was about. They, the Elder, the Younger, the children and his father's wife gathered and read.

DEAR FREEK PEOPLE: LET ME START OFF BY TELL-ING YOU THAT I KNOW WHAT YOU DO IN YOUR HOUSE. I KNOW THAT YOURE KIDS ARE A BUNCH OF INSEST BABBIES AND YOU WORSHIP SATIN. I WANT TO TELL YOU ALSO THAT I HAVE A KEY TO YOUR HOUSE AND I ALSO HAVE A GUN. YOU CAN AVOIED DEATH IF YOU DO EXACTLY WHAT I SAY. PLEASE LEAVE $100 ON THIS PLACE AT YOUR DOOR EVERY SUNDAY. IF YOU DO NOT FOLLOW MY INSTRUC-TONS, I WILL HAVE YOU ALL SHOT. REMEMBER. I HAVE A KEY AND I KNOW MY WAY AROUND YOUR LAND VERY WELL. HAIL SATIN FREEK FUCKS. YOURS TRULY THE KEEPER OF THE KEYS

The letters were sticks, like a child first learning to write. The Keeper of the Keys was left-handed, for the ink, blue ballpoint, had smeared to the right and upward as the note went on.

"It's a kid," his oldest sister sighed.

"Whose kid?" His father's new wife, who was just twenty and five years older than his oldest sister, narrowed her eyes at the horizon. "None of the neighbors have kids. It must be a town kid. I wonder what he did, did he hitch a ride all the way out here, I wonder?"

Enda peered at the note. "Did he mean Satan?"

His youngest sister, who was six, asked, "What's an incest baby?"

How his father had hardened. And how the earth had trembled.

Enda squatted over the drain and thought, I HAVE BEEN HERE FOR A THOUSAND YEARS. I AM THE STUFF OF TITANS. I AM MADE OF STONE. He came in peace. He would make the earth tremble, if needs must. He was the anointed, the Divine, the worshipper of Satin. Look upon my works, ye mighty, and despair. He had never been smaller.

Footfalls, giggling, a croak, "Gogmagog." They were nearing, and the wait was awful, nearing the ultimate terror of entering the bathroom where they would sniff, find nothing, turn, and leave him alone. Floorboards, footfalls, a creaking, a creeping. There was a sort of anteroom directly outside the bathroom's other door that led to the rest of the second story, where the floor slanted and a big oriel window protruded, giving anyone who walked there the impression of being on a ship. The voice that giggled gave way to squeals of surprise, followed by thumps of feet mismatching in an otherwise patterned gait. The door from the anteroom was open and the feet righted themselves. The bottoms were bare; Enda knew this because they sucked and popped on the linoleum, cotton-muffled bump-bumped on the terrycloth bathmat just outside the tub, scraped at its dirty selvedge with long toes when their host sat down on the toilet. Pee percolating, the bowl echoing empty; it reminded Enda how long it had been since he had used a proper bathroom. The one on the toilet did not flush, instead padded toward the tub. She wanted to wash her feet and told this to no one in particular.

But Enda, poor Enda, knew there was nowhere for him to go, no good would come from screeching. What more could he do but answer? "Okay." And he shut his eyes, for the curtain had torn away.

THERE WAS A public park that used to be the property of an oil tycoon, a hundred or so acres donated to the city upon his death, still marked by the millionaire's grip on it; there was a gatehouse and a drawbridge, a king's view of the bend in the river from the house, a grand castle three stories high, worked from fieldstone so it had the look of having always been there, the grounds and exterior mimicking the survey of a feudal lord. It had played host to Frederick Douglass, the Marx Brothers, the Grand Duchess Olga Alexandrovna of Russia, Anais Nin, and Truman Capote. Nowadays, the local department of energy and environmental protection unlocked the place for guided tours and wedding receptions only, though it was very much still lived in. The junkies who did not have anywhere else to go knew where the master keys were kept and made copies of them. They knew how to jimmy locks and windows and how to silence alarms. They went in and they were not guests. They played that the place was theirs. People who had nowhere else to go, sober and sobering, went to the castle and found peace. Most of them were folks who had survived Woodstock and, reflecting on the halcyon days of be-ins and back-to-the-land, called the castle and its environs the Ashram in the Park.

The junkies gave the best sermons. These were not parables, but monologues. They were portions of the internal scream, articulated from the back of the throat, hoarse, congested, never risen above a mumble. You might be tempted to hear this voice and find it sarcastic or perhaps just sour. Either way, it tended to grate. The thing to remember was that it was like a thorn thicket around the Holy Grail; you had to keep cutting away at the brambles to get to the gold of the story.

The one whom they called the Son of Man was known to drop in from time to time. He was a user, too, had taken too much, had died and had woken on the third day and now materialized in public libraries, community centers, Valero parking lots, and any causeway that led to a beach. He answered to nicknames, much in the way he might have answered to a gilded title. He was Babe. He was thirty-three and lived at home to get clean and did landscaping for the local cemetery. His spare time, now that he was meant to be getting his act together, was spent reading in the library or cooling his feet in the low tide.

His stepfather (who never did know what to make of him because Babe did not and would never really belong to him) wanted to get him treated as an inpatient somewhere. He asked the Son of Man why it was so difficult to stay on track.

Babe said, "The worst thing about smack is that it brings out the best in me." And it was true. He smoked, typically, combining it in a bowl with tamer things. He wanted everyone to see what he saw, hear what he heard. He did not experience the sticky lethargy he might have otherwise felt because the hash he cut it with made him overcompensate. He remembered where he was, walked the painted white line on the shoulder of the road to show to himself he could do it.

He told stories to any who would listen and thought of it as a real bonus if he could make his audience laugh. He knew a guy. He knew a guy who knew a guy. Last Memorial Day weekend. Last year. A couple years ago. This one time at the corner store. This one time when he was mowing at the cemetery and thought he saw the one he helped bury get up out of the casket and walk away when everyone's back was turned. He said that in life, his old life, the dead man had always left without saying goodbye, why should he start now? The punchline: "Because you can't get rid of anyone that easy. Especially not that motherfucker." What Babe meant was that no one is ever truly gone for good.

Another routine got him in hot water. He performed Friday nights at Blue Jeans and liked to sometimes begin thusly: An entrance made wearing a crown of thorns fashioned out of plastic autumn foliage from Joanne's. He stood and said, "Jesus Christ walks into a bar. A bar pretty much like this one, from the lime rinds in the ashtray, the rerun of that one Alice Cooper album, to John, who has the bizarre need to keep the men's room door open during this discourse."

John had run to the gents' in haste, overactive bladder as a result of his diuretics, banging the door behind him, not knowing it had bounced open again. You could hear the splash. The routine picked up.

"Jesus Christ walks into a bar, wearing his crown of thorns. The place is a bar where mostly hipster kids hang out these days. Like, where the old hard drunks used to go, they've been pushed out by these bratty kids. Because bratty kids know everything, I can promise you that. Make no mistake. They can tell you that they know how to do calculus and they don't know how to count. How many apples are there, Johnny? A million. Little Johnny's all sour because you're talking down to him. You tell him, No, buddy, there's just three. One, two, three. Real slow, so he gets it. And's he's giving you this look of such chagrin, as if to say, I feel so sorry for you. You belong at a vivisectionist's, but I feel sorry for how dumb you are. Clearly, it's a million; I won't tell you that, I'll let you play with that idea. Those kinds of kids. They all look like

Miranda Priestly these days, I got shaded by a two-year-old at the Circle K, earlier. She didn't like what I was wearing and told me so. She told me I looked like Puck. And they know Shakespeare nowadays. I had to look up Puck; he's a fairy, or a pixie, or an elf or something. From *Midsummer Night's Dream*. They did an adaptation of it for a Netflix kids' special. I had *Pee-wee's Playhouse* when I was two and not much else. They did not want us growing up cultured when I was coming along. And we're let to breed and we've become just smart enough to know how dumb we are, and we don't want to pass that on to the next generation, and we have them learning Spanish and French and shit in the womb, so they'll come out bilingual. And they can talk about iambic pentameter. And I can't. And neither can you.

"And now your kid's smarter than you and you have no one to blame but yourself. This kid got away with insulting me. She told me I looked like Puck. For a minute, I didn't get her reference. I thought she was telling me I sucked. She kept pointing at my what-have-you here, and saying, Puck, Puck. I told her to go puck herself. And her mom tried to follow me. I think I lost her; that's part of the reason why I'm here tonight. I'm hiding.

"And despite this passive aggressive takeover, there's still one or two hangers-on from the old days, when the bar was the place for real men, working men to stop at after a sixteen-hour day, hard, out in the fields, a day of lumberjacking and bear-wrestling and field-dressing their moms' Pomeranians. Stuff that men do. He points to the crown." Babe pointed to his. "And he says, 'I'm going to get killed for wearing this.'"

At this part, the older ones who knew who he was, what kind of people he came from and what he was up to even when he told his own mother he was clean, left. His poor mother. The younger ones, curious, knowing where it was going, or peeved and ready for a fight.

"Because those bastards killed their moms' Pomeranians. If they can find it in them to kill a Pomeranian, they'll have no problem doing anything they want to me. They're crazy."

He had another routine in which he pretended to read from a

list of his anecdotes, sorted on index cards by their first sentences. "Last week," "Last year," "Last (insert holiday here), sub. Allhallowtide, sub. Halloween, etc.," "That time." This portion of the act was known as "I'm really a hack." Upon reading the first sentence, he then wadded and tossed the index card into the audience, and another and another, the audience playing along, waiting to catch them like baseball fans at a televised stadium game. Someone would invariably start a game of Keep Away, and Babe suspended any narrative at any time to see how long the wadded index card could go around the old dance hall. The record was eighteen minutes.

His mother asked him if he remembered that video they had. "We had to tape it because you loved it when it came on. It was this Georgia O'Keeffe documentary. It must've been made in the seventies, everything about it sounded very Bob Ross-y. She was talking about bones and how she saw through them to the colors in the sky." A PBS special, soft flutes and a guitar, her home in Abiquiu. She wore black like the oldest grandmother. He liked her talking about bringing home a barrel of bones. "I said to myself, he's going to grow up and be a stoner. Some people look at their kid and say, that kid's going to be an artist. That kid's going to be a politician. That kid's going to be an axe-killer. That kid's going to be a stoner. He'll have something nice to look at when he's stoned."

After that, the Son of Man received for his sixteenth birthday a book cheekily called *102 Things to Do When Cooking Oregano*. It suggested things like listening to "Everybody's Free (to Wear Sunscreen)" while on the treadmill, or trying Thai food.

He was there the day his mother met his stepfather. He liked to credit himself as having brought them together because he went to work early, never having formally gone to school. The cemetery was a grand one and an old one, home to the remains of colonists and slaves and their descendants. There were mausoleums like follies at the Petit Trianon, there were hydrangeas that bloomed blue and deep purple. People memorialized spouses and partners and children on concrete benches: DANIEL MICHAEL

ROSENBERGER. 8/31/1942-10/7/2009. ALL IN GREEN WENT MY LOVE RIDING. His stepfather hired him as a caretaker, which had him trimming bushes, mowing, planting, replacing withered bouquets with blooming ones at the feet of new headstones. He never dug graves and he never placed a body in the crematorium. He maintained the pond and looked after the ducks his stepfather kept at the time and now let run wild. They were Muscovy ducks, mostly; they were frightening animals, faces mottled red and bulbous, clawed paws, demonic, but very sweet when you brought them things to eat from a bag. The Son of Man gave them names: Butch, Bastard, Hemorrhoid, Meatwad, Bubo, Stool Sample, Orgonon, Mondo Trasho, Hepatitis A, Hepatitis B, Hepatitis C, and Big Bird. Babe had a sign put up, urging visitors not to feed them bread crumbs. SEEDS & OATS PLEASE. FROZEN PEAS ARE A BIG FAVORITE.

He overheard his mother say to his stepfather, as if for the thousandth time, though this was the first, "You stuck with me. For the longest time, it was just me. Then me and Babe. Now it's Babe, you and me." So, it was all right.

His stepfather asked Babe if he remembered saying time was a ring, in that primitive barbarianism is scraped away to make room for an Enlightenment and, falling into its pattern, the Enlightenment is then scoured and replaced by the old barbarianism again. "You must've been a kid still. I don't know why I say that, I'll think of you as a kid if you live to be a hundred. But anyway, time as a ring. I still think about that."

His mother asked if Babe remembered having told her about his dream house. "And you said you didn't want a house. You wanted to be somewhere that sounded like the south of France." That wasn't quite true, but he hadn't known how to picture a house, save for angles seen from wide windows. He had the feeling of modesty, though it might have been a castle, for all of him. He saw fields and sky, deep gold at one end, bloody twilight at the other, 6 a.m. there, 6 p.m. here, the best hours of the day framed east and west. He used to be afraid of full dark when he was younger and saw the gloaming as a dreadful ticking down. To shake himself, he held out until the last red smear before sundown, as if to say, "Not until the last bat of my eyes. You won't get me while I'm awake."

Babe asked his Blue Jeans disciples, "Does the word wannabe sound like an insult to you? It never has to me. It's always sounded to me like a nice little marsupial, cousin to the wallaby. Look," he demonstrated, cooing, pointing at a guy in front, "it's a wannabe in its natural habitat. Isn't that the best thing you can be, though? Wannabes want to be something. Wannabes want to make laws and make love and make shit happen and save the whales and the trails and the snails and the kales. And I like a wannabe's future. I wannabe in a place where there are laws that allow me to make love within sight of trails which lead to thriving whales and healthy snails. We'll make shit happen and eat a bag of kale."

WHEN THE CURTAIN pulled back over the tub, there had been three faces instead of just one. Enda, who found himself unable to move, could not shut his eyes against anything and was able to consider each of them without any subjectivity, for the stuff inside (the chemicals that tell you to smile, laugh, run for your life) seemed to have frozen up, too.

LC did not think. LC followed whatever impulse had come in that instant, and turned on the faucet. To everyone's surprise, it worked. Rosemary would later guess she hadn't used the upstairs in at least six years, saying, "And if the water down here is on the fritz, why isn't it on the fritz up there?" Nonetheless, it burst full into Enda's scalp, roaring, icy. He squealed under it.

They had him and, like they were the guards and he the condemned, they took him by the hood of his new sweatshirt and led him through the hall. He was grateful they did not let him trip on the stairs. He was grateful, in fact, someone had found him. He looked forward to punishment in the way he used to at the old home; there was nothing in the world like a good smacking, waiting, having to count them out, the winding down to where you could see the slate being wiped clean. It was never preceded by the Elder's averted eyes and his silence, and the telegraphed agreement that everyone else in the old home was to do the same (even the lowest of his father's children, the ones who worked in the fields and could not read, the ones Enda did not often speak to). Better to come back bloodied than to have everyone pretend you were nothing more than a bad smell.

If he were at home, the Elder would have given the sentence: "Fools' names and fools' faces always appear in public places." The younger ones would watch.

He was thinking of the letter from the Keeper of the Keys. No one had left any money at the door, and he realized no one would, however long Enda the Younger waited, eyeing every opening and shutting from his place at the table in the study, from a thicket of cedar where he thought he'd hidden himself well. He wondered if they knew. The Elder knew the number of hairs on his head, and the thinner, pubescent ones besides. The Younger was right-handed, made to switch when his father taught him his first letters. It was a sticking-point in his memory, wormed into the muscle of both hands: grabbing for the pencil with his left and drawing it back almost as soon as he had thought to do it, anticipating a slap, the right hand moving forward, unprepared but willing, forming a big E (two hundred times!) until it looked like his father's Spencerian example. He copied passages from the Psalms and from Ovid, and the benedictions and epyllions relinquished their beauty to the fussiest curlicues. He hated penmanship.

It dawned on him now that the laying of hand to cheek, hand to buttocks had only ever been for venial crimes. Nothing he did was really that bad if he knew he could be scourged. And he was relieved. He thought of what all they might do to him. Will you spit in my face? Will you pluck out my nails and then my eyes? Will you break every bone and reset them all so I heal crooked and hobbling? Will you humiliate me after and have me empty shovel waste? I can do that. Just don't tell me to leave.

"Behold," LC giggled, presenting him to the big room. "A boy."

The room erupted gently, chuckles from the back of the room surging forward and lapping, warm, at Enda's feet. They were more relieved than he, it seemed, and about as shabby and dirty. Holly, recognizing him, crept as fast as she could and sat before him, reaching to play with the drawstrings of his sweatshirt, and he did not flinch when she grabbed his finger. He allowed himself to look at everyone, and he smiled.

RL asked, "What do you call yourself, young man?"

Enda told him "Babe" because it was what the babies at the old home, himself included, were called. He had a thin memory of a mother saying it to him in particular, whether it was his own mother or another of his father's wives he didn't know. He knew no one would believe him if he told them his name was Divine.

ET, standing with Rosemary, watched her for clues. Ought we to be angry? Or do we let this event pass as a close call, a mountain out of a molehill, and welcome the trespasser, albeit at arm's length?

LC echoed, "Babe." He looked like some of her children, but he didn't look like her.

AJ swallowed, for the boy was beautiful.

THE SON OF MAN had a routine in which he began by opening with a song. Usually, it was Steve Miller's "Fly Like an Eagle." He would begin with one of two declarations, that he loved the song or that he hated it, and would try to mimic the laxity of the seventies, slurred and out of sight. And he would laugh at himself, insisting it would be the funniest thing anyone in the audience would see that night. He laughed at the audience and they laughed at him because the sound was hysterical, out of breath, caught in his chest until he freed it with a braying, full-bodied "HA HA HA." It would be captured on his first album, *Hail Satin*, repeated at his last recording, *Live at the Ashram in the Park*.

He said he looked forward to the day he saw God at last because he never used to believe. He said he'd never had enough proof, despite the terrestrial splendor of changing tides and the sun and the stars, which in themselves were miraculous. He'd always asked himself what more he would need, and asked of God the same. When the time came, Babe said, "I think He'll moon me.

At the end of the day, I don't know what else He can do."

His stepfather asked him, "Do your jokes have to be so crass?"

ENDA GAVE HIS knapsack to Rosemary, who made a quick inventory of what he had. The canned food she was thankful for and said he could stay as long as he liked, if he was willing to play with Holly. "And," she added, webbing her hand and placing it over ET's belly, "we'll have another little one around here soon. We'll need all hands on deck when the time comes."

She returned the knapsack to him. He checked its secret pocket, pleased. She had not found the daemon box.

ET told him, without waiting for the question, that it was going to be a girl. And she wondered why she wanted him to know at all, for the idea felt flimsy to her now and she was filled with the need to say it again and louder. But the boy's eyes were sharp. He asked, "Is he the dad?" pointing at AJ.

ET told him he was not.

"Then who's the dad?"

"She doesn't have one."

"She doesn't have one."

"She doesn't need one."

"She doesn't need one."

It was not quite mockery. ET had forgotten that about youth, that confidence of knowing just enough. At thirteen or fourteen or fifteen, things fall apart. You are betrayed, not bastioned. There is no God, there is no good. Everyone is a liar and you will not be played for the fool again because you are too old for that—and you are the only one who seems to know it.

LC did not seem to know it either; she seemed to think he was a toddler and tried to force a sweatshirt she'd found over his head. He folded his arms, scowling, protective of the one he had until he saw the lettering on this one, white block on navy. ENDERS IS-LAND, it read. He stripped *Home Alone* and pulled the hood snug over his hair. He'd very nearly told her ENDER was almost ENDA. Instead, he asked who Ender was and how come he had his own island.

"He was an insurance man," AJ put in. "Rich enough to buy it from nuns. Then he died and the nuns bought it back."

He had gone there himself once to recover by the ocean, within sight of the blue Marian grotto, the chapel where they kept the arm of Saint Edmund of Abingdon. It was a foul-looking thing, black with still blood, all knuckles and fingernails, wrapped in a sleeve of bishop's purple. The Society of Saint Edmund kept it, along with other bodily fragments, locked in a glass case at the back. (It made AJ think of roadside attractions from the old and gritty days. SEE THE FEEJEE MERMAID. SEE THE BEARDED LADY.) He'd had many questions and regretted never having asked them: Where was the rest of Saint Edmund? How had the arm been acquired, for what coin or what service? How did the Society of Saint Edmund know it really was the arm of Saint Edmund? He'd had such headaches then, sharp enough to make him drool. He hadn't done much talking on Enders Island; he made an effort to meditate, under the care of a priest who knew his father and knew of AJ's work. He was a good fellow, bravely admitting he'd come to the clergy twenty years ago to battle his love for another man, hearing confessions face-to-face instead of through a screen, and when he said he'd pray for you, he meant it. AJ took his meals in the Silent Dining Room. He didn't know if anyone, with the exception of the counselors, would have wanted to speak to him anyway.

Blessed is he who loves and does not therefore desire to be loved.

He might have repeated all of this to the boy, then, hearing the priest as suddenly and as sneakily as one might hear a demon in their ear, realized it would have been inappropriate. Inappropriate. It was inappropriate, even, to look at this boy, even now. He thought he'd taken care of that. But still. STILL. What you don't outright desire you still appreciate.

Instead, he told the boy he'd had the same sweatshirt once.

Enda shrugged. "Maybe this is it."

AJ shook his head. "Too small."

ET told him to come away with her, into the kitchen, another room. They found themselves on the veranda, the screech of the screen door making him jump. He was thankful for ET. She knew what most did not, never having to ask, never angered nor disgusted, though she was irascible. She saw and lifted and separated and waited until you were calm. It was why LC called her "Mom."

She held his hand until it was still. She said, "You know what's wrong, at least. That's a start."

He might have said everything, there and then. Heaven knew he wanted to; the burden, even now, weighed worlds. How do you mimic fevers? For how long do you claim constipation and dry-mouth, nausea when you're famished? He was not so skilled an actor. On paper, AJ was in treatment for opioid addiction—that was what sent him to the hospital, anyway. He looked the part, but he did not feel it. His hands, though shaking, were warm and dry. He wouldn't have known fentanyl from foot powder. He ate like a rat, hurried, picking at his portion until everyone looked away, when he could gobble it down. Unlike many of his kind, musicians and otherwise, he had never been anything more than a teetotaler. Left to his own devices, he would sooner wait out any storm in the cold grip of sobriety. This alone made him a freak; to wallow in a chemical purgatory would have been, at least, an admission of guilt. But he was not guilty, only of thought, not of action, and he knew his hands (those hard-wired tools, quick to preserve) would move to strangle himself before they touched a hair on a pretty young pupil's head. *I made a covenant with mine eyes.* And so, the rest of him rebelled, the headaches that crept from the back of his neck and through the corners of his mouth. His father said, "Take this," and he took it. It kept him soft and quiet.

Once upon a time, you could buy paregoric over the counter. In this day and age, you had to know which doctor. Or, in less savory circumstances, you had to know a guy who knew a guy. He knew a guy who knew a guy who kept him supplied with enough OxyContin to do what he must, and a little left over, bundled in ET's knapsack in one of its hidden pockets, should the three of them fall on rough times after the hospital. It sold for close to a hundred dollars at eighty milligrams. They'd not had occasion to hawk it, not yet.

ET, in the grip of it, tried to give him some measure of what she had, her fingers squeezing his. He let her lead him as they went walking around the neighborhood. Up the hill was a juvenile detention center, chain link and wire, grassy and Grecian, low security, to accommodate the kind of people who might one day want to buy eighty milligrams, controlled-release or immediate-release. There were bushes that bloomed hydrangeas in the spring, an athletic field with soccer goals and the gritty oval of a track farther down the valley. The chapel there, Protestant brick, summoned the miscreants to evensong with automated chimes.

Lord, now lettest thou thy servant depart in peace according to thy word
For mine eyes have seen thy salvation,
Which thou hast prepared before the face of all people

"Rachmaninoff," AJ murmured.

ET wanted to see the hydrangeas, though it wouldn't be warm enough for them until May. She said she wanted to pretend they were there, for the baby to be near them; she said they reminded her of home. She was not from around here, AJ knew, nor was she from Connecticut or Cape Cod or any of the other places where he knew they grew. It was not home as per the usual definition. He thought he knew where it was she meant. He thought most people might know where it was she meant, for there were moments (not even those) in which he could smell it, feel it, idiocy or infancy, always looking up instead of down, into the sky with the sun in one corner and the moon in the other, the ecstasy akin to riding his father's shoulders on a long walk. Though now, he had no need for anyone else to give to him that bliss; he could do it himself.

Was that madness, that bliss? Or was it everything building up to it?

And then it fell away, coming to the hydrangeas at the edge of the chain link fence, bare, now that it was colder, empty stalks, save for a few papery bunches that hadn't dropped off yet. ET was looking at them as though they were blue, pretending. It made him sick. He could see why she put up with LC; it was better to play a game (knowing it was less likely to end) if you had two people. He looked at her belly, flat; he could tell its void through layers of clothing. Mirabel, a dream, a doll. What lark, what lunacy. He wanted to ask ET all sorts of things. Why insist you were with child when you did not like children? Why not break down, admit how far gone you were, know your own frailty, and say FUCK IT?

He'd seen ET broken and it was awful. He could not do what LC could do, looking in the way she could, transcribing vibrations. All he had at his disposal were tears, sorrow that went from its initial horror to nullity in a matter of minutes, the harrowing of hell preceding the outer darkness. She would not let anyone near her in that first stage, her face wet and running, never quite breathing, everything squeezed shut or pulled tight. Then nothing. What remained were small eyes, blooming open and red, belying the demon that had taken her and shaken her and still curled around her heart to see how much more from her it could suck. The nurse told her to let the good voice in her be the louder one. She took ET's head in her hands and said, "The ugly voice can get pretty plain. It makes it easier to hear. That doesn't mean it's right. Let the good one be the louder. Let the good one be the louder. Let the good one be the louder. The good one is what makes things happen. It sends people to the moon and writes symphonies. It makes people get well when everyone else says they're supposed to be dead. Let the good one be the louder."

"They're pretty," he allowed, playing along.

He wondered what they must look like from outside. What would he do if he were to meet himself, right here? Can you ever really say you've met yourself? It's a constant architecture, you're always building and collapsing.

He did not want to say it for ET's benefit. She knew in her way, in the same manner in which she knew she was with child, when she was in the grip and full, as she knew water was wet and day turned to night. She might have been with him, in soul if not body, when he stepped into his bathtub.

"It didn't hurt," he told her.

"I know," she said, the edge gone from her voice. *Is any among you sick?*

"Eighty plus cabernet. I was numb all over," he told her. He did not remember how much he'd had, of either substance.

"I know," she said. *If he has committed sins, he will be forgiven.* Then she said, "It could've killed you."

"I wish it had," he told her.

"I'm glad it didn't," she said.

In his mind's eye, as clearly as the day it had happened, he took a kitchen knife, filled the bathtub with water like lava and himself with red wine and blues, thinking not of the castrati but of the Skoptsy, though he could not bring himself to bear the "greater seal," as the sect called the outright removal of testes and member. He thought he might shout and he took precautions, a ball of athletic socks oozing in his teeth. And all was still, save for the glands that bobbed in between raw blooms. His legs were jelly. Not his body, not his burden. The small bathroom had smelled of pine and rosemary and he was somewhere else. It was the first time he'd felt the grip of it. *He that is able to receive it, let him receive it.* He dreamed he was a nesting place for a thousand doves, all preening and courtship, his arms alight to accommodate them all, his beard full of feathers. They cried, *Wooo-OOO-woo-wooo.*

THE SON OF MAN said, "I'm here all week. What am I saying? I'm over thirty and I live in my parents' basement. I'm here till I die." He paused. "Knowing my habits, I've probably only got a week left. So, yes, in fact, I'm here all week."

LC WATCHED ENDA dream and saw what he saw. It was night, thick cedars, his path lit by a flashlight that seized on and off. The things it lit upon might have been branches to the waking eye, though here in this infernal sect of the mind that could and would twist anything at any moment, they were alive. Soon, they would make themselves known. They would writhe into brilliant green and open their jaws for him. He was locked outside and had to find the way back to the house; he could see it and LC could see it, a flicker in between branches, a lighted window. The flashlight, its battery faulty even in sleep, went on, then off, then on, like the most brutal joke. The idea was that it had been given to Enda on purpose, the giver knowing how frightened the boy would be.

LC could see it, but could never change it. It was someone else's dream.

So, her hand on his shoulder, soft, then hard, she shook him awake. "You were making noise," she whispered into his popped eyes, green as the snakes were going to be.

He moaned, rubbed one eye. He was in a sleeping bag on the sitting room floor, wrapped in an afghan, a plush dog pillowed under his head. He righted himself and reached around for it, embraced it. It was an enormous thing, overflowing his lap, blue and purple, droopy-eyed and long-eared, a grand prize at a carnival game. Tucking it under his arm, he took it with him, following LC, stepping over dozing bodies on the way to the kitchen.

It would look dark, they both knew, if they turned the light on and did their best to scrounge semi-blind. In the east, the sky was gray, the shadows blue. Soon, there would be sun. Enda found a box of shredded wheat, plain and sealed, filled two huge mugs (one marked HIS, the other HERS in black curlicues), and poured water over them from the faucet. There was a bowl of sugar on the table, too, and they both sprinkled their cereal with it liberally. He had HERS, she had HIS.

He'd been here for maybe a month, enjoying himself, despite never having had a full night's sleep. At the old home, it was bedtime at nine, up at five, a blank slumber all the way through. Here, he woke at midnight, again at half-past two, again at three, again at a quarter to five. LC often woke with him and they would share these secret civil twilights, not saying much, keeping company all the same. Sometimes, they would sample the records and tapes and CDs on Rosemary's shelves, clamping on the heavy, puffed headphones, absorbing with eyes squeezed shut, then trading. They were both a little sick of Joni Mitchell at this point, and went for the more robust work first, Mozart's *Requiem* and *Apollo et Hyacinthus*, the Turtle Island String Quartet playing "Julie-O." LC liked Carly Simon, "Coming Around Again" fused with "Itsy-Bitsy Spider. Enda liked Jimi Hendrix, "If 6 Was 9" and "Little Wing," and had Steve Miller's "Fly Like An Eagle" memorized; he was surprised to hear himself humming the little intervals, "*Tick-tock-tick, do-do-doo-doo*," sounding, he thought, like a dove. They shared for Toumani Diabate and Ballake Sissoko's Malian kora, one ear for each headphone, cheek to cheek.

"Have you ever been to Mali?" Enda asked.

"I've never been anywhere," LC said. "Have you?"

"No."

In the daylight, when everyone was up and about, they watched the old television Rosemary kept in the corner, covered most of the time, though she was willing to make an exception, so long as ET hovered nearby to make sure the movies weren't too violent, the shows too foul. They watched a lot of PBS and, under ET's eye, a lot of standup comedy. He learned you only needed two things to get a laugh out of someone, and these were spontaneity and the clear, plain light of day, things everyone seemed to know about but never had the pleasure of watching fall out of a blue sky. Mitch Hedberg asked, "Do you believe in Gosh?" and Enda nearly wet himself. Holly crept over now and then to join them, laughing when they laughed, though she couldn't have understood. He learned Holly had a larger vocabulary than he'd thought, just eight or nine clear words, the most used being "Ma." For a time, he refused to believe this was the extent of what she knew; if he could talk a blue streak, why couldn't she? In truth, she understood far more than she could articulate, in the manner of one who reads a second language better than they speak it. Enda did not know this.

Nevertheless, he tried a joke on her. He sang, "I wanna fly like a beagle." And she laughed, and LC laughed, too, because they knew beagles couldn't fly. Enda snorted, covert, the way you do when you don't want to laugh publicly at your own humor. But what could he do? Laughter itself begets laughter. Look at LC, how her face gathered together, holding her breath, releasing in long, veiny gasps that made her sound like a tea kettle. And here's

Holly, who looked human, giggling removing her disability and twenty years so that anyone else dropping in (if they overlooked her twiggy extremities, good only for crawling) might think she was another one of them, nothing miraculous, nothing pitiable. He drew in air, and crooned, "I wanna fly like a beagle, let my big ears carry me—" He took the blue and purple dog and made its ears flap.

Imagine that. A dog with ears like wings. A dog that took flight like a bird, but because beagles are known for their chubbiness, it would undulate once it was airborne, up and down, up and down, blue and purple, its round little bulk going one way, the ears the other. Like a cartoon. Absurdity is what makes comedies of tragedies.

He came to believe the blue and purple dog was what his daemon might look like. Somewhere in its place beyond the veil, it lay in friendly repose like a sphinx, like a dog waiting for its master to come home, the way its plush rendering did now in his lap. It had a red felt tongue sewn to the place where its mouth should be. He called it Dorothy. When Rosemary poured wine (Cisco Strawberry, syrupy, brought by a guest) and let Enda have some ("Just a tot because you're still young.") he dunked its snout into the mug to let it have a taste. It was what you did, he remembered, and what his father did, leaving a cup of homemade cider in their orchards before the frost. Dorothy wanted more and Enda obliged, and soon the daemon's snout was pink and so was Enda's chin. It helped him laugh. It helped him sleep.

"That's it, that's enough," ET said and made him rest, Dorothy pillowed in her lap for his head. "Rosemary's got too much going on to look after one wino. I'm going to be keeping an eye on you."

Enda snorted. "Wino." It was one o'clock in the afternoon. It was like melted candy. He turned to look up into her face. "Any ideas for baby names?"

ET blinked, once. It seemed silly, but she wanted it to be true, despite everything. She blinked again. "I haven't decided," she said finally.

"Well, what's your last name? You need to know how the first

106

name will work with the last name so they'll flow."

She told him, for it was common enough and there was no need to lie to him.

Enda grinned. His teeth glowed pink. "So, there's a lot of options." He made a list on his fingers. "There's Christmas Jones, there's Casey Jones, Jughead Jones, Basketball Jones, Grace Jones. There's Agent Smith, there's Ranger Smith, Winston Smith, Septimus Warren Smith—"

"You're just trying to wind me up."

"—there's Will Smith, Stuff Smith, Soapy Smith—"

"You better cut that out."

"I'm just trying to help."

"You're being a smartass."

"I'm trying to help."

"I know." Without quite knowing what she was doing, she kissed him, firmly, gently, on his hairline. Did he belong to her now? "Try to breathe through your nose and get some sleep."

WHAT SHOULD SHE tell her? Mirabel (the name sounded sillier every time she said it to herself) might come in another month. She might come in a decade's time, like those curiosities known as stone babies, dormant calcified bone that can only be coaxed out by their host's natural gases, parasites expelled. Because that is what they are; that is what babies are.

ET was empty now, as empty as she had been in ages. This was the sum of things: poor of money, poor of spirit, poor of body. Did ET want to go back to things before? She thought of everything as pre- and post-hospital, and was under the impression life pre-hospital was not something to which she wanted to return. Not that there was anything particularly wrong with it, and therein was her puzzle. There had been a job, not generous in its salary, but certainly enough for her to live on (and, in this day and age, who could boast that?). There had been a place to live, with hot and cold water, air conditioning and central heating, a Netflix account, a good used vehicle. What do you do when there is nothing wrong? What do you do when there is nothing wrong and nothing has happened and there is no concrete language for the way things have grossly changed, albeit *sub rosa*? For one, the light was too bright. Noise, from sirens to the faintest tinkle of a xylophone, was too much and too full of static, nothing clear or bright or beautiful.

When she was a girl, she thought, as Teresa of Avila and Therese of Lisieux seemed to think, there was the world on top and the world within. There was the rich, interior castle in which you dwelt, carefully walled, its gardens full, its windows tinted ruby and blue, grand and high rooms you muralled in your best energies, your most wonderful thoughts. And you looked out from your castle into the world on top, and you were protected. You looked out from your castle and you thought the world on top couldn't be so very different.

This was the beginning of feeling full. Fullness was a complete accessibility. You knew more about the world than the sum of its parts. You were resolute in its clicking decisions because there was no *click* to be felt; events were seamless, as threads in a tapestry, for now in this floral clarity, you could see the shape in all of them.

Emily Dickinson said, "I could not see to see," in reference to mourning. William Carlos Williams said, "Must you have a part in everything?" in reference to smelling.

Then, like that, it was gone. She did not know if things had grown darker or if it was merely in comparison to what she had felt before. Was that a symptom of the mind's tightly winding or its unraveling? Or was this, the warmth and becalming, the ruby and blue, meant to be the end goal beyond riches? This was her first true glimpse beyond the veil. She had only touched it for a minute. This was not what one might call happiness, for the word only described one of many colors this fullness held. Contentment? Perhaps. She knew everything she had known before, that there was no God, that she and everything she had known before would die and replacements would stand where they had all stood. These ought to have been easy enough to process in any state of mind. The difference now lay in the removal of conceit. And she thought everyone would be much better off, the equation could at last be worked, if everyone stopped and smelled the flowers once in a while.

People thought Georgia O'Keeffe was trying to paint pussy.

Was it better to say FUCK IT and disappear? People did it. Before Rosemary's, the trio had stopped at an underpass where a neighborhood of tents and shopping carts had been erected. Among those truly down on their luck and those like themselves, refugees whose terms of treatment or parole dictated they no longer needed around the clock care, or who had been left to the elements when hospital funding was cut, there were folks who had allowed that kernel to burst and here they were now, moving from underpass to vacant lot, some in tents, some in fully converted vehicles (vans, buses, once an ambulance, another an ice cream truck), who had also said FUCK IT and lived without an address.

Babe, a growing boy of twelve or thirteen or so, slept with a purple and blue dog and sucked his thumb. She knew a little of where he'd been before, thinking of what he'd had then and what he had now. These were, more or less, the things a child ought to have: shelter from the storm, the expectancy of a good meal and a place to lay their head. The rest was guesswork, a yes or a no gleaned from offhand tact. Yes, Babe did have brothers and sisters. No, he did not miss them. Yes, his father was alive. No, his mother was not. No, he was not the oldest. No, he was not the youngest. "Just the youngest boy," and that was how he left it. No, he did not miss his father.

"I live out here now," was how he put it. Always the funny hesitation when he used those words, "out here." Did he think of the old home as within the magic circle and the rest of the world as what? The outer darkness? The outer limits? The Twilight Zone? *"It is the middle ground between light and shadow, between science and superstition, and it lies between the pit of man's fears and the summit of his knowledge,"* as Rod Serling said. The implication was that out here was not what he thought it would be, and ET did not believe it was her imagination when she heard one or two bright notes in those words, escaping the gritted teeth and stingy distribution of yeses and nos.

He was happy out here, wherever this was. Happiness was a

start. She hoped it could retain itself, devolving (for it would never last) into contentment.

Mirabel was coming; Babe would be the dummy.

"Let's go walking," she said, and they went around the neighborhood, through town, stopping into the Starbucks where police, peeved at no emergency, had once come and gone, bought refreshment to go (a Pink Drink and a bacon and egg and cheese sandwich for Babe, a Violet Drink for ET), and followed the first of many cats that had colonized the garden of the Ashram in the Park.

"Don't get in their face like that," ET called. "They'll swat you."

And he heard, discarding the leaf-feathered stick, and sitting so they might grow curious rather than cautious. There were orange cats, brindled cats, black cats with a triangle of white on their chests and white paws, prancing like little men in tuxedos, gray cats with coarse, tufty fur, plump cats, cats without tails, without teeth. They were timid, they were affectionate, they were amorous, they were grouchy, they were bossy. They nested in his lap; they rubbed his knees. They were no different, really, than dogs. Babe took up the leafed stick and began naming them. "That's Henry, that's Kelso, that's Edith, that's Mink, that's Blanche, Rose, Dorothy, Sophia—"

Neither of them knew what to say to each other. ET had never been much of a conversationalist and, as it turned out, nor was Babe. In her old life, as in this one, ET had loved hearing gossip more than spreading it. She recalled the pleasure of the phrase "You're not going to believe this" and all its acidity, and sucking it all down, digesting, eventually excreting to make room for more. Someone else's outburst, someone else's idiocy or ineptitude, someone else's duplicity. Someone who thought everyone else was talking about them and now, as a result, they were. Someone whose man had cheated and was now hellbent on trashing his reputation in petite, petty ways. And ET was a merry audience because none of it had anything to do with her. I am not you or you or you, you bunch of dingbats, I know better, I deserve to revel.

No one did much of that in this life, for everyone lived day to day. Nevertheless, people found things to talk about. You talked about what? The weather? The traffic? She had never been one to give her own trials; she had thought about it, in this life as in the old, and nothing ever seemed to have the substance.

Babe's questions came with appendages. No yeses or nos. What did ET do before? How old was she? Where did she used to live? Why had she been in a hospital?

What could she tell him? You don't go to a hospital when you're at eternity's gate, do you? There are criteria to meet. Headaches, loss of appetite or gain, inability to sleep or insomnia, reduced sex drive, tightness in the throat, difficulty breathing, difficulty reading, difficulty concentrating. The hospital had the Goldberg test: Do you feel guilty for things over which you have no control? Do you feel trapped? Do you feel unable to enjoy hobbies or interests? Do you often think of suicide? Do you often think of ways in which you might commit suicide?

Yes. No. Yes. Yes. Yes.

What could she tell him?

Instead, they watched a wedding party, the ceremony less than an hour over, the couple less than an hour old in holy matrimony. The forecourt of the garden filled, scaring the cats and sending any interlopers toward the fringes, now the audience for a sacred pageant. It was two brides in twin gowns with sweetheart necks. One wore a veil, the other didn't. There were cupcakes iced in blue buttercream, candles on the tables, a choice of salmon or steak, California rolls, portobello kebabs, tuna and wasabi, an instant pot and a copy of *Mastering the Art of French Cooking* tied with white ribbon, wooden spoons, waffle iron, Elton John and Natalie Cole, the Macarena and *Footloose*.

Enda had never seen a wedding before, and he told ET so.

"Were you ever married?" he asked.

"No," ET said. "I was a flower girl once."

"What's that?"

"You follow the married people around, tossing rose petals."

When his father married his most recent wife, Enda the Elder had the youngest girls trail the bride and groom carrying bulbs of garlic, from the start of the ceremony to the start of the wedding night, to abandon their charge only when the groom lifted the bride over the bedroom threshold and shut the door to the stink and foul serpents. Perhaps what they'd needed all along was rose petals. The flower girls here seemed to have emptied their baskets long ago, though they kept their chaplets in their curled hair, this one in firstfruits, this one in daisies, this one in tinsel, as Feronia, Flora, and Fulgora, the harvest, the foliage, the summer lightning. Enda recognized them, pointing them out. (His sisters had dressed as them. His father had seen them in glimpses. His oldest brother said everything was batshit.) He wondered if someone in the wedding knew what he had known at the old home, or if it was just a bit of theater.

They were startled when a gentleman in a clergyman's casual black strode up to them, not in the way of someone who means to ask you to leave. He held out his right hand to them, his left balancing a tray of hors d'oeuvres and two cupcakes.

"We couldn't," ET said.

"She's lying. Yes, we could," and the boy angled for a shrimp vol-au-vent, cramming it and another into his jaw.

"I'm sorry." ET sighed. "His manners, not mine, are atrocious."

"Thank you." This, thickly, through a wedge of cake.

"You sound like a damn Muppet."

"It's not easy bein gree-een," crooning when his throat had cleared. "Ma'am, I'm not sober."

"Excuse me, please. Forgive him and his unorthodox humor. Pretend he's not here."

And everyone laughed a little, because it was a funny situation. Enda discovered he could hold his Cisco well, in strawberry as in other flavors, and could pass for a goofy, if bumptious, brat. He had hidden his habit, doing what he could to keep it mum, particularly in front of ET, who had become more of a cozy bitch in recent days, snappish but all in good fun. You almost wanted to be the butt of her jokes, and went for it much in the same way you might fish for a compliment.

The pastor wanted to invite them to the reception. The wedding party felt guilty for cutting their stroll short, and they looked like such nice people, a mother and her boy.

"And another on the way," Babe added, and his eyes went sharp, lids low, brows high, a bit of drama that could cut to the quick, when ET turned to glare at him. She did not want to admit this was a look she had given him more than once, a look her own mother had given her, and it still inspired conniptions. It was a look that had you by the collar, and it did not matter if you were caught in the act or perfectly innocent. It was your pride. You ought not to be treated this way, you were not a child, you were not stupid, you were not a liar. "Cramping your style," as they said in the 50s.

The pastor congratulated her and looked to her belly. He asked when she was due.

"Anytime now," she told him.

He thought she was joking and laughed again, and they followed him to the reception. The brides shook their hands, one warm, the other lukewarm, and Babe thought of a way to make the former come around to him. ET observed from afar, always at hand, should her boy's charms exhaust the guests too soon. He managed to sample the champagne and the cabernet and the Sauvignon blanc, with a ginger ale chaser in between. There was a photo booth and a pinata. There were courts for bocce ball and horseshoes. He danced with the father of the latter bride, the one whose idea it must have been to invite him and ET in the first place, and then with the former bride's cousin, a girl his own age with beach-curled hair and a great laugh and who did not seem to mind his tendency to insert "cumin" for "human" when an instrumental remix of "Human Nature" played, or when he told her people vomiting was funny to him.

He would say at Blue Jeans, years later, "I don't like observational comedy. I like wit and I like stories. I hate it when that's what you have to go on in your bag of tricks, *Toast, what's up with that? Am I right?* But if you can't find the littlest things funny, you're just a bunch of dead people inside. I saw someone bite into this big wedge of red velvet cake and the spray of crumbs across their face made them look like a wild animal, and the cake was their kill. I've never seen dessert look more primal. And it actually scared the hell out of me for just a moment, mostly because it was ridiculous. It's only cake and it so happens to bear a passing resemblance to human gore when its being crammed in there, when someone's that hungry. It makes you think, if they can do that to a piece of cake, what could they do to me? I could be the second dessert. I am known to be sweet, and I am low fat and high protein. I am not safe. And that just got me going. My impending doom is a laugh a minute. Rage also, that's a big one, rage is hilarious to me. Have you seen that really trippy movie? *Waking Life*? And Alex Jones is in a car and he's bellowing about the corporate slave state and I don't know what all into a bullhorn and he's driving around downtown Austin, and as he approaches the climax of his testimony, his face deepens in color, because it's in rotoscope, so everything looks like an acid trip, going from pink to purple to blue, pretty gradually, and then suddenly BRIGHT RED and he's shrieking, this steroid shrill. About DESTINY and BASIC HUMAN FREEDOMS. And the funniest part was that this was probably the only coherent thing he's ever said. Everything else he does now is about lizard people and it's not funny. I thought Alex Jones was a comedian until someone corrected me. I thought, he's got a surrealist thing going on, he's a satirist. But no. You know, that horror when you stop and it becomes clear: Boy howdy, he really believes in this stuff. Tinfoil hats and lizard people. That just made me lose it. It was even funnier than cake gore."

Impotent rage and cake as kill.

A minute, a flame. Both never hoped to last, though at least he had them.

He tried to remember which bride was which, as he'd never learned their names. The cupcakes were topped with plastic letters, L+S. The S was blue, the L purple, the couple's favorite colors. He figured L was the one who invited them because she was also the one with a tattoo in purple letters along the inside of her left forearm: *This magnificent refuge is inside you*. He asked her if it hurt, getting it. "Not too bad," she said, pushing back her veil and, finally, face red, undoing the bobby pins and letting it rest in her lap. "I mean, it stung. But I'm glad I got it." He asked if she might get another one, and she told him she was thinking about it, possibly another quote. "Like *DON'T PANIC*, just in big letters. Maybe on my other arm." She was a bit drunk.

HE PAID HIS hosts just as he had at Starbucks and at the houses before. He went to the table mounted with gifts and, in between the Keurig machine and the towel set, placed one, two, three, then four coins from the daemon box.

"Will that be enough?" ET asked. She was as yet a skeptic about it.

"I don't know." Enda was feeling warm and soft and blissed. He steadied himself on ET's arm for the walk home. "It could buy them a house, for all I know."

"It didn't look like very much. They did let us come to their wedding."

"Last minute. We didn't know they were going to be there. They didn't know we were going to be there. I didn't have coffee mugs on me, I'm sorry to say." One or two, then four and then five cats trailed them back to Rosemary's.

He had heard what ET had not. The former bride, the one who kept an eye on this funny pair until they left, who approached them more than was necessary to ask if they were having a good time, and who made excuses to hover at intervals around the gift table to make sure nothing was missing, found the coins as she took the final inventory of the evening. She waved to her wife, who looked, uttered, "Holy shit."

"I know," the other breathed. "This settles everything."

Her bills, her loans. Absolved.

At Rosemary's, ET put Enda right to bed and he slept, out cold, waking well into the part of the night that was darkest, his clothes wet and stuck to him. It was the witching hour, which is midnight or three a.m., depending on who you ask. He'd been dreaming of the old home, to a part of the land not far from the house they called the crater. It had been a manmade pond years ago, filled with rainwater collected in tanks. It was a project that had to be maintained and was now abandoned, the drought revealing the earth, made fecund by animal scat and the little rain that came their way. Grass worked its way in between cracks and its slopes were home to milkweed clustered in washes of coneflower. It might have looked like the poppy field outside the Emerald City, though it had in its first incarnation been an ocean floor. You could look into the white dust and find stamped into the earth the whorls of urchins and snails and trilobites. In his dream, it was not the ocean floor, but the surface of a dead planet, Enda the Younger and the Elder its sole occupants. He was sitting in the crater, having run from the house, and could run no more, too tired to do more than sit and wait, for his father could see him whether he was in plain sight or under a rock and had only to appear.

AJ woke him this time.

In Rosemary's house, Enda drew his hood over his face and pulled the strings tight until all AJ could see was the tip of his nose. He did not want anyone to look at him.

Through his hood, made of thick stuff, Enda could barely see him, and he peeked through the hole, finding AJ at the other end of the room. He had shaken him, Enda guessed, and then sprung across the floor. The man never quite talked to him; he addressed the boy's elbow, his foot, the space just above his head. Enda tried to imagine what he must look like now. He'd tucked his arms into the sleeves and hadn't a face nor appendages, wondering if he was doing this for himself or for AJ. ET tried to arrange things so Enda never found himself alone in the same room with him; Rosemary invented chores for the boy, distractions for the man until it was clear that, for any communication between the two, it had to be in glimpses.

Was it because, at last, the Son of Man was in the house?

Lotis became a lotus, and Priapus was foiled.

Pitys became a pine, and Pan's plan was spoiled.

Enda wondered if this was where the greater God and the lesser gods came from, instead of the ether. He reasoned for the first time that if you imagine violence as slapstick, it's easier to look at, if not think on. The fact of it was they were not nymph and demigod, but bodies with hearts that could be bruised and broken, still working after injury, still going.

AJ wanted to tell the boy, "I won't hurt you."

Enda wanted to tell AJ, "I know you won't."

On the floor beside him, ET, deep in a dream of her own, did not quite snore.

To Enda's shape, AJ said, "I heard you crashed a wedding."

It was like talking through a tin-can telephone. But Enda wanted to try. "Invited interlopers," parroting what ET had said of them.

For a moment, a headache caught him, pick end, above his right eye and drove deeper, and he forgot where he was. He knew, without having to ask, what it meant to be full, what it meant to be empty, in the grip or in the outer darkness. It was the first time since leaving the old home he'd met emptiness in its stark providence, its cold lines, fireplaces full of ash, stained windows broken and murals scarred. The interior castle, gutted. It might have always been in shambles; it might have collapsed just now in a matter of minutes, forever. He swallowed, mouth gummy, wondering if what he needed in order to make it all bearable was to go through the cobwebs and the vermin in the walls with a veil dropped over his head, everything a little golden, like looking through a mist. It fled, not instantly, retreating down a black hole that grew smaller and smaller, and Babe watched it go. But it left behind a terrible feeling of being trapped in his own skin. He itched, he wanted to throw up. Benevolence, obliterated. Cisco Strawberry, and Red, and Orange, gone. What do you do?

His stepfather would say, "I thought all that humor came from on high. But you've been flying for three days."

He asked AJ (with chagrin, because he knew he could) if he had any money on him. AJ said he did not. "Why?" Everywhere, from the supermarket to the Starbucks, was closed, but not the Circle

K.

"Just going for a Powerade or something."

AJ weighed it, recalling impulses, if not true stories of his own, telling his father he was going here when really he meant to go there. No wrongdoing, just thirty minutes of wasting time. When would he ever know that feeling of being pleased with his own mind, of not wanting to be anywhere else or anyone else? He'd come to accept it was too late for him in that respect, and followed the straight and narrow path until he died.

But he knew the Circle K sold bad wine and, at two a.m., did not discriminate. Babe knew the body language of a much older man, growing into it until, at thirteen, it became a natural thing to walk with his knees a little stiff, his voice a little hoarse, his vocabulary economized, calling everyone Man. Having left his ID at home, it was no problem, was it, to get just one bottle of something, this once? A waste of time, a click of his teeth, Babe had nothing to hide, don't make him stand here by the Hostess cakes and the rotating hot dogs and the Top 40 tinny overhead. And in that buzzing light, it was easy to believe what Babe might look like in ten years, in twenty, sallow, lined, thin-lipped, his big teeth less rabbit-y, the gap between eyetooth and incisor suggesting a permanent loss (FACES OF METH; THIS COULD HAPPEN TO YOU; JOIN ADDICTS ANONYMOUS TODAY), rather than a pretty defect.

It was what kept AJ on the straight and narrow. He knew what men like him did, men who lived without restraint. Dolores Haze was old at seventeen, having lived a lifetime as a slave and a pet and a prisoner, and that was only fiction. Colleagues and clergy defiled their young charges in minutes, leaving them slightly hollowed out, not afraid but deflated, wondering why anyone would want to do them a small generosity, what it might one day cost. Jack Wild (never stated, just assumed) was a drunk at twenty-one and died at fifty from cancer of the mouth, a piece of his tongue cut out. And that was the Artful Dodger, the one who could take anything; it was too awful to think of what happened to the Olivers of this world. It was too awful to think of them as real people. You could never do it, could never quite recompose their kid designs into matured likenesses. They were always dwarf grandmothers, gray-haired pucks with hair growing out of their ears, seventeen or seventy-five, but not grown-ups.

AJ looked behind the boy, where his mother slept. ET was out like a light these days. Once, in a two a.m. fugue like this, Babe had tickled her under her chin, drawn a moustache and a goatee on her face in blue pen, shouted "FIRE" into one ear, had LC shout the same into the other. And still, she did not wake.

"You don't have any cash?" Babe's voice leaned into a whine.

"Don't you have your own money?"

"Emergency funds. I can't eat into those."

"What kind of money is it supposed to be, anyway?"

"Mickey Mouse money, for all I know. So, you don't have any cash?"

"A few dollars." AJ ducked into his hip pocket, pulled out a ten. It was all he had, but he didn't know what he was saving it for.

Enda grabbed it. "You want anything? While I'm out?" He tugged his hat down over his ears, one foot in the doorway.

"You're just going to the Circle K?"

"That's the destination." Implying there might be stops along the way there and back, completely incidental. "You want anything?"

AJ considered a V8 juice, decided against it. "No, nothing. All set."

Unlike LC, the distance AJ placed between himself and young boys (himself angling toward the ballpark of ten to fifteen years of age) was imposed by no other authority than his own mind, the same place where desire also burned a path. He did not love this boy. He had never been in love, not of the kind wherein he could expect it of the same tenor in kind. You were another species by now, the language of springtide forgotten. Everything was simple in springtide, you had to be subtle, you had to be a snake. They babbled, angled inflections, furred, rudimentary creatures. You demanded, they recoiled. You had to be ready with a strike, a trap, a dupe. It was a devil that lived too closely to his surfaces, sometimes winking, other times flashing, always blurred by this or that commotion. AJ had hidden it so well, and he knew that one day, in spite of everything, it would kill him. LC and Holly were the only ones who looked him in the eye now. ET, though sticking by him, developed the habit of looking at him sidelong, and only after she had finished talking.

Mirabel was going to be a girl and Babe was going to be a man. In these things, he had to believe. *Credo in Deum et in Filium Dei unigentum, Deum de Deo, Lumen de Lumine, Deum verum de Deo vero.* Now and at the hour of our death. He didn't know what else to grasp.

Through the window, he watched Babe's hat, its red tassel dancing, grow smaller and smaller as he moved in the streetlamps. Before he could disappear completely, AJ knelt and prodded LC, who woke and shrieked in ET's ear, muffling the sound by padding her mouth with her hands and howling directly into the pink canal. And she turned on her side, and she yawned and murmured something about cats ("Don let um in. Keep tha door close—"), and was out again.

They were a Man without a Heart and a Girl without a Brain. They trailed their Dorothy all the way to the gas station, keeping a distance, canopied in the natural dark as well as in the shadows. The streetlamps in this part of town were always on the fritz, work crews gutting the road all hours trying to repair them. The local consensus was that they were too dim for the area, which was thickly wooded; someone's daughter, someone's son, a freshman at State, a Ford Taurus, Cisco Red in red cups, a little back road at seventy miles per hour, a deer or a dog. Still, people blamed the lights. They could tell Babe's movements from his shoes, a pair of Rosemary's, actually, loafers as mules with sling backs, furry imitation calf in red, black stitching, a man's seven, and so his feet slapped and scraped along the pavement as he walked. They were alarmed when they reached the Circle K, for the boy had darted out of sight for a moment behind a bush, and hopped out again with his shoes in his hands, silent but seen, red cap bright. In the store they edged the shelves and refrigerators toward the back, Babe padding here and there, never quite seeing them and thus failing to recognize them, building an armful of items, two bottles of water, a box of Cheez-Its, a granola bar each in blueberry, honey, and peanut butter, assorted fruit snacks and candy bars, a bag of Skittles, a V8 (for AJ), a Powerade in lurid blue. He was sick of the vegetable regime at Rosemary's and too smart, it seemed, to try and fool a gas station clerk. So far, he still looked thirteen. Overhead, it was not Top 40, but Jackson 5, a declaration, *All I do is think of you* or *All I do is dream of you*. AJ and LC moved to the lunchmeat and dairy, watched as he made his exchange at the register, taking everything in a bag which twisted and untwisted around his wrist. They were especially antsy because they were sure ten dollars would barely cover what he meant to buy, if at all. But it had, more than enough, so it seemed, and the boy left with a bag which twisted and untwisted around his wrist. They were close enough behind him when he left that the automated sliding door did not close again and did not chirp, though they managed to duck behind a Taurus, and Babe was none the wiser.

He followed the streetlamps, murmuring *All I do is think of you to keep company*, counting steps and moving directly into where the light was brightest, two lamps that flanked a great arch, scrolling granite, meant to be solemn with its engravings of the Alpha and the Omega and scripture across the top: IN MY FATHER'S HOUSE ARE MANY MANSIONS. I GO TO PREPARE A PLACE FOR YOU, and its copper plaque beneath, greened by the elements: THE MOUNT HERMON CEMETERY ASSOCIATION, EST. 1918. It was designed to bring comfort, and it did. Here, in truth, were many mansions. The punchline came in its obelisks, its benches, its headstones marking the wipeouts of families and whole neighborhoods from the time of its rising, the first year of the Spanish flu pandemic, the last year of the Great War. The wealthiest patrons could afford eccentricity; there was one gravesite that did not have a headstone, just a sculpture of a male nude, greened copper, that urinated into its own tiny pond when the groundskeeper flipped a switch. It collected snow in winter, bugs in summer, you could imagine the poor green fellow shivering or itching, along with the more classical erections of angels and virgins, making mourners think the weather was much colder than fifty degrees, that their arms crawled with invisible gnats. Enda wondered which god it was. (It was a replica of an installation at the Kafka Museum in Prague. Its commissioner was a life-long library patron, bookworm, and weirdo. When he died no one got the reference, but his sons obeyed the articles of their father's will and told the funeral party they didn't get it either.)

He had never seen *Night of the Living Dead*, never seen *Thriller*, and did not know to be afraid. The dead knew nothing, though there were signs nailed to trees, reminding living visitors that drinking, loitering, picnicking, camping and hunting were prohibited. (SMILE! YOU'RE ON CAMERA) He bent to read epitaphs. Most were elegant, excerpts from Revelations or from poetry. Many wanted to get in one last laugh. He recognized Rosetti's "Death of a Wombat" and the last words of Augustus Caesar: "THE DRAMA'S OVER. APPLAUD." There were others that made him laugh: "GOOD GAME," "I TOLD YOU I WAS SICK," "THAT'S ALL, FOLKS!" His favorite was "ALL DRESSED UP AND NOWHERE TO GO."

He laughed because he knew now, fully and hugely, that he would die, too. It made him laugh because it was absurd to him, that he had never known anything but the immediacy of an itch, the first throb of a headache, hunger, thirst, the need to urinate, the stuck-pig feeling of diarrhea, swallowing tears, trying not to blush, lighting the cold steel of fear underneath with a weak but dancing flame (that semaphore, I AM NOT AFRAID), smothering snickers like he was doing now. How do you imagine the opposite of all that? His father's house was a life of studied quiet, until his brother told him it was all batshit. Out here, he was astonished to find the general rules still applied: Added to no drinking, no loitering, no picnicking, no camping, no hunting, you might as well add no laughing, no crying, no wanting, no fearing, no rambling, to be practiced under a certain governance, not just in the Mount Hebron Cemetery. You could not laugh at a funeral, for example, but you could laugh at Divine's political speech in *Pink Flamingos*, which opened with the words, "KILL EVERYONE

NOW." You could not be afraid of the dark after the age of five or so, but you could spend thousands of dollars to wire your home with alarms and signs that read SMILE! YOU'RE ON CAMERA.

From her place under AJ's arm, LC imagined seven markers, inlaid cement bricks so low and so small that not many would have seen them even through well-moved grass. They were not here, but their names were, jumping at her from otherwise anonymous resting places and rearranging themselves in a straight line far away. The scene was clearer to her now than it had been in years, though she could not approach it with anything other than her coldest faculties, as though she were a tourist. They were Alana, Helena, Portia, Dovie, Rose, Jeremy, Mirando. When she called for them, she used to squeeze them all into one word and they came in a bounding pack. There were a lot of people who were called Alana, Helena, Portia, Dovie, Rose, Jeremy, and Mirando, and it would have been nice to see what her bearers of those names would have turned out to be. Would Helena have become Mrs. Handbasket, mother, mathematician, mate, dead at seventy? It wasn't much of a summary, but they had to put something. All those people who looked like you, a nose, a jaw, a smile, it frightened her, almost as much as hearing one of the other ones (the ones who did not call her Mother) curse, because hearing a child curse correctly was the most frightening thing of all. She had yet to hear Babe curse, but then, he was not her child and so it did not matter.

Enda went on and so did they, staying on the gravel path until it ended in a rather messily kept chain-link fence at the edge of the woods. The boy chose to hitch himself over while his protectors opted to look for a hole or an unlocked gate. In a moment, LC found a hole, one made last Halloween by feral teens and not yet filled. They ducked, tore their clothes when caught, seeing this was where the gravel path met the beaten-dirt path of the park and they were not completely lost. Babe was a noise in the distance, his gait cautious, tripping in the dark over this and that, hissing when he stumbled, an occasion nearly prompting a curse ("GOD——", petering out, a sigh). He slowed, the bag on his wrist rustled, they could hear the burden, the V8 and the treats, swing out and smack against his thigh, a pattern that made AJ think of a yo-yo going out and back.

There were wedding scraps in branches and bushes, growing thicker as they neared the park and the house and the ashram, deflated balloons, ribbons, fanned cupcake wrappers, a seating card that read DOROTHY CLOUD, AUNT. LC foraged and suggested AJ do the same. They soon forgot their charge and grew quite busy stooping and gathering items of interest. AJ found a whole collection of single earrings, in pearl, turquoise, amethyst, opal, and aquamarine, finding also an anklet in gold, a bracelet in sterling silver, a tie pin of a dog. LC found rose petals, a diamond earring, an inhaler, a retainer, a jade-studded barrette, a table candle, a dessert fork. She loved the drink coasters as they neared the venue, stopping to read them when she found them: ALL YOU NEED IS LOVE; LOVE LOOKS NOT WITH THE EYES, BUT WITH THE MIND; GRAVITATION IS NOT RESPONSIBLE FOR PEOPLE FALLING IN LOVE; THE BEGINNING OF LOVE IS THE WILL TO LET THOSE WE LOVE BE PERFECTLY THEMSELVES.

"Let's see," LC mused, "—the Beatles. This one's Shakespeare. Einstein. Who's this last one?"

AJ looked. "Merton."

"A lot of people have a lot to say about the same thing."

"I guess so."

AJ thought that if only his chemistry had taken another route, perhaps he might have loved LC. He did not know how old she was. He did not know her name or her ancestry or her education. He did not know her organs or her bones. He knew she could be all things bright and beautiful, living moment to moment, joy in clouds and in crisp air, wanting to pet every dog, see every show, taste every crumb. Her mind, despite her years, was still a tabernacle with room enough for all manner of congregants, demoniac and devi side by side, not as yet unreconciled. Isn't that the thing about children, that they know not what they do?

"I don't think they're here," AJ told her.

LC nodded. "Oh, I know. I know that. They're likely at the old home."

"Are people allowed to do that? Bury on their property?"

"I think so. I don't see why you shouldn't, if it's your people." She paused. "You're allowed to bury a dog."

"I guess."

"In my next life, I'm coming back as a dog."

"I don't think you can make that decision."

"Sure, you can. I'll come back as one of the Queen's corgis. That'd be something."

"It would." AJ read somewhere the other day the Queen of England no longer bred corgis, and that only two mixed-breeds of the original herd were left. He decided against telling her. He told her instead about meeting the Queen once, years ago, pre-concert, Covent Garden. She had brought Monty. "He peed on all the seats in the royal box."

"Territory," LC sniffed, and they made an inventory of what they'd gathered, and pressed on.

INTO MURMURING, INTO movement, they were in the company of others like them, not much more than shapes in daylight or in dark. Shadows became articulate, ghosts ambulatory, winnowing through the park's paths, through woods and pavement, *over hill, over dale, through bush, through briar.* They had, all of them, in their minds, come so far. And now, they were relieved, they removed their shoes, dumped their knapsacks, shed layers, for the ashram in the park was warm due to an ongoing error at the power company, wherein the heat never shut off completely.

Enda was the only kid, though there were others his age or younger. He stood for awhile behind a fellow no taller than him, though his hair was gray and his breathing labored, it seemed, through a pulpy, pulmonary swamp. The fellow spat and bent to kick off his shoes at the door, straightened, and there was a flush of pink in his cheek, like a baby's. Enda watched him pad toward the window, to open it, and to lean out so he could light a cigarette.

Enda's father smoked a pipe, but that was rare and toward the end of the youngest son's time at the old home, he had given it up. He had seen his brothers smoke pilfered cigarettes, and he knew they traded for them, discreetly, when they were in town. He had always liked the smell, for it reminded him of a bonfire, of burnt sugar, and his father called them filth. And Enda supposed this was true, but it made this fellow look old enough and mellowed enough to make him think nothing could touch him, and still a boy, just like himself.

He remembered, *Fear no more the heat o' the sun/Nor the furious winter's rages*.

He remembered, *All go unto one place*.

And he sighed, excreting demons and guilts and devils of someone else's making. No one watched him. No one thought less of him. No one added his name to a shit list. So, he asked the old boy if he would be willing to trade for a cigarette.

The old boy coughed, said, "You can have this one." And gave Enda another from the pack in his pocket. Canadian Classics, the box read, with a moose and a blocky warning that cigarettes cause cancer. The boy caught him looking and told Enda he liked the cigarette boxes from Canada because of the pictures.

"Of moose?" Enda asked.

"No, like lungs and stuff. They're big in Canada about that, making sure people know what they're getting into. So, they put really gnarly pictures on the boxes of lungs and teeth and tongues that are all rotted out."

Enda started when an ash fell to his bare toe. He coughed and eased into it; the boy, for his gray hair and red eyes and watery voice, did not look rotten. On the contrary, he looked very well-preserved. "Have you ever been to Canada?"

"Once. Quebec."

"How was it?"

"Oh, I dunno. Nice." The fellow spat again, and there was a runner going from his nose. His eyes were wet, too. "Everybody speaks French up there."

"Why'd you come back?"

"Too cold up there. It snowed six feet before I left."

Enda watched how the fellow smoked, rounding his lips and issuing hazy rings out the window, into the dark. Everyone here obeyed the sign, where, among the prohibitions of food, drink, and alcohol, smoking was also forbidden. He tried a few times to work his mouth into the right shape, but never got the hang of it. He asked the fellow, "How old are you?"

"Thirteen."

"Me, too. It's my birthday today."

"Huh." In spite of himself, the fellow's eyes brightened, the joy of finding another Scorpio, another Aquarius, another Leo. "Quel coinkidink."

The foyer and then the rest of the house warmed and filled with bodies and their smells. Someone found the thermostat in a back office that had been left unlocked and raised the heat to seventy-five. Layers shed, clothes piling behind Wainscot chairs and music cabinets. Some were nude, others retaining their modesty in t-shirts or underwear, never both. The house filled again, this time with sighs, suggestive of burdens laid and aching limbs relieved. We have come from so far, and now, here we rest. Watery sounds, thinner than breath, reduced to moisture, issued from people who had forgone all nourishment, comfort, acumen, in exchange for these hours. These were Matins, Lauds, Vespers, one after the other, the world fallen away for a warm oblivion. The devotees nodded like the heads of flowers. Some went still.

Enda asked why this place was called the ashram in the park. The fellow told him, "Hippies. You ever seen the movie *Hair*?"

"No."

"You know Woodstock?"

Enda knew the Peanuts Gang.

"Jesus." The fellow told him about people with long hair who wore beads and dropped acid and saw eternity. "Hippies used to live here and then the state cleared them out and made the house nice and put a plaque on it. They pretty much just hung out here and grooved on it all. My mom used to live here, she told me about it. She used to be a groupie." He went into his pocket and found

127

his wallet, green Patagonia with Velcro. There was cash in fives and ones and a ketchup packet from Burger King and a picture. "That's her. Back in the day." Long hair, sure enough, beads, big glasses with round rims, a smirk for the camera. In fact, it was a photo of Janis Joplin, cut from a magazine; but the fellow thought she looked like his mother and so he kept it and believed and one day the thought stuck and became true.

Enda asked, "Where is she now?"

"Dead."

"Mine, too."

"Do you have a picture?"

"No. What's a groupie?"

"You know Jimi Hendrix?"

"Yeah."

"She fucked him. You know Jim Morrison?"

"Yeah."

"She fucked him, too."

"Are these people hippies?"

"No. They're smackheads. They don't live here; they just stay the night."

Hippies saw eternity and smackheads oblivion.

Hippies waited to tell you what the trip was like when they returned from it, never at the moment at which they found themselves truly behind the veil. They might have told you about the things they saw and heard, fractals in the rug, the beauty of water on your tongue, the depth of Sun Ra's *Super-Sonic Jazz*. Those were the ones who had approached the veil. The ones who went beyond said much the same thing: a city made of light; light as language; a notion of familiarity, a return, clarity, and over much too soon. You compared it to a near-death experience or to an alien abduction, maybe being born. You only needed to do it but once or twice, in a lifetime or in a year. For some, once was enough. It showed you everything and your place in it. It absorbed you and warmed you, and you were comforted by the knowledge it knew what you were and did not belittle or chastise. It suggested a common knowledge, planted in the worm of every human brain, lost at birth and needing but a nudge or two to call it out from the fog. A lot of hippies showed up at Rosemary's.

Smackheads told you everything because it might be the one and only time they would have the chance. They did not talk about the trip because there wasn't one. This was beyond the veil, far beyond the light language of the magic city, from even its glow, no one there and you were gone, too. There was the memory of your pulse and its ebbing radiance. There were sighs, having come from so far. And now, we rest. *This is the light of the mind, cold and planetary*, as Sylvia Plath said. *Cause de river's quiet/And a po', po' gal can sleep*, as Langston Hughes said. It held the same odor of despair, the same pleasure you find in wallowing because you knew you might not have to do any of this (bathing, eating, speaking, waking) again. This, too, was a return, expiration being the same state as pre-conception. Smackheads talked about their time on earth, knowing the possible distance they would take from it, remembering what they could while they could. A few of them showed up at Rosemary's, too.

"Do hippies go to Heaven"—Enda thought out loud—"and smackheads go to Hell?"

The fellow started. "Do what?"

Enda repeated the question.

"I think you all go to the same place. It's all brains and chemicals. There's an idea somewhere that we're all just brains in jars, anyway."

"Then, who's in charge of the jars?" Enda asked.

The fellow snorted. "And where's he getting all the brains from?"

"From the brain forest." Enda wondered if he'd heard "brain forest" somewhere before; it was so good he pretended he was the one who'd thought of it.

In the next room, restored to its former grandeur, its oak polished, its shelves full of first-edition replicas and china fauns and nymphs and sylphs, its davenports and ottomans reupholstered and stiff, hung with signs bidding tourists not to sit on the furniture, its windows colored and clean and casting gauzy greens and reds across faces in daylight, cushions were removed and repurposed, humped up against the fieldstone columns and the wood-paneled walls, laid in low cots along the floor where the people rested and nodded.

Hippies saw the empyrean and smackheads the void.

The empyrean was easy enough to imagine. What, then, about the void? Neither boy could conceive of a time in which there had not been impressions, a color, an odor, a pinprick, a shout (whether it was for one or the other of them or not), an idea that built itself so securely into the brain it felt tangible in the way places long collapsed and gone feel tangible still, having been, could continue to be, if in another embodiment.

Enda thought, I just want a little quiet.

He asked the fellow if he'd ever gone into the next room while everyone rested and nodded. The fellow told him he hadn't, not yet, for the sighs frightened him, and Enda knew this was true.

The fellow's eyes were wet, Babe's dry.

Babe poked him. "Ashes to ashes."

The fellow poked Babe. "Dust in the wind."

Babe thought he and the fellow might go on this way forever, speaking in code, a free association of things they liked, translated into what they knew and saw and felt. He hoped one day he might find a way to use his own words.

They sat.

Someone with a phone put on Jeremy Irons reading "East Coker." Babe heard part of it, up to the line "*O dark dark dark. They all go into the dark*" and felt his head aflame, then cool, the heat turning inward with the rest of him, right from the nostrils, grazing the back of his throat with icy fingers, dropping away and writhing up again, but only momentarily, in his bowels. Now it was quiet. Now it was still. He had gone back to the womb. He devolved, blind, curving inward and becoming a tiny knot, feeding on a supply of blood that was his own, then shared, then, with the knowledge he was sapping another being of her heart, ate of it anyway. This was the void.

Would anyone save me if they knew?

The Son of Man asked, Would anyone save me if they knew? Or am I better off dead? It would be as simple as that, he reasoned, to vanish. Nothing since the womb had been more plushed.

He had heard somewhere, something on TV at Rosemary's, a round table of talking heads, intellectuals, academics, a Democrat, a Republican, a Libertarian, a feminist, a rabbi, a priest, a mushroom shaman, a Bhikkhuni, that the only thing America seemed to truly contemplate anymore was suicide and that all other decisions were sort of shot from the hip. It led the discussion down a pessimistic path, each party blaming the other for the fall of a nation, once great or yet with the potential to be great. He'd half-listened. The Republican wanted to talk about kids today, as did the Democrat. The Libertarian wanted to talk about taxes and the housing market. The priest and the feminist wanted to talk about family planning. The mushroom shaman and the rabbi wanted to talk about addiction. The Bhikkhuni wanted to talk about health care.

The Son of Man thought, Shouldn't all these people be walking into a bar?

Beside him, the fellow sniffed. Enda felt for his hand, squeezed. Both of them were chilled.

"What's your name?" Enda asked.

"Cher." The fellow nodded, sniffed. "What's yours?"

"Babe. Your name's really Cher? Like THAT Cher? *Love after love* Cher?"

"No, fool. Like the French word. It means 'dear'."

"What's your real name?"

"What, Cher's not good enough?"

"No, just—what's your real name, is all. Babe's not my real name."

Cher closed his eyes, wiped his nose on a pillow's plush. "I figured that."

"My real one's Enda."

"Ender?" Cher pointed to Enda's sweatshirt. "Like that?"

"No, Enda. It means 'bird'."

"What is it, Australian?"

"I don't know."

"Maybe it's French."

"Maybe."

They closed their eyes in tandem and, hands still laced, listened for awhile to a fellow talk about his grandfather's time as a soldier in the second World War. He had been in England long enough to carve his name into the wooden snug at a pub in Brighton before going into Germany, where he had been captured by the Nazis, nearly shot on a roadside in the darkest night, survived a prisoner of war camp and lived his days in New Mexico until the government moved in to conduct nuclear testing. His other grandfather had been in Japan at that time, having watched a kamikaze pilot crash an American ship that had been emptied of men and supplies, having been chosen as the one to notify the families of the enemies killed, having to bear humility and hospitality and green tea until he could be alone to weep. "I was in Syria," the grandson said. "My grandfather told me not to join up."

The woman next to him added that her grandfather might have been held in the same German camp. "Did your grandfather wake up one day to find everything deserted? All the guards gone, no one there but the POWs? Did your grandfather ever tell you about the flyers? On the day all the POWs woke to find the camp deserted, there were these papers, these flyers all scattered around, like they'd been dropped from the sky. My grandfather kept one. It basically warned the Germans that the Americans were coming, and that everything had better be in keeping with the Geneva Convention or they were sending the German POWs back in pieces. They didn't say word-for-word, *We'll cut off your kraut boys' toes and pull out their teeth* or anything like that, of course. But whatever they said—"

"Was your grandfather in a castle? The Nazis made a lot of old castles into camps."

"No."

"Oh. Mine was. He kept the telegram they sent to his mother about being captured. He went kind of batshit when he came home."

"Yeah. Mine was in a hospital for a year when he got back. He stopped voting, too."

On someone's phone, Jeremy Irons intoned, "*Datta. Dayadhvam. Damyata/Shantih shantih shantih.*"

ET WOKE AND wondered, Where is my boy?

Inside her, Mirabel stirred and turned.

LC STOOD OVER Babe and watched him dream.

They'd found him inside, not too long after he'd fallen asleep. Next to him, Cher had slipped from Babe's hand and now both boys lay with their backs to one another, fists knotted between their knees, reflecting the postures of all present. There was little breath to be heard or felt, and the gray dawn did not touch the colors in the glass, so everyone sleeping, everyone dreaming took on a smooth, clean look under the light. It might have been a mausoleum, a tomb of ancestors, for these were not people, but sarcophagi, carved from marble in poses from life, as the Etruscans had done. But out of the blue, someone would shake themselves awake and they would rise as the sun did, porous and hollow and, what's more, alive for every burning inch of daylight, bringing them to their former positions, though now they moaned. They had succumbed to Vesuvius, heads on fire, and here was what remained.

Enda dreamed he was thirty years old and visiting with an old fellow who lived in one of the huge, turreted houses along the main drag into town. He'd always, it seemed, been under the impression that because the houses were so grand the people who lived in them must be so rich. As it turned out, the old fellow was the grandson of the house's architect and first dweller. It was a sprawling, solid place, the veranda interchangeable with the ivy, apple green in its heyday, now the color of fume, windows lashing open like eyes through the storied leaves. They used to say you could squint on a windy day and the ivy turned into dollar bills. As it turned out, the old fellow had not seen the real gold of this fortune, having watched it spent away by various relations, investments that went bust, et cetera. By the time some real lump of it came to him, it arrived in the form of this house. The electric was iffy, the plumbing was poor, the wires a hazard. It was a danger to turn on the television. "And nine times out of ten," the old fellow said, "I don't."

The Son of Man asked him what about that one time out of ten. "I'll tell you what. *SVU*, son. I don't miss one show, not for as long as it's been going."

They sat, Enda on the sofa, the fellow in a wide armchair, and watched until LC was standing over Enda, years and years ago, telling him to get up.

He woke.

LC whispered, "Get up. We have to go."

He yawned, turned to his other side. No heaviness, no leaden jellyfish creeping in one ear and out the other, solidifying mean-time into a headache. There was no headache at all, in fact. He could spring to his feet, in fine fet and fettle. He only wanted a little quiet.

LC repeated, her voice pulled tight. "We have to go." She was thinking about going home, not to Rosemary's but somewhere she knew and Babe knew, where they might not be let to return if an-yone found them missing.

Babe wanted to find that quiet again and worked the parts of his brain that might take him back, burrowing into his sweatshirt, curling his toes. He dreamed again and was thirty-two and his mother asked him what he meant when he said he was going to the beach. "We're a hundred miles from any beach."

"We have to go—" LC had said it more than twice, growing hoarse.

People were waking.

"We have to go," LC shrieked, then mouthed the last word.

Coughing and crusted eyes.

LC moved when everyone else started to. She looped Babe's arm around her neck, tried again when it slipped, tried a third time and hissed when his nail scraped her nose. Babe played possum and went stiff, then limp, save for his mouth, which squirmed from one end of his face to the other, rearranging, making itself small enough to disappear into a knot, to burst when he could not take the joke any longer. He wanted to wake Cher. He wanted Cher to come with them.

Of every time he had seen lips as blue as these, of the babes who came before him, boys who did not survive a night, did not survive the transition through the canal, he had looked at each of them with something like disappointment. And, with every passing baby boy, it felt as though his expectations could not be lowered any further. If he could do it. If his sisters could do it. If the boys who had come before him could do it, though his father had declared them disgraced, not damned outright. All had survived. Enda the Younger wanted to be damned. He wanted every new boy to carry the burden and the knowledge, all of it, for it could never be a load that was equally shared. He wondered if he would have gotten a new name, if any boy had lived. He wondered if every boy sired by the Elder had once been called Enda.

Cher, dead, looked like a baby.

LC laid one finger on him, at the bow of his blue lips.

Enda thought about survival. AJ thought about it, too, letting Enda take his arm. Survival was the paring down of living for one day, maybe the next. And both thought, What could be better? Imagine having to concentrate everything to immediate proximity, the way that wild beasts and professional foragers do. You have what you have, not much more.

It sounded like a facet of hell, but only at first, when you remembered how things were in your old life.

The smackheads moved on Cher at once, searching his clothes for things. Someone found two alligator finger puppets. Another found a Tic-Tac container, empty. A bottlecap, a menu for a local pizzeria folded into the narrowest accordion. A Free Tibet sticker. A sticker in support of a local politician running as the Republican candidate and its twin for the Democrats. A magic marker in orange, a Sharpie in red, and both still worked.

They asked Babe if he wanted to take anything. "From your friend there."

They had gone in together and kept one another warm in a cold night. Pared in this way, that made Cher a friend. Enda said aloud, "I don't even know what was in his stuff."

ET ASKED ROSEMARY a few times what she would do if Holly died, using different language every time so Rosemary wouldn't give her the same answer. *If Holly were gone. If Holly became ill. If Holly vanished in the night.* It was something she did with her own mother. If her mother gave her the same answer, she wanted ET to go away. "Stop asking. It's not going to change however many times you ask. Go find something to do." You could never guess which was the real answer because they were all the same.

Rosemary was different. She could be unlocked.

What would you do if Holly were gone?

"I would try to find where she went to."

If Holly became ill?

"I would care for her the best I could."

If Holly vanished in the night?

"Get her to unvanish, I guess. Wasn't that an episode of *The Twilight Zone*? Where the little girl gets stuck in another dimension or something? With her dog?"

If Holly died?

Rosemary said, "I'll die first, though, won't I?"

ET allowed that while this was the usual way of things, it didn't always happen. "My mother is dead," she pronounced. This was not true, but ET had not spoken to her mother in nearly two years, and the absence was beginning to solidify.

A few days later, she asked again.

Rosemary said, "I'd bear up as best I could."

Rosemary said, "I don't know."

Rosemary said, "I don't like to think about that."

Rosemary said, "I'd want to die, too."

The last was the true one. It chilled ET and elated her. She tried to relieve herself with the knowledge Mirabel could never die. She could never die, ET reasoned, so long as she was never birthed.

I have no children. I am with child.

Now, waking at the witching hour, it was a curious thing to find herself thinking not of the bloom in her belly, but of, "My boy. Where is my boy?"

ENDA WALKED WITH them so they were three abreast, AJ at his right, LC at his left. He held on with the ridges of his fingernails. His knees were lousy hinges, and he buckled twice before they left the cemetery. Still, AJ told him, echoing his own father's tone and distilling it to its best and most thunderous, "Get up. I'm not carrying you." In that moment, he was any other man, shaking his head at a wayward youth. Any other man thought, This is a child, not yet human, half-formed and smelly, sweet in its stupidity and its ability to mimic what it sees. A child is entertaining, if only for so long, if only before it makes a mess. It is a creature in need of discipline. Would you desire a dog? Of course not.

LC said she could carry him. The boy was as tall as she, though she outweighed him. Muscle memory saw her through the effort, and she had him cradled for a few steps before the ache in her arms made her rearrange him in a fireman's carry over her shoulders. His head lolled into the crook of her neck. She could smell his crown. He could smell her. They did not recognize each other, though both caught the instant of familiarity and sought it beneath these layers, cotton, wool, flora, fluid. He smelled mostly of cheese, she of onions.

Babe moaned. "I'm hungry." He wasn't really; he'd grown tired of saying "I want to go home."

The void was home.

Years later, when he grew from a scruffy kid to a scruffier adult, he heard what people said about him. The Son of Man was thirty years old and still lived with his mother. The Son of Man couldn't get his shit together. If he wasn't in rehab someplace, he was in jail. If he wasn't in jail, he was using. He would be six-foot-one, one hundred and thirty-eight pounds. He would have long lashes. He would have long arms. His innards would glimpse the skin's surface as fish in a pond. He carried transgression and vice and disease and disappointment. He would bite his nails to the quick. People looked at him and felt better about themselves. People made jokes. Before he got famous, while he was still living, not many knew what his voice sounded like, though they had been his neighbors for as long as they could remember. Kids in the south part of town saw him and did Towelie. Kids north saw him and did Beavis.

"Well, if that's what you must do," he would say, "if you want me to be a cartoon. Fine, I'll take it. But understand: there's plenty of other drugged-out characters. Characters I'm sure you've never thought of. Bugs Bunny had those carrot butts. Droopy was on whatever I'm on. An aside: I don't know what I'm on half the time. I just know that he's on what I'm on. The dead obvious one is Shaggy. Shaggy had charm, everyone loves Shaggy for all the same reasons. Like, when you're thirteen, you get the joke. And you try to be very louche about it when you point it out to your church-going friend, *You know why he's scarfing down all those hamburgers?*"

For my yoke is easy, and my burden is light.

Enda Martindale was thirteen years old and he knew what he would be.

Babe had already traded the candy bars and the rest of the junk from Circle K.

AJ found the bottle of V8 in Babe's pocket, the thing no one in the grand house wanted, and told him to drink. He kept the cap for himself, caught the boy under the chin with the bottle, upsetting red down his front.

Babe coughed. "That's yours."

AJ told him, "Drink."

Babe countered, "I hate that stuff. I only got it for you."

AJ said it had things the boy needed. "You don't eat right."

"Rosemary doesn't put salt in anything."

What did Enda eat at the old home? He remembered apples cooked on a stove all day in cinnamon and nutmeg and butter and salt. He ate them with cream on top. They had eaten of their own cows, mincing them for meatloaf, smoking pounds to strips that filled an envelope, boiling the bones for stock. His brothers worked with the meat, his sisters the garden. They got bulk flour and select canned goods (tuna fish, beans, coffee) from the supermarket, brought to the gate by a hired man. His father took all deliveries, paid all bills, accounted for every cent, never dipping into the daemon box for daily needs. Once, there had been some confusion and they had gotten items from someone else's groceries among their own. The Elder sent back most of them, turning one moment and back another, never having made a full inventory of what was theirs and what was not. He caught Enda, spoon in hand, eating from a large jar of peanut butter. He did not ask him if they had ordered it, though its place in his home, in his kitchen mystified him. Enda saw this and said his father's wife had added it, last minute. And his father, mollified though blurred, said no more about it.

He didn't know whether to be sorry or to try again.

They got halfway through the cemetery and now the gate was in sight. They stopped a minute because LC's shoulders hurt and Babe was coming around, and they sat awhile. The arch was rounded and the sun filled the curve on a clear morning. It was dark yet, blue, so you could catch the impressions of things. You saw movement. You saw a quick procession, one that might have been solemn if those in it walked the right pace, going out from the cemetery, not in. Instead, they scurried, as quickly as the idea of mourning might allow, all angles and bowed heads, while their legs propelled them in funny tip-toeing that kicked up the dirt. Two mourners, slower than the rest by their burden, brought up the rear. In their care, held by wrists and ankles and swaying like a middling full sack, was Cher. Someone coughed. Someone whistled, was told roughly to stop by another. They carried rucksacks and duffels and sleeping bags, too. At the house, everything was as it should be.

"What will they do with him, do you think?" Babe knew, but he wanted to hear what LC and AJ thought.

"Put him in the woods," LC thought.

AJ thought of telling the boy about the way Mozart was buried (en masse, wound in a sheet, dusted with lime). Instead, he found himself telling Babe the Poe story of a live burial, hoping to frighten away the melancholy. Babe's attention was short and all were relieved by tales of ghoulish things. AJ's father had liked to read ghost stories to him, and as a boy, AJ had thrilled at this new color of fear. M.R. James and Charles Dickens, spiritus fog at Christmastide, blood under the door, grinning in the hall. Ghosts were not quite one thing and did not make sense. It was just this side of pleasure to be afraid.

Babe laughed.

Down the way, the procession slowed, ticked, listened. Heads turned, looked up, recognized the troupe up the path as more of themselves, and started up again. Cher's bearers had trouble getting their footing on the gravel, and the stones made the one holding the wrists slip and made the one holding the ankles trip, and soon one let go of one ankle and one let go of one wrist. The one in back tripped again, putting out both hands this time to break his fall, causing his partner to haul Cher by the feet like a crash test doll. The one in back hurried to keep up. He bent and groped. He hissed, "Shitshitshitshit."

After they took everything from the body, they would bring Cher into the woods, as LC had predicted, and leave him there. They would put him in a thicket of cedar where the needles covered him well. In another day, a family of razorbacks, creatures blended from wild boar and domestic pigs, huffed and pushed the needles, turning and peering at what the juveniles had found. Already there were marks, made by pigs who could not wait. A taste, a testament. Blooms above the bone. The meat was slim, but it was young and good. When this was pronounced, they knelt and they ate.

Here, on this morning, in this place, there was a pond full of ducks. AJ noted one unfurling itself in the overhang of an oleander. The three watched as the first duck, head feathered green, shuffled to the lapping shore, turned for its mate, dowdier and beige. The dowdy one took her time, let the green one go first, paddled in when he upended himself, green head under, popping up, going under again, rubbery feet pedaling.

"Those are the ugliest ducks I've ever seen," LC announced, a little loudly, as though she wanted them to hear.

The beige one, starting at the sound, hissed, and Enda squinted. "I didn't know ducks had teeth," he said. The beige one held her beak open and her tongue wagged, and they could see that it was serrated up and down both sides, not exactly teeth. The light had purpled and the funny, bubbled skin around the ducks' eyes and beaks was brighter than their plumage. The beige one hissed again, stared quietly, a warning, not turning as she sauntered into the pond, pushing off and gliding toward the center, still watching.

"Maybe there's eggs," LC said, and made a move toward the bush, yelping when AJ pulled her back by her hood.

"Someone coming—" AJ ushered them behind a small mausoleum.

Headlights, exhaust, a radio going in and snuffing out when the vehicle parked. A shape descended from the cab of the truck, whistling through teeth the tail of what the radio had been playing. The bed held an assortment of tools, talons of rakes and faces of shovels, and sacks of woody manure. The shape became man and he shook in his fist a large plastic Baggie. It sounded like cereal, and it summoned curious and quacking miscreation from the underbrush, feathered green and beige, brown and black, pretty as paintings if you didn't look them in the face. Bulbous here, warted there, closer to toads than ducks, monstrous with their spurred tongues, peering out at the world with small eyes.

Babe was not yet out of his stupor and did not understand he was meant to be quiet. He scrambled from under AJ's arm. "I want to feed them—"

"Quiet—"

"Fuck off, I want to feed them—"

"Sit down and be—"

Babe had already slipped out of his fingers and was striding up the path. His eyes were heavy and red and wet and a runner dripped from his nose, pooling in the bow of his lip. His hair was in oily smuts under his hat and his clothes were in layers; people knew his texture from far away.

AJ and LC had not taken account of their own appearances for a while. They wondered at how they must look, not through a mirror and not through one another, but through someone else.

Babe knew nothing but the difference, even at this age. He did not know to be afraid of it and he never would. He was talking to the man with the Baggie. "Are they wild?"

The man whistled (Enda knew the song, "Fly Me to the Moon," Rosemary had some Sinatra), stopped. "I guess they are by now. I'll have to get some kind of licensure from the state."

"What do they like to eat?"

"I don't know, little things. This is Wheaties flakes here."

The man held the Baggie out to the boy, and soon they had moved toward the pond's bank, and AJ and LC couldn't hear much more.

ET USED TO like to play house, well beyond an age where it could be deemed appropriate or funny or eccentric. She did not have the charm needed to make anything funny or eccentric.

Her idea of house did not include other people and so no one else could ever quite enjoy the game with her. The objective was not role-playing but routine. At one o'clock, you swept the floor. At half-past, you prepared an invisible lunch. At quarter-of, you painted the walls and redecorated, and at two, you planted flowerbeds alongside the herb garden. The next day at that hour, you put in a koi pond, then scrapped it for a hedge maze.

Later on, when she had her own place, she made a habit of walking up and down the road where she lived, stopping when the contents of a lit window intrigued her. She would look the house up if it was on the market, and move from room to room, angled from the farthest corner so as to widen the space, looking at the kitchen as it was meant to be seen. Houses were built in 2002, 1970, 1880. They had hardwood floors, new tile, wall-to-wall carpet. They included refrigerators, glass-topped stoves, washer-dryer sets. There were good schools, dog parks, conveniences. The

Clutter family lived there, Katharine Hepburn lived there, the Manson family lived there.

And now you live there.

She imagined it, and could not conjure the necessary furnishings. There were no chairs, no tables, no rugs, no electronics, no bed. What about her own artifacts, her books and jewelry and clothes? In her mind, they did not feature. It was her, her odors, her echoes.

Could a house be haunted if its ghost was alive?

And then I'll live there.

She wrapped herself now around Mirabel and wanted her boy to come home. Her belly stirred, she knew it.

THE SON OF MAN asked if anyone knew what the most comforting thing was. "Knowing that one day, tomorrow or years from now, we're all going to die." It was a joke that garnered some measure of distaste, prompting his stepfather to implore him, not for the first time, to write things a little more positive.

"It is a positive thing," the Son of Man argued, after the show when they were all home.

He brought up that medieval motif, the *Danse Macabre*, in which a king, a beggar, a cleric, a maiden, an infant go to the grave in a long and blissful procession, full of quick steps, hand in hand, like a game of Following the Leader—a leader that is all but the bones of any and everyone, moving toward the common hole. "It always made me laugh," the Son of Man said.

"I'm not laughing," his stepfather countered. "This is not funny. This is completely unfunny."

His mother tried to tell his stepfather what her boy was getting at. "I don't think he wants to get a rise out of anybody."

"Can ANYBODY hear me?" His stepfather rubbed his eyes. His stepson's humor had, for all its bleakness, a cleanliness to it, a softness that did not judge, belittle, or pervert. No one came away from the ashram or from Blue Jeans in anger. Something lifted, and the burden was not so great. "Can anybody hear me? Can ANYBODY hear me in this HOUSE? That's not what I'm talking about. He's not well."

The Son of Man ducked his head under the kitchen faucet, slurped. "I'm still here. I can hear you." He wiped the dribble from his chin, the wetness from his eyes.

The French called it "yellow laughing." Through the black, the Son of Man thought, that must be the light. It was the thing that burst to the forefront, for all your efforts to contain it. When you went to a funeral, when you approached the edge. It was the thing that brought you back to multitudinous odors and tastes and sights and you remembered, suddenly, what it was like to walk barefoot along the shore. Imagine: you, who have little in the way of money, who may never have had your name in the paper, who might be known, if only as an example of what could happen if you didn't stay in school. You, who might be the beggar, who are also steeped in the joy of being alive, moment to moment, color to color, are let to walk the same shore as the king.

"Either this wallpaper goes, or I do," as Oscar Wilde said.

"You can't kill this tough Jew," as Rod Serling said.

The Son of Man said, "I can't do it forever. If I did it forever, who else would you all be laughing at?"

His stepfather sighed. "That's what I'm talking about."

LC AND AJ had the window seats on either side in the pickup's cab, and Enda sat in between. AJ pulled him in after and LC wedged herself in by his right.

Their driver, having introduced himself as Ranger, drove an even fifty miles per hour on the highway, citing his poor night vision, exited at twenty exactly, and took the road toward town at the recommended speed of forty. Enda asked him at the pond if Ranger was his real name.

Ranger told him, "No, just a nickname." His real name was Pliny, after the place of his birth in some back wood, and he suffered for it as a kid. His father had the same name, making him Pliny Jr. "So, I am become Ranger."

Babe asked, "Like *Walker, Texas Ranger?*"

Ranger clucked, eyes on the road. "Now, that's a little before your time, isn't it?"

Babe said, "It's on TV, isn't it?"

"Well," Ranger slowed for a yellow light, "I haven't had a TV set in ten years. I don't aim to get another one. You're lucky you all caught me when you did. I have a hundred pounds of mulch back there that's going to feed all the bushes at Mount Hermon. I hate to see a dead azalea, don't you?"

LC remarked that his truck was very tidy, and that he seemed very tidy, too.

"I like my moustache trimmed and my 'I's dotted," he said. "Where am I letting you all off at?" He piloted the truck at the same easy pace, looping around the center of town, the YMCA, the shelter.

It was at this juncture LC began to shake, her leg bouncing on its ankle, knee knocking against the door. AJ saw and leaned across. She emptied without warning, he knew, deluged in panic while he and ET buoyed in despair. It might have been a word, a sound. Her hair bristled, her skin erect, her face tight. You never knew what she might do, for she lived moment to moment. He caught her sleeve before she could leap from the cab. It was a lucky thing Ranger drove at a crawl. Nevertheless, the passenger door flying, the tires screeching only a little, he brought the truck to a groaning halt, right there at the intersection.

"Almighty. Goddamn—" Ranger exhaled, lurched forward, five miles slower. "What? What? What was that about?"

Behind, AJ held fast to LC. Enda held his breath, pinned beneath AJ's arm.

"I don't want to go home," LC announced.

"Don't listen to her." AJ tried to take her hand. "Make a right, then another right at the next light."

"I don't want to go home." Then, again and again, an emphasis on the last word, as though everyone ought to know what she meant, "I want to go HOME."

The radio, snuffed. The truck, slower, slower. The wheel, turning and turning, guiding the party into the parking lot of a Wag-a-Bag. The sky, now gray, almost day. Ranger, perplexed. He craned his head around to his passengers, neither frightened nor angry. "You want to go home," he echoed, "you don't want to go home. Where do you want to go?"

AJ waved to Ranger, pacifying the air with an elegant hand. He asked LC if she meant the hospital.

"No." She sniffed.

"Rosemary's? You don't want to go to Rosemary's?"

"I want to go to Rosemary's."

"Well," AJ sighed, "that's no problem, because that's where we're headed."

LC eyed him over one shoulder. "You're sure?"

"Absolutely."

It was difficult to imagine LC having any other home. AJ knew a little of ET's pre-hospital days, as ET knew of his. (ET would never tell, though there was nothing, really, to tell. He had done nothing, and swore on his life to ET that he would do nothing. There were her furrowed eyes, the idea he hadn't done anything, as yet.) LC's ailments were too big to be tamed. Her offenses could be forgiven by God, only tentatively by a jury of her peers. The orderlies knew all about her; they pitied her, spoke to her loudly, kept her at arm's length. She was one of the ones who would never leave, not even on a day pass. Here, the defense pronounced, was a plain example of the mind turning against itself. She did not know what it was she had done. The transformation had happened in an instant, so quickly she had not felt the shift. She was all eyes and raised fur, capable of anything. Where could you picture her? In a wilderness, crouched in a cave? Under brush, under branches, like a boar overtaken by hunger, fright? What did you do when you were no longer human?

And so, AJ was the one who held her hand and kissed her and comforted her in her emptiness, for he, too, was all eyes and fur.

Ahead, Ranger nodded. The headlights lit upon a poster in the window of the Wag-a-Bag, COCKATOO LOST. ANSWERS TO THE NAME OPIE. WILL COME IF YOU WHISTLE ANDY GRIFFITH. On that morning and the days before, a little old man had treaded up and down the main drag, thinking of,

146

without meaning to, a faraway place with one traffic light, moonshine and lemonade, a fishing hole. Ranger had seen him, a little old man whistling on a loop and looking into all the trees, and thought he must be senile.

He put the radio back on, Paul Simon, and they all sat for a while so LC could collect herself. AJ coached her through one breath, then another, easing the air through her pursed lips, emitting, quite by accident, a whistle, getting a chuckle from Ranger. Babe joined her, wolf-whistling. Ranger pointed to the poster in the window and noted there was a hundred-dollar reward if you could catch that cockatoo. "All you have to do is whistle Andy Griffith."

"Is a hundred dollars a lot for a cockatoo?" Babe asked as they turned back onto the main road.

"Is a hundred dollars a lot?" LC echoed, in part because she really did want to know.

"They live to be a hundred," AJ remarked. "And they're clever mimics. My father had a macaw that he taught to sing the Litany of the Saints."

Here was where the light of day lay upon their neighborhood. In the dark, the old houses were lit from inside, and all you could see from the street were luminous shapes in the air and the cozy clarity of the people inside. Now, even at this early hour, you knew the white paint had grayed and flaked, the deep-eaved porches were larded with bloated black bags and overstuffed couches.

"Welcome to Sesame Street." Ranger pulled up beside Rosemary's and insisted on seeing them all to the door.

A face in the window, a darting curtain, thumping feet around a corner, and ET met them before the screen door could slap behind her. She looked at Babe, her hands twitching, still, twitching, still, as though under restraint. It was Babe who went to her, his head at rest on her shoulder. "I couldn't get to sleep," he said. "I didn't want to wake you."

Her arms, limp at her sides, remembered their purpose and wrapped themselves around her boy, one hand in his hair.

LC kissed ET's cheek, AJ the other. They intoned, supplicants

147

in echo, "Sorry, Mom." It made the air around them gauzy and warm and contagious. From his distance, Ranger shifted on his feet. He peered through the embraces to look into ET's face directly, remarking to her that he did not mean to be forward, but she looked to him like a gal who was very well-loved. "And in need of a good night's sleep," he added.

ET blinked, and saw a little man with a trim moustache and a bright flannel shirt. She told him he looked to her like a very nice man. She thanked him, and asked where he found her boy.

"Mount Hermon."

"The cemetery?"

"It's not as ghoulish as it sounds. Yours truly is groundskeeper thereabouts, and my work has been featured in *Better Homes and Gardens*." He huffed. "At least, I think it ought to be."

For the next couple of days, Enda commented on the new and constant rose in ET's cheeks. When he played with Holly, he chanted one of the rhymes he learned from LC, making Holly laugh and AJ smile with his own modifications.

Ranger and Mama sitting in a tree
K-I-S-S-I-N-G
First comes love, a baby carriage,
Then comes Ranger with a diamond and marriage

"That is not funny," ET snapped, redder. "That is completely unfunny."

"But it's true," Babe sang, and Holly echoed the tune.

Later, he begged to go out again, and ET obliged, walking with him down the hill toward town. It was a fine day, one in a long line of fine days since; ET suspected this was an illusion, assigning meaning to something when it meant nothing at all, and so on. She kept one hand on her belly. Mirabel had, in these fine days, squirmed and wormed, not a burden but a flowering, akin to delight, the anticipation of your birthday, of Christmas morning.

Babe walked backwards so he could look at her. He'd stopped snickering over the miracle baby, perhaps resigned to what was coming, perhaps humoring her. He asked why she was in the hospital. "Were you sick?"

She, as tight-lipped as he, allowed that, yes, she had been sick.

"And you all," one finger circling to include AJ and LC, "were in the hospital together?"

"Yes."

"Were you all sick with the same thing?"

ET paused and, deliberating, maneuvering him toward the curb when a car came too close, said that, yes, more or less, the same thing.

"Are you contagious?"

"No." She thought of the episodes throughout history in which one thought caught the fervor of entire villages. Choreomania infected a Christmas Eve Mass in Bernburg, Germany, causing the congregation to leap to their feet in the sanctuary and dance until they dropped. The Salem witch trials. Satanic panic at nursery schools.

"Are you batshit?"

"What?"

"Batshit."

"What?"

"Are you a crazy person?"

"What?"

Enda tried again. "They have hospitals for crazy people, don't they?"

More than half the folk who turned up at Rosemary's were crazy people. He wasn't being unkind. It made ET want to sit down, which she did, right there on the curb, one hand, as it always was, starred atop her belly. She saw what he could not, what others could not. That was that.

Babe sat beside her. He picked a crumb from the corner of his eye. "My dad's batshit. My brother told me."

"I'm sorry for his troubles."

"He wasn't always crazy. My brother told me that, too."

"That's sad."

"He said that the world outside was going to burn."

"A lot of people think that, and they're not crazy. Some of them are on television all the time."

The compound was three hundred acres, fenced all around, miles from anywhere. They grew and preserved and stocked their own food. His father took one wife, discarded her, or mourned her when she bore his child, then another. The boys worked the land, the girls the hearth. One day, when the world had burned and they were all that remained of their elevated species, they would rebuild society in the model of the great and heavenly kingdom. Enda the Elder christened the compound Martin's Valley, because that was what the family name meant; he uttered it with reverence, and it became synonymous with all the other words that referred to Paradise. There was one God, a layered thing that peeled away into a fecund multitude, scattered here and there, in trees, in water, in the beasts of the field that unveiled themselves with a look, a word only the Elder could hear. He had the proof of the ancients. He had dreams. He had visions.

George III of England greeted a tree, believing it to be the King of Prussia. Saul declared himself divine, then damned, soothed only by a shepherd with a harp. George III died a drooling cripple, blind and babbling. Saul fell on his own blade, having slain his thousands, but the shepherd his tens of thousands.

Enda the Elder told Enda the Younger that his mother had been carried off by that licentious slime, that clever snake that could hide in clouds, as well as grass, and his mother had known its name. You had to watch your humor, your words, the tour of your thought. You could be seen. You could be heard.

I can't see you if you can't see me. Not in the void.

He felt as though he had been to the Roman forum, the temple, the great cathedrals. Though these things were ages gone, their solidity of time and place lay beyond the fenced three hundred acres that had been his own crumb of the world, and he had not been told to expect so great a difference on the outside from the Elder's stories. When he got to Rosemary's, he saw *Jason and the Argonauts* on her TV; it was nothing like he'd pictured it from the epic, and kept saying so until Holly howled in his ear and

Rosemary snuffed the TV. You have no choice when you see it for yourself. It is only you and what you've been steeped in. Was it awful? It could be. Was it beautiful? He had seen it in glimpses, in a look or a word. That ought to be enough for anyone.

"What do you call it?" He pointed at ET's belly, flat to him.

She looked at him sidelong.

"I'm not making fun. Really. What do you call it?"

"It's a she, first of all."

"No boys allowed?"

She reminded him that he promised no jokes.

"You're right, you're right."

Exhaling, breath a golden haze. "Mirabel."

"What'll you do when she comes?"

MEANWHILE, AJ PUT LC in the upstairs tub. Rosemary and a few of the others kicked and cursed the boiler into shape so she could have a proper hot bath.

Holly peered around her mother's shoulder and guffawed into her neck when the pitch of the chorus reached a crescendo of blind rage. The basement was dark and reduced everything in it to scattered limbs and gnashing teeth. She was never frightened when any of her visitors fell into a passion. Nor did she cower at her own mother's break, rare as they were. It was something, she thought, to see the blurred smiles and adoration and kisses pull away to reveal the beast they hid. Tantrums, tears, goddammit, goddamn you, goddamn it all, as though you had the authority to call upon your Maker to fix a shifty boiler. As though the boiler were the source of all your troubles. It was better than a cartoon. She liked it when Babe did impressions of these episodes. He wagged his tongue, his face reddened, then purpled, his lips peeled back to let his teeth become an ogre's grimace. He had seen a fellow on the street with a bullhorn, howling about the pending results of a local election. The fellow recited that chapter of Proverbs, one that Babe and AJ both knew and found humor in, if only for its verse of a dog returning to his vomit. "—SO A FOOL RETURNETH TO HIS FOLLY," the fellow shouted when the police arrived.

Babe knew the passage and did the whole thing for Holly when they got home, faces and all. How she had laughed and laughed and laughed. Rosemary had asked what the fellow was so angered about. AJ guessed it was because of the dog catcher, the only office that mattered. (The town had elected to merge the position of dog catcher with that of the local police department, who had, unbeknownst to all of them, seized the fellow's dogs from his home, all fifteen of them, on his half-acre lot.)

Panting, Rosemary bounded upstairs, Holly on her shoulder, LC in the tub, AJ on the toilet seat, LC's clothes in a heap on the floor.

"It took a year and a day," Rosemary huffed, "but I think we got it."

There was a rubber covering over the faucet with a seal's fat face. Rosemary filled the room with steam and the tub with foam. She entrusted AJ to keep an eye on her.

LC sat and breathed and, after a while, she splashed.

"We had to boil water on the stove at home," she told AJ. It was one of the few, true times she'd said anything about the old home.

LC was a grown woman, as dictated by her age and the growth of her bones, dentin deposition. Her hair, still dark, was threaded with gray, as Holly's was. Her eyes were bright and starry lashed, and they often made AJ think of those fair little flowers that bloom at the center of peyote buttons, petals like daisies, an eye that unwound in desert rain. Hands, small; arms, long. Her breasts, pendulous, the areolas blossomy and brown. Layers kept her without sex and without shape, and he had never seen the lines of her thighs. Hers was a belly that bore one world after another, expanding, contracting, lunglike in itself. She had not trimmed her toenails in weeks. Her legs were coated in ape's fur.

He handed her the shampoo (tear-free, brought by a visitor) and told her to wash her hair, and she quickly made a mountain atop her head, smelling of green apple.

"I'm Marie Antoinette," she announced, pursing her lips. A gulp of air and she disappeared, sinking and coming to the surface with a pop. "DON'T TOUCH—"

There was only a moment of chaos. AJ wedged towels around the bottom of the tub to catch the spill and eased her back in. She'd caught him folding her clothes so they would be stacked and ready for her when she got out. She'd caught him holding the pillbox.

"I was going to put it back," he murmured.

She sighed, her voice thick. "Don't take it from me."

"I would never." He placed it on top of the tidy pile, patted it with one finger. "What's inside?"

"It's mine."

"I know that. I just want to know what's in it."

"You keep things in your pockets."

"And I told you what they are."

"You should get rid of them."

"And I will. I promise."

She was at peace, pink. "Okay."

"Can I have a look?"

"I don't want you to lose anything in there."

"I won't take anything out. Scout's honor. Just want to take a look."

"You were never a Scout."

"It's an expression. I promise."

"Okay. Don't take anything out."

"I won't."

Babe had a daemon box and LC a dybbuk box. ET told her about them in the hospital. Dybbuks were not daemons, nor were they ghosts. A soul was not a ghost; it clung in death as it clung in life, warmed by a beating heart, which it sapped until the heart shriveled. Its opposite was an ibbur, a soul that settled in the heart like a good deed and grew until the deed was done, and the heart was made stronger for it, the ibbur, too. LC had always liked that story.

He popped the lid and looked. He counted one two three four five six seven eight twirls of hair, infants' first shearings, dark like hers and tied with ribbon, pink for girls, blue for boys.

"I thought you only had seven kids," he said.

"I lost one." Her hand splayed and starfished over his, the palm warm and suckling. "They took him while I was asleep."

"I won't be cursed now that I've opened this thing, will I?"

"No."

The lid snapped, making a bright, golden noise, and all was well.

All was well, but not all had settled. The air remained thick.

AJ asked if she'd thought about a disguise. He spoke to her plainly, fairly, slowly, the way the orderlies had. "You're not supposed to be out, you know. I'm not trying to scare you, I'm not telling stories. We ought to be serious for a minute. I don't think you'll get an appeal if you're picked up somewhere. I don't think you'll go back to the hospital. This isn't like before. People are afraid of people like you, even if they have no reason to be."

Pondering, LC squeezed the moisture from her hair, marveled for a minute at the shine. Meanwhile, the water had darkened and the foam depleted. "I won't hurt anyone."

"I know."

"I never hurt anyone."

It had happened too quickly. Her aim had been precise. A technicality, they had not suffered. This was true.

AJ sighed. "I know that, too."

"Will I have to wear a mask?"

"Something like that. I was thinking more in terms of a wig."

"Marie Antoinette." She again piled the thinning suds. She held her head high to balance the burden. In thick, Franco-German mimicry, she uttered, *"No harm will come to me. The Assembly is prepared to treat us leniently."*

"Let's be serious now. We can't stay here forever. I'll have a talk with Rosemary about that, too."

"There is nothing new except what has been forgotten."

"Let's be serious."

"The King of Prussia is innately a bad neighbor, but the English will also always be bad neighbors to France."

"Please. Let's be serious."

"I have seen all, I have heard all, I have forgotten all."

"For the last time—" AJ plunged his hand into the tub and the plug came out, the water and the suds moving toward the eye of the drain in one big rush. "—for the last time. This is it. Let's be serious."

Perhaps she had no choice. He had to remember that. LC was the most touched of them all. He was waiting for her to give that most flippant of proclamations, "*Let them eat cake.*"

Marie Antoinette never said that, and he knew LC knew that much.

Her hair still larded with soap, her belly and legs lined, her hands small, her arms long, she stood and with resolution stepped into the waiting towel. Her head, high. Her enunciation, divine. She said, "*I should be very sorry if the Germans disapproved of me.*"

THE SON OF MAN said, "I thought about being Catholic at one point. The word *Catholic*, for those who don't know, just means *universal*. As in, God is found in everything and everyone and your time alive is spent trying to find it. Yes, there you have it. I called God it. Because the idea of God as a person makes me think of what it must be like to live with someone who's either passive-aggressive or manic depressive, who can't handle criticism and just can't take a joke. And the temper is explosive. And you know how I am about tantrums. I'd never survive if there was a God; I'd laugh too hard at every little hissy fit He threw. But God as a feeling, as a commonality. I like that idea, that's something I can get behind. That turned into one of many things I'd have to tweak if I was going to join up.

"I thought, Can I be Catholic and not have to answer to the Pope?

"Can I be Catholic and just sit, and not have to do that aerobics routine, sit, stand, kneel, sit, stand, kneel?

"Can I be Catholic and not have to buy all the stuff at the souvenir shops that they have?

"Can I be Catholic and not have to give them money—which might be going to some crooked lawyer to keep a crooked priest out of jail?

"Can I be Catholic and not keep the sabbath—because I do like my beauty sleep?

"Can I be Catholic and still be an atheist?

"Can I be Catholic and still put an Occupied sign on the confessional door? I think I'm the only one who finds that funny.

"Can I be Catholic and not go to hell?"

ENDA DREAMED AND AJ dreamed and they met tonight in the same place. This was the universality that Babe, known also as Enda, known also as the Son of Man, would come to look for for the rest of his days. In a dream, contrary to that wished-for notion, you do not do and say whatever you want; you do and say whatever you do and say. In a dream, there is no room for deceit, amongst the flying and falling teeth.

In their shared dream, they were in the crater at the old home. It was daytime and there was a storm coming, the sky gunmetal green. The coneflowers swayed. The air was not indicative of a summer storm because in the waking world it was almost winter and everything felt thin and static, translated by slumber into a rumble above.

They were both unclothed, inches from one another, though they wore many layers and slept now in separate rooms, AJ with the others, Enda with ET in Rosemary and Holly's shared place.

"WHAT HAPPENED."

It was not a question, and, face to face as they were, Enda felt he must shout, as you do across a canyon. His voice carried, high in cathedral vaulting.

AJ shook his head, shelled his ear with one hand.

Enda tried again, "WHAT. HAPPENED."

AJ, knowing what the boy meant, looked down. He, from his end, understood himself to be the monster, and if he were the monster, that must mean this was a nightmare. His understanding of monsters was that their ferocity came from having more of something, more teeth, more heads, more limbs, skin as scales, a protrusion of horns, a tail. He was not ferocious. He had two of everything.

Enda, howling. "WHAT HAPPENED."

AJ covered himself. "DON'T LOOK."

"WHAT."

"DON'T. LOOK."

"WHAT."

"TURN. AROUND. RUN. AWAY. GO. HOME."

Above, the gathered clouds were turning and turning, inward and upward to form a puckered orifice. They understood that from there, this was where the thunderbolt would come and, following the thunderbolt, the deluge.

The old home was on the hill, its peaked roof, one light winking.

"I DON'T LIVE THERE ANYMORE." Enda moved to take AJ's arm.

"DON'T TOUCH—" AJ spoke as LC, but it came with great difficulty, squeezing her high voice through his throat, which had become a tight straw.

"YOU'LL DROWN."

"WHAT."

"YOU'LL. DROWN."

The storm held and churned, retained by the contractions of the orifice. Enda thought this must have been the time his father had gone mad. It was his understanding that all had been blue and bountiful, one or two spatters that signified nothing more than daily distress, a shower that would come and go. And really, wasn't that all a summer storm was, too, writ large?

But you couldn't tell him that.

In a minute, the rain would come, and Enda knew it would be forty days and forty nights before it would calm. He did not know how he knew, only that the knowledge had descended and had begun to crystallize, while reason and attitude, those rivers that keep the mind afloat and moving, began to slow, cool, freeze. If he allowed this last, awful stage, they would be stuck here. In another minute, the crater would fill. In another minute, they two would submit to the chill of the deluge, the water squeezing from all sides, and when they woke, they would follow the pattern of their monstrous crystal. Enda would hate. AJ would lust. They knew the play of that pattern, as clearly as though it had truly happened in some other, far less buoyant truth.

If they drowned, AJ would wake first. He would cross the room, stepping on clawed toes over snoring congregants, shedding layers. His appetite drove him, his nerves the cracking reins. He had wider eyes and a tail, following the dark until he loomed over the boy, who was still hissing, still dreaming. Imagine Saturn devouring his son. He does not want to but he must, according to the twist in his gut. Imagine his surprise when a curious light darts (from a torch, from a flashlight) into this corner and that, looking for the bathroom at two a.m. and finding instead his rounded, blinking eyes, his thrashing tail, the boy halfway down his throat.

And Enda, poor Babe, dead yet though he lived, without laughter, without joy, for what is the point of madness without laughter?

Where could they go before the orifice opened?

AJ pointed to the house on the hill.

Enda shouted again, "I DON'T LIVE THERE ANYMORE."

"GO. HOME."

Enda knew the Elder was there. This knowledge, divine as it was, plain as it was, he knew that if he left the crater, in AJ's company or not, if he trudged over hill, over dale, through brush, through briar, he would enter the old home and he would never leave. He would wake and rise, stepping on pawed toes over snoring congregants and he would leave all behind, save for the daemon box, that wealth hoarded forever. Imagine the half-drowned dog, soaked to the bone, fur as matted as his lashes, retracing his steps to the old home and there he would stay, chastened, bitter, without laughter, without joy, without love. For what is the point of love when you know everything? What is the point of wealth if it is never spent?

Where else was there to go?

To the Empyrean, fantasy of Rosemary's hippies, of acid and Mirando City mescaline?

To the void, lair of smackheads, of poppies and unhygienic needles?

Back to the hospital?

You could not remain in any state for very long, as settled as you may believe yourself to be. And here, an impending flood, a collection of green diarrheal cloud, a serpentine thunderbolt.

Knowing, Enda, poised to grab AJ—

LC DID NOT dream, though she was in the same place as they and could hear them from the house on the hill. She was wide awake, AJ twitching beside her. This was memory, wherein you entered a fugue state and all else falls away so you may practically find yourself there in that place, with the heat on your neck and the grit between your sandaled toes. In a memory, if the conjurer is true and the image as clear as the day it happened, you can only say and do whatever it is you have done and said. In a memory, there is no room for deceit, amidst the sentiment and the idea that things would have been different, if only.

In the memory, she was on the hill, looking down into the crater, which was empty, under a summer sky, which was blue. She was a girl and a new bride and her husband was almost forty. He was surveying the land that would be their home and telling her about how he was going to work it. It was trailers and cedar and dust now, land given them by her father as part of her dowry. He had been thinking, he said, of the future.

She, bright eyed, nodded.

"I mean, of the world." He had been reading, scriptures and Ovid and ancient prophecies, and he understood this blue valley of theirs to be a sort of paradise. "You can almost taste it. It's more fertile than anywhere else around."

She agreed, wholehearted. She came to him from a large family, introduced, betrothed, and wedded to him by her father, dressed and veiled by her mother, who drew her close before the new couple was to retire after the wedding feast, "Remember: *To be sober, love thy husband and thy children.*" She was fourteen. She had lived on a compound herself, smaller than this one, and farther away from anywhere. At least this place was close to a market, and she could see a neighbor's house if she climbed a tree. Her father read the scriptures and the ancients, too, and did not send his children to school. At home, she and the others had been versed in everything, from Genesis to Aesop, and she understood trees to have been nymphs in hiding from a lesser, lecherous god, that a dragon would one day but not to-day come to precede mankind's final judgment. Magic was a matter of course.

Her husband had a plan, and he placed his hands on her shoulders. He had a great ambition. He had her help in it, didn't he?

He did, of course, he did.

"Well," he picked her up and she rode his shoulders, and she bathed in the blue, "how do you like the idea of mothering the brave new world—"

"—*that has such people in it*," she finished, for she had been made to memorize it and had played Prospero in family pageants, a cotton Moses beard hooked around her ears.

She was never meant to grow up.

ET THOUGHT ABOUT the future. It came to her in flashes, as it did when she was at her fullest, when the burden felt light and she capable of anything. She had been awake since half-one, thinking about her baby. Mirabel turned and prodded and played in her blood, as she did when ET thought about Babe. Was Mirabel jealous? And ET thought this couldn't be so, as she had read that creatures in utero respond to certain stimuli (music, laughter, motherly chitchat) when said stimuli is positive and nurturing. Rosemary said herself that Holly had kicked when she thought of, quoting Peter Pan, "lovely thoughts." "All I had to do was think about, I don't know, walking on the beach or something, and off she'd go." Holly would never walk, on a beach or anywhere, as Rosemary knew also. "But she could kick. She just wanted to get started."

In the future, if you look it full in the face and remember the old idea that no one is perfect, there is no room for deceit. You will say and do whatever it is you will say and do. In the future, she would watch her boy (my baby, my boy) kneel in the grass by the front steps, which would still be overtaken by fire ants, despite her husband's (my husband's) many attempts to get rid of them with sprays and traps and angry blasts from the hose. Her boy would kneel and sink his hand into the whirring red nest, in full and violent preference to the knot in his gut. He would weep. He would tell her he could not sleep. He would tell her, when she asked, that he did not know what he was doing. She would tell him she had done the same thing once, years and years and years ago, long before his time. She, too, had wept. She, too, could not sleep. She did not know what she was doing then, either. She would remember his joke, her favorite of his: "God didn't become man to show us God. God became man because we asked Him to get His high and mighty ass down here and see for Himself how hard this is. *I had no idea. I'm so sorry. If I ever say JUST SAY NO again, please slap Me.*"

"You, too?" he would ask.

No, she would tell him. "Not in the same way. I just did the same thing."

He would huff and snuff, sneering as she dressed his hand. It would be covered all over in the tiniest welts which would, in time, have the look of pustulant acne, then dry into scabs, then flake away with a little prodding from a fingernail.

"I had nightmares," she would tell him.

"Of what?"

"All kinds of things. Of being in school and a project was due and I hadn't done it. Or I was at a doctor's office and he came in wearing just dirty underwear and was getting ready to shoot me up with poison."

"That's it?"

"Well, when I was awake, I'd read the newspaper. There was a story about a groom who'd been beaten to death by two drunk party-crashers at his own wedding reception. There would be a thing every other day about somebody shooting up a Walmart or someplace because he didn't know how to talk to chicks."

"That's it?"

"Actually, all of that was okay. I thought all the time about what other people had and how they got it. I didn't want all that but I knew I was supposed to want it."

"Ranger said you jumped off a bridge one time."

"Yes."

"It was on a river near a golf club or something."

"It was a big deal. There was this tournament going on. I think ESPN was shooting it, Tiger Woods was there, all that. There were cuties in stilettos and fat cat sugar daddies all up and down the road, limos everywhere. Bumper to bumper traffic, everyone was late going to work, everyone was late getting home. A twenty-minute drive turned into two hours."

"Were you just out walking or were you in traffic?"

"In traffic."

"And you just got out of the car?"

"Yes."

"Was it on TV?"

"I'd be surprised if it wasn't. They were shooting live."

"Did Tiger Woods jump in and come to the rescue?"

"I doubt it. I assume the police."

"Goodbye, cruel world, and all that?"

"Yes."

Still, he would say, "That's it?"

"Yes. That's it."

"You were going to let Tiger Woods push you over the edge?"

Her son, heaving in the pink predawn, would put his greatest exertions into peeling a clementine as a mug of water carouseled in the microwave. The objective would be to have the skin of the fruit in a single, swirling ribbon before the timer went off. It would be just about impossible because he had bitten his nails to nubs. Ranger would tell him to use a knife, which would break him, and everything would turn into Pandemonium as the timer sounded. ET would fish the half-peeled fruit from the trash to divide into wedges, ringing a saucer; her son would take the hot water in sips, a teabag bobbing.

And Ranger would come huffing in, scraping dirt from his shoes. "Someone en't living right around here because those ants are liable to chew through the foundation of this house."

Babe would wave to him with a cottoned hand. "Piranhas," he would say.

It didn't sound like a hell of a lot, did it?

She did not want, she knew, anything else. It might have been the biggest setup for despair she would ever have, for what would she do if she outlived them both, son and husband? What would she do without her boy? Rosemary had said of Holly, "I'd want to die, too."

They slept but a foot from her, breathing in the same bed. When Holly woke (without fail at first light), Rosemary would wake, too. Rosemary was the heart, Holly its flame.

She decided she might sleep on it and she did for a solid, shimmering, spastic hour, curled into a comma on her right side, then left, lips quivering, perspiring thickly behind her knees and chilled to the bone. When she woke, her bladder was full and her everywhere from belly to groin felt as though it had been taken in her sleep by a large hand and squeezed. It reminded her of her monthlies, when the cramps were so awful she had to run a towel under hot water and drape it over the delta. She had not had a monthly in, well, months. Redundancy made her smirk, then smirk crumbled to grimace, the vacuity chancing on pulling in the rest of her, beginning with her eyes. Rocking and shut, she returned to the fetal comma, neither empty nor full, inhabited first and foremost by another entity, hot and conductive in a way only flesh can be. It seemed it would last forever when it didn't, as though it had decided its host had had enough for now and, pitying her, began a lingering exit, like urine through a catheter.

ET realized she had never tried to imagine what Mirabel might look like.

She opened her eyes and saw her boy. He was still at that age, still unformed, wherein he could go either way, matted lashes and big eyes. It was what used to frighten her about children, having come from an era in which you had to be one or the other. Her mother used to put her in dresses.

But he's not me. I'm not him. We live together in the same house.

(Was this what God was, having found yourself in the same place, at the same time as another person?)

The Son of Man woke, smiled, said, "Hey."

Then, blinked, sat up, kicked out of his blankets on the floor. From her bed, Holly sighed and stirred, her mouth agape, heavy eyes following him as he went to the other room where everyone slept, ears alert for his steps over dreaming heads.

ET entreated Holly to go back to sleep and, rubbing her eyes, followed him.

Babe had woken when AJ had, if not in the same place, at the same time. He found the older man's empty pillow, indented with the weight and fluctuations of a head that has been too full and, popping up when it did, left behind the moisture of a night's foul visions. A red hair spiraled down one side of the wet flannel. LC, not having slept at all, left little mark on her pillow. They had both folded their blankets and taken their knapsacks, leaving much of the junk in them behind and in tidy arrangement. AJ had left a note in his copperplate hand, which looked out of place on note-paper. *For Holly*, it said.

There was a point to them, or there had been at the time they'd picked them up, from the ground or gutter. A tiny yo-yo that whirred with colored lights. A pillbox full of fortune cookie scrolls, a decade's worth of collecting. Salt and pepper shakers shaped like an avocado (salt) and a red chili (pepper). A carnival prize plush monkey, furred black with pink paws, a pink face and a pink belly. An Indian doll with string hair and floral skirt, dusty-smelling. TV aerials. Blue glass insulators from telephone poles. Bottlecaps. Like statues of saints or family heirlooms, these things had their places on shelves, ringed high around the room, rimming the ceiling's molding, and soon Rosemary would add their contribution. It was why, ET thought, Holly liked to look up so much. They were worth nothing to anyone, pennyworth, gumball machine treats, save for this small creature for whom bright colors and pretty shapes and a good word could win the day.

If ET were empty and if Babe knew a little more of what the average house was meant to look like, they both might have thought of the place as a shrine, then, after the initial glow had faded and its dirty congregation came into view, as the parlor of a cretin's interior castle.

Are we all of us batshit?

AJ had taken his King James Bible and LC her scarab box.

Babe started when ET knelt as if seized, and wanted to know why she was going through AJ's pillowcase.

She looked up, the empty pillowcase sagging on her arm. "Did he take his coat?"

"I don't know."

"Go look for his coat."

Rosemary kept them by the stairs. His was missing.

In his coat was his own hoard, a plastic bag full. OxyContin could be sold or swallowed. LC would have no one if AJ were gone. ET reviewed the possibilities as she pulled Babe out the door, still open and swinging into the house's lopsided angle. Who would make sure she washed herself? Who would remind her of blue hydrangeas and dogs? Who would feed her? And what of AJ? Who would comfort him? Who would listen to him play and read? ET decided it would be impossible to find one without the other and Babe agreed they could not, assured her they would not. They had woken at the same time, but not in the same place, and such things would happen if they could not meet.

Enda, following her, itched. He did not want to admit to a stranger, much less to himself, that he felt the loss of that plastic bag more than its owner, more than his home, more than his own father, and was ashamed by the delight and agony of how full it was. Aching, he passed ET and pulled her after him.

THEY WENT UP the hill, where the Son of Man recalled how, a couple of years later, he would know to go there if he wanted a quick supply of Klonopin. He would spend six months there at fifteen, possession with intent to sell. The juvenile detention had a number of inmates, eleven-year-old maniacs, fourteen-year-old insomniacs, sixteen-year-old alcoholics, who could convert the worth of milligrams into dollars. They ate their meals without relish because everything was defrosted or rehydrated. They were not allowed to curse. Everyone called the place baby jail.

He bought from, then kissed, a girl he had danced with at a wedding once.

"So, how do you end up here?" he would ask.

She told him she'd been caught selling at school and her customer, a boy in eighth grade, had seized during a math test, gone into a coma, and was now a vegetable. His parents were going to unplug him and demanded the highest condemnation when the police traced their boy's purchase back to her.

"I want to go to Florida," she would say by way of explanation.

"There's psychos down there," Babe would tell her.

"There's the Hemingway House in Key West," she would point out. "They have a whole colony of six-toed cats. My aunt lives there, too. She works at the Sugarloaf Hotel. It's nice, it's right on the water; I caught a shark there one time. I'll go live at her place."

"Far out."

"Yeah."

"What's wrong with here? Not *here*, I mean here, in general."

"I'm fucking up here."

"Well."

"I can't keep my head straight."

"In Key West, you'll get your head straight?"

"I don't know. I'm just fucking up here."

"When are they letting you out?"

"Next month, depending on my hearing."

"Are you going home?"

"No. I told my mom I wanted emancipation, and she said, Go for it. I don't know if she means it or if she's playing head games. I don't know what she wants."

"You could come stay at my place. You'll have to sleep on the floor."

"Where's that?"

"Down the road, believe it or not."

Both shook and shivered and sneezed and sweated.

The girl said, "I don't even know your name."

"Babe."

"Like the Styx song?"

"More like, *I got you, babe.*"

"It's *I got you, baby.*"

"No, it's babe. You're Lady."

"Whatever. You could be a psycho killer."

"My mom's a psycho, but she's not a killer."

"Are you a psycho?"

The Son of Man would be pronounced manic depressive and prescribed lithium. He would wander unclothed into the cafeteria and make a habit of urinating in the potted plants. He had once tried to jump from the boys' dormitory roof to the maintenance outbuilding; he would fracture his leg the first time, then make it on the second attempt, crediting, he would boast, his ability to think lovely thoughts. He slept for three hours a night. He would let anyone love him who would have him and bear the inflamed carbuncles of their passions. His anus would rupture. His eyes would crust. His veins would thread. His hair would gray. His teeth would yellow, edges pellucid as fine china.

I don't know if I would have left the old home if I knew it was going to be like this.

Now. Here I am.

He never seemed to run out of money. When it looked as though he might run out of dollars, more would appear, spent just as quickly on things for friends; he had a knack for making new friends. He met John in line at Starbucks. He met Andy waiting for the bus. He met Jimmy in the locker room at the Y He met Lee buying mushrooms from Pete and covered Lee's costs. He dubbed them all with nicknames; never again would they be John and Jimmy. They would be Yeti, Ondine, Uncle Feather, Mothman, Gumberoo, Monoceros, Pooky, Cornholio, Werebear, Thunderbird, Lounge Lizard, Champ. He whistled "Won't You Be My Neighbor?" and invited them all back to his stepfather's house to watch Eddie Murphy on the TV.

"I come in here from a ten-hour shift," his stepfather hissed through the wall, "and I have some individual by the name of Sasquatch on my couch."

"Did you just call him an individual?" the Son of Man called, as though the last word were a curse. "I can hear you."

His stepfather went across. Everyone had gone.

The Son of Man rubbed his eyes. "Good evening," he croaked.

His shape filled the light in the hall, snapped the bedside lamp awake. "Satchmo, Sasquatch. What have you. Somebody sucking down some science experiment from my coffee mug, and with his goddamn tennis shoes on my couch."

"Oh. Yeti. I told him to use a Dixie cup."

"Doesn't he have a home?"

"We'll call it that."

"Don't they miss him there? Does he have a name, a real one?"

"Like Ranger, for example?"

"Don't his people miss him at home?"

"His people are nice people. So, naturally, they kicked him out. I'm being serious. He had nowhere to go."

His mother asked him in the morning, putting a mug of hot water in front of him and a peeled clementine, "You're not going to join the 27 Club on me, are you?"

The Son of Man assured her that, No, of course he was not going to join the 27 Club. He amended this, adding that the Under 40 Club was much more illustrious, having Mozart and Chris Farley as members.

"I love you the most, you know that." His mother looked away when she said things like that, as though sentiment were a creature that might bite.

"I know." The Son of Man blew his nose. "And he loves you the most." He jerked his head toward the back of the house, where Ranger had his study. There were old consoles there, left over from the days when computers were the size of refrigerators, vacuum tubes and Geiger counters, a ham radio that screeched demonic code to fellow operators in Colorado, Cameroon, New Zealand, India, Iceland. Ranger trolled surplus stores that took the stock from laboratories that went defunct after the Cold War. He found a gag can of plutonium and gave it to Babe as a stocking stuffer. He gave Babe's mother a mug that read ONE BOMB IS TOO MANY. He had its twin, WELCOME TO THE BLACK HOLE, the one he'd caught Yeti drinking from.

They listened for awhile to the duet of tap-tap-tap, beep-beep-beep through the wall.

"You think you could use one of those things for a séance?" his mother asked.

Babe told her a story he remembered hearing at the ashram in the park. Everyone there was close to the thin place and thought they might as well relieve themselves of the things they might have otherwise taken with them to the grave. He was listening to a girl he'd danced with once at a wedding a long time ago and whom he'd met in baby jail. She had been one of the ones who had died a few times and revived, on the first occasion in a bathtub full of ice water, the second at her mother's house after the two had reconciled, then quarreled. At the ashram, she told Babe about having once been filled with such anger, such rage as she had never felt before following a terrible fight with her mother that when she heard about a shooting at a sidewalk sale in Santa Fe, twenty-five dead, ten of them tourists seeking sunshine and mesas, she thought of nothing else at the time, save for these words that seemed to have narrowed her heart and her mind to a single, stinging pin-prick, "I get it now."

"Not that I would ever do that," she added quickly. "Just that we deserved it, is all." In this narrowed state, it was easy to accept this as her fate, a name among others, memorialized for a moment by news stations, in thoughts and prayers. This is how we cull the herd, until the herd has gone extinct. Don't we all deserve to die? She had been out when the story broke, come back when her mother had descended into her own pit and cast the worst flames when she saw her daughter step over the threshold. "She just lost it. I wasn't all the way inside yet, and she went off." Here she was, the parasite, foulest thing let to live, whom a mother would be ashamed to introduce in public. I can smell you from here. "I turned around and walked right back out. She said, I'm talking to you, you're not going anywhere. I said, Watch me."

A sidewalk sale in Santa Fe, twenty-five dead, ten of them tourists. The gunman a lone wolf, unwell, unruly.

I get it now.

"What I didn't know was that her closest friend since—I don't know when, they grew up taking baths together, that's how far back they went. This was someone whose house she'd go to when things got out of hand at her place. My mom wound up living there through the end of high school. She was maid of honor at my parents' wedding, my mom was maid of honor at hers. College roommates. Blood buddies. I called her Auntie, the one in Florida. Well. She and her boyfriend went out to Ghost Ranch, then into the city. The news already had a list of everyone dead."

I get it now.

"I walked around the block a few times. Then, I turned around and went home. I couldn't leave her alone like that. She'd hurt herself." She breathed, shallow, watery. "She broke every dish in the house. She was okay, but we were eating off paper plates for a while. We went to Pier 1 and I got her a whole new set."

IS IT MADNESS to want to find an answer when there is none?

Is it madness to look for logic when everything feels like a dream?

THEY WENT TO the places where LC and AJ ought to be but did not find them there. It was early yet and many places in the business district were still closed. ET held Enda's hand and did not think of the winding in her gut. She compared it to the days when she used to bite her finger, mandibles driven deeper by the wrong mantra, IT DOESN'T HURT IT DOESN'T HURT IT DOESN'T HURT, because it didn't, and rationalized it by reminding herself so long as the skin did not break, she could do this and keep herself from shouting inflammatory nonsense, condemnation, contrition at people whose circumstances had nothing to do with her own. It would be about as useless as lighting a fart on fire.

Now that her baby was coming, she was not ready.

Enda tugged.

Her belly wound, swelled.

Enda tugged.

Her belly swelled, twisted.

"Mom."

"Stop that." She pushed him ahead. "You're too old to be doing that, you're slowing me down. Walk on your own."

How she hated looking at him, this boy. She might have pitied him, like a dog you have kicked, if he had met her eyes with that powdery horror animals have when they are hurt. A dog never deserved abuse; he was only hungry or afraid. A man was too clever to fear or hunger, they knew these as pretext for uglier things. The boy looked ready to bite. He shook, bared one tooth, a furled lip. He made a foul gesture with his finger and kept his head turned away when he did it—was he angered, or was she not worth looking at? He obeyed her, nonetheless, jogging ahead until he appeared to her to be moving on four legs instead of two. She could see the ear flaps on his cap going up and down.

She remembered something her own mother said to her: "Rosemary had a better baby than me." It was said in half-jest, maybe even three-quarters.

Would the Antichrist have been a better baby than me?

And she thought Rosemary, her Rosemary, was the lucky one. Rosemary with a baby that would never walk but who could never talk. Perhaps, she thought in a moment of all wickedness, Holly's affliction was her mother's blessing. Perhaps a foul mind was reflected by a fouler form, curses as cooing, slander as smiles, having to sit in your own mess as punishment for what you could have done had you been born with all your faculties. Rosemary called the girl a miracle. "My miracle baby," she said, bending to kiss Holly's crown.

"HA," crowed Holly, on all fours.

Joseph Merrick, the Elephant Man, lived his twenty-seven years as a human gargoyle. He had a leg the size of a tree trunk. His skull grew spurs and left him half-deaf and his speech muffled, as though he were talking through wet cloth. He liked to quote Isaac Watts, *'Tis true my form is something odd/But blaming me is blaming God*. Almost a century later, John Hurt would wail under prosthetics, "I AM NOT AN ANIMAL. I AM A HUMAN BEING," and earn a nod from the Academy, and viewers would wonder at how anyone could have been so cruel to that poor, maligned little man.

Could I create myself anew/I would not fail in pleasing you.

ET covered her face with her hands. She would not call this empty, nor would she call it full. Full was when you knew things, beautiful things. Empty was knowing nothing at all. Full was seeing the composition in the chaos. She stood still on the side of the road, one eye open and seeing Babe stop, too, his hat a red speck. The pain in her belly and groin was great. She could not stand. She wanted him to turn around, and he did. She wanted him to come back and, without her having to call him, he did, half-walking, half-jogging. She had thought he would keep going and not look back, as she might have done to him, but he had not. He knelt beside her and she thought of what an embarrassment it might have been for her, had she been in his place, to have to cater to someone on all fours on a dark roadside.

He put his hand on the back of her neck and told her to breathe in through her nose, out through her mouth. "Does it hurt?" He could not keep the astonishment from his voice, even now, the mild amusement. He still did not believe how real it was, that if he did not feel it, why should she?

He asked again, "Does it hurt?" This time without emphasis on any one word.

Her womb contracted, gathering the flush of her blood back into its home, knotted in her gut. This was the motherload, winding and winding, and her skin felt like hot dough. This was not a matter of seeing as understanding, much like the feelings of fullness and emptiness, in which you knew things, as they shifted, to be as they were, without explanation, without calculation, having always been, so they will be. She did not look like a woman pregnant. But what do you do if you know yourself to be one? What do you do when you've seen it in a dream and feel it in your flesh?

Phantom limb, Parkinson's, restless-leg syndrome.

At the hospital, she had known a woman who had ants crawling under her skin.

She had known a man who had grown angel's wings

LC had grown a tail.

She knew herself to be swollen in breast and belly, reddened and throbbing to the touch. She knew of her veins and of her ballooning pink feet. She knew she was turning into a great, grunting sow, about to birth a passel of piglets squealing in the mud. It made her think of that Pink Floyd song, from the album with the oinking and barking and baa-ing: *Mary, you're nearly a treat/But you're really a cry*. She'd imagined, curled up on her bedroom floor at fifteen, a pig called Mary being hauled off for slaughter, going from live thing to bacon, ham, pulled pork.

Babe's hand was dry and cool. He told her to breathe in, then out.

She vomited. Then, as you often do once you've vomited, she felt much better. She was wet through her clothes, but she could stand. Mirabel had not come yet. She pressed Babe's palm to her cheek in gratitude. He, though perplexed, did not pull away. They stayed as they were for as long as ET wanted, before they had to get up and go again.

AJ MANAGED TO thumb down a truck and they rode for nearly ten miles when LC suddenly and earnestly told the driver to take the next exit, then right at the light.

They had been going toward the city, where there were shelters aplenty and fewer possibilities for either of them to make trouble. AJ would find a women's shelter for LC, then a men's shelter for himself. He did not want to abandon her, but as most overnight facilities accommodated women and children or men and never both, he would have to leave her in another's hands. He knew no one knew her name, as she did not remember it. He knew no one knew of the tenets she must now live by, which included a specific distance from children. But she could not help that. He knew no one knew of the tenet he had laid upon himself. He knew he could not help that either. He had his hoard, gripping it in his pocket.

What do you do when you are inhabited, without knowing how you have invited the demon? How long before the demon has the workings of all your faculties and, before long, wears your skin like an ill-fitting suit?

"Neurosis: bad for me," Tommy Tiernan said, in a special Babe had watched. "Psychosis: bad for you."

The driver this time spoke little English, though he mentioned where they were going was not far from where he lived. LC peered through the window, cracked despite the chill. She recognized it and she did not. Here was the market on the side of the road, its signs for pecans in season and beer, now a new ad for CBD oil. Here was the parking lot that had built itself up in the years she'd been away into a gas station, a HEB, a pizza parlor, a dress shop that filled its display window with formal gowns, for homecoming, for prom, for quinceaneras, for sweet sixteens, for bat mitzvahs, a commotion of chiffon and bling. LC had never worn a dress like those in the window. Here was the farm that sold peaches and blackberries when it was warm, apples when it was cool. Here was the sign for the Church of Our Lady of the Sacred Heart. Here was the sign for the Covenant United Methodist Church. Here was the sign for the Redeemer Lutheran Church. Here was the sign for the Church of Christ. Here was the sign for the Sweet Home Baptist Church. TURN HERE, they said. LC had never been to any of them.

She told the driver to keep going straight.

"We'll pass by my place, then," he said.

Where there had been houses that were once grand, then gray, then empty, and were now warm and filled again, though not in the same way as their first incarnation. Like Rosemary's neighborhood, they were Queen Anne castles divided into apartments, split into duplexes. There were cars at the curb, trucks in the drives. There were shoes on the porch, from grandfathers' boots to kids' sneakers. There were scooters in the grass, roller skates on the steps, inflatable wading pools in the summer, basketball poles in the winter. There were chain link fences that corralled panting, grinning dogs and the children they nannied. There were colored lights in the windows, or potted plants, or blue TV glow. There was the aroma of grill fire, of stew on a stove, of weed smoked discreetly in a backyard. A laugh, a wheeze, an exclamation, a snatch of a song on a radio, *"Babe, I love youuuu—"*

"Babe, I love youuuu—" LC echoed. She played with the scarab box, snapping the lid up and down through the pocket she kept it in. Then, echoing Ranger, she said, "Welcome to Sesame Street."

AJ did not stop her when she wound down the window. He did not stop her when she emptied her knapsack at slow, generous intervals along the road and into the highway. The driver, who had been eyeing the shoulders for deer, heard, slowed, mouth squared, brows together. "You're not suppose to do that," he called into the back. "See the signs? You're not suppose to do that."

There were two signs, one on each side of the road among those reading TURN HERE. LITTERING IS UNLAWFUL. FINES $200 UP.

And now, a trail up the road of unlikely treasures, valuable to those with the right kind of eyes. The kids behind the fences found ways out, legging over top, wriggling through holes their fathers meant to repair but hadn't gotten around to yet, worming in trenches dug by clever dogs. None were old enough or tall enough to reach the clasps on the gates. The air was crisp and it was Halloween and the children came clamoring in costume. Most were dressed as birds. Here were two blue peacocks, a horned owl, a falcon, two gray doves, a yellow canary. Here were two dogs, a brown hound and a black mongrel, who galloped in a cross-pattern into the road for the joy of running and back to the shoulder where the trinkets were. Their mothers had made their costumes by hand and the children were proud of them, ready to wear them to school and into the night. They picked up things, thinking they were candy, then, holding them close and seeing what they were, eyes wide and marbled, made quick work of finding what they could and putting them into their pillowcases that would also hold M&Ms and Milky Ways. The hound had an emerald earring, real. The owl had a diamond ring, fake. It was all the same to them.

They did not forget to wave.

LC waved back.

"We're going home," she told AJ. "It's all right. We're going home."

AJ closed his eyes. He did not know what that meant and would not try to shape it. He opened his window fully, let the children tear into the King James Bible when it landed in the dirt some distance away from the shoulder. The birds pecked, the dogs sniffed, all recognizing it from their parents' shelves at home. None wanted it, though the superstition was already thick and they all stood and squabbled awhile about who would be the one to take it, because it was bad luck to leave a Bible out in the elements. But then a mother called, then another, a grandmother, a father, and they scattered, dogs ahead, birds behind, or they would be late for school.

"Lucky there's no cops out here this early," the driver sighed. "I'm not paying you all's fines."

RANGER'S HOUSE WAS a lucky thing for him because it came with his position as groundskeeper. It was well-kept, one hundred and ten years old, the home of all the groundskeepers who came before and lived under its gabled roof. Someone had commented that it was a Cape Cod house, eyeing its brown shingles, while another called it a strawberry box house. The first commenter was from Massachusetts, while the second was from Nova Scotia. Ranger, being a local native, had always thought it looked like a renovated bunkhouse. Everybody called it a cottage.

It was a short walk to the duck pond, which he could see through the kitchen window, thought it was partially cloaked by the pendula of the weeping birches, white and copper, around its fuller, pregnant end. He'd put in the birches himself, ages ago, when he'd first started. His predecessor, an angular fellow who went in for starker pines and red-berried possumhaws, arched an eyebrow and said, "Really? First order of business, weepy trees?" It was sentiment, yes, but not what the fellow thought. They were a veil, not tears, through which you found yourself in another,

176

stranger, albeit familiar place, the way you did in dreams. You went into the pendula of weeping red birch, which was a porthole, to the beginning of a great quest, mapped for you and only you. You learned you were really a long-lost prince. You learned you were really a god, hidden among the cows like Krishna, and you discovered you could play the challenge of mysteries and ordeals as you would a game.

In India, they called it *lila*.

In Rome, they called it *ludus amoris*.

He put on the radio, tucked into the windowsill, turned it up loud enough to be heard from outside and shook a bag full of Wheaties. Santana, *"Ellos tienen que jugar, ellos tienen que jugar . . ."* The ducks responded more readily to the music than to the sound of the bag. Ranger had seen their heads sweep at the click of the dial, heard padding of rubbery feet up the bank and into the grass. Tails twitched. Wings clapped. He whistled, tossed handfuls, made percussion with his lips and maracas with his teeth, spraying spit. It was seven o'clock in the morning and many a jogger had caught him doing his little thing, calling him sweet or calling him batshit.

ET came through the pendula and thought he was sweet.

Babe came through the pendula and thought he was batshit.

Ranger, catching them, stopped, for he had not gone through the veil into the dream, it seemed. Here was the dream come unto him, tattered strangers beamed through from another dimension, colored blue in the pale light, eyes a touch too bright and too large, dressed in approximation to what people wore, t-shirts atop sweaters atop sweatshirts when they could just put on coats, shoes that did not fit, not quite from this world and they were here for him. Ranger was not the prince, after all, and he'd never really wanted to be. Better to be the sidekick, who is always still around long after the quest has ended.

Babe hollered and ran across the pond to him, scattering ducks.

ET trotted behind, rosy beneath the blue.

Ranger dumped the rest of the Wheaties and, moving forward, said, "Now, I was thinking I hadn't seen the last of you yet. I speak of the devil and two devils appear."

LC HELD AJ'S hand through brush and through bramble, over hill, over dale, walking a mile from where she'd told the driver to stop ("Stopstopstop, please stop. Hereherehere.") on a rough road of white clay. She led him to a creek so he could drink and rest. She told him this was where she used to live.

AJ asked, "What, here?"

"Right here."

It was hills and cedar and scrub as far as his eye could see. The horizon held a thin ink of barbed wire, and from here he could make out the notice, stamped on tin with crude lettering, just as it is found on every rancher's property line, PRIVATE. NO TRES-PASSING. This one elaborated, OFFENDERS WILL BE SHOT.

Now that she was on this side of the fence, did LC offend? She remembered having always been on the correct side, never having strayed a fraction of an inch from where the demarcations that divided this world from the other (for there was always another) lay. She had expected—what? A wasteland? Bare trees and rocks? Barren wintertime, cold and damp, and nothing to eat? That was what she had been told to expect, anyway, and by degrees, this was true. It was the notion of eternity that had thrown her, at first, for when she went beyond the fence it was summer here, just as it had been there. And it was winter here and, identically, winter there. Life went on, it turned out, no matter what or whom you tried to bar.

What if

What if I, the offender all along

What if I brought winter?

I had to, I had to because serpents sleep in winter and none could survive the frost if I were to—

She whistled to quiet herself, making giant's steps over the tall grass. She had liked that song at Rosemary's, Carly Simon singing "Itsy-Bitsy Spider." Long Island, 1991. She had never been to Long Island and she did not know what year it was, nor did she know the passage of time. To her, as it had been when she was

178

small, a life in its entirety was simply one long day in which many things could happen. When you died, you began another. That was what she had liked to play at, anyway, and if you play at something for long enough, it becomes real. She could be one hundred years old, for all of her. Her sentence had been, as AJ had repeated to her, despite ET telling him not to, for the remainder of her natural life in a state psychiatric facility. When she asked why and when ET told her not to answer the question, AJ told her what the staff had said, "Because you are a danger to others and to yourself." Now, usually, the words in that statement went the other way around: *You are a danger to yourself and to others.*

I was once put to death at the guillotine. I was called Maria Antonia Josepha Johanna. I was entertained by Mozart and wore the finest trappings by Rose Bertin. I had a palace and a garden and a little snorting dog called Mops. When they lifted my head I could see vulgarity for miles. I was a pearl diver, too, off the coast of Japan. I could go forty meters deep for the biggest pearls in the most secretive oysters. I greased myself head to foot, filled my ears with greased sponges, to block the chill, and embraced a great, mossy stone for the descent. I dove into my elder days, and it seemed I would go on and on, when I surfaced too quickly and went back under.

At some point, "Itsy-Bitsy Spider" segued into Carly Simon's original piece, about coming around again, "—*who knows where or when, but it's coming around again.*" Here was someone who understood time as LC did, in that, time was a ring, a revolution, a repeat, a restart, a reformation, a redemption.

She did not see the headstones all at once; she caught her toe on one, because it was so low to the ground and the grass had grown so thickly, then on another, on her opposite foot, realizing there was a row containing seven of them. She combed her hair out of her eyes and hooked it behind her ears, alternating these gestures until she grew angered and pulled at it. She rubbed her nose, her wet eyes, she swallowed. She understood her bladder was full and, squatting, relieved herself and, now that she was at the proper level, saw the stones were marked, stamped into concrete and left to the elements. The dates at the bottom were too small to be read, though the names at the head were lettered largely and heavily, and it would be some time before they could be obscured by concrete or moss.

DOVIE. HELENA. PORTIA. ALANA. ROSE. JEREMY. MIRANDO. Five girls, two boys. These were those in one row. Behind them were more, all of which were a little grander, left with the crumbling remains of flowers or pillars of coins, noting the visits and tributes made to the deceased, ENDA THE YOUNGER, of which there were many. She counted at least fifteen of them. Never before had she wanted so badly to be a bird, for it could only be from a bird's eye view that she could grasp the meadow as a whole, its span and its fullness, the intervals of stones marked ENDA THE YOUNGER.

And she was seized by a notion that evolved full-bodied and breathing, and she was no longer full nor empty. Something, however, had fallen away. She did not remember her name, if only where she was now and a little of what it would mean.

She bent and read the stones, looking for the date. Finally, she dropped to all fours and crawled between the rows so the search would not be so cumbersome. She, for a moment outside of herself, had the look of a lizard, or some other servile thing that crawled along on its belly, grazing the dirt. She ground the heels of her palms into her eyes, filled her mouth with her sleeve, knowing there was little point in looking for a date if you could not recall the present year. She howled, but her throat ached and it came out in a thin squeal.

"Which one is mine?" her voice, high, rumbling with phlegm. Then, a deluge, "WHICH ONE IS MINE?"

AJ, who had been gathering what he could of the coins, looked up. It held, to him, the same tenor as, "I'LL SLEEP OUTSIDE." He pocketed his findings which, to an indiscriminatory eye, could not have held more value than common dimes, and bounded to her side, knocking his knee against innocuous corners and scraping his calf. He had lifted from graves before and made a point of never reading the names of the deceased, and he had told the same to LC.

Her mind, like cobweb, could catch hold of any notion and it would be ages before she might be relieved of it. Perhaps she was like that famed imposter, Anna Anderson, who, after a failed suicide by drowning in the Spree, woke in a hospital among misinformation and rumors and fantasy. Someone declared her accent was Russian; it was Polish. Another recognized her as the Grand Duchess Tatiana; she was too short. Another modified this to mean that if she was not Tatiana, she was, nevertheless, a Romanov; she was a factory worker named Franziska, who was known until her death by the name Anna.

Madness, AJ reasoned, is about impressions. You catch hold of a notion and, because you are a creature that has evolved to recognize patterns, you let it tangle in the webbed, sticky proteins that have also caught *this* article and *this* memory so nothing is smooth, nothing is processed, nothing is rational. And how much worse if no one in your immediate environs is capable (or willing) to straighten out the mess. You conclude you are the surviving heiress to the Russian throne. What else do you have? The streets? The Spree?

It doesn't sound like a hell of a lot, does it?

Lavender's blue, dilly dilly
Lavender's green,
When I am King, dilly dilly
You shall be Queen.

He approached her, slow and from the side, one hand for her shoulder. He knew the song from an opera, Benjamin Britten, *The Turn of the Screw*, the Metropolitan in New York, himself at the piano. LC had always liked it and he tried it on her now, a newer, lovelier impression to replace the ugly one that was superimposing itself, growing tangible, getting tangled.

Because it had worked before, it did not mean it would work every time. The thought had already caught and already stuck. A great wave in her had drawn itself up, crested with horror that, whether true or phantasmal, carried itself high in her blood, crashed over her heart, bringing her to her knees, weeping as though this heart of hers, which was real and truly drowning, might break, too. And AJ felt a little of his own reason lapse, and he heard himself giving voice to a favorite saying of his father's, "There are no atheists in foxholes," calling on golden divinity to descend or appear (for gods descended or appeared) in his time of need—all this amidst LC's repeated howls, "WHICH ONE IS MINE?"

YEARS LATER, IN the process of dying, the Son of Man wondered what it was about him that made his mother think of him as special. There was nothing much he could do and he knew, having witnessed it firsthand and putting up his friends because of it, that many other parents would have lost their patience with offspring like him, long, long ago.

He tried to think of the things he liked or things he had some aptitude for. His stepfather had a few sayings, to "Think positive" and "Do the easy things first."

To know what you were good at and what you liked was to remember who you were, first and foremost. He had gauzy notions about gods, of having seen one, or of having run from one—more likely having dreamed of one. Was he born in a garden? Was he born at all, having begun life knowing how to walk and to talk, to read and to write, more than half-formed, the way the first man came to be, more or less sculpted?

He told people he was adopted because everyone noticed he and his mother looked nothing alike. And it wasn't untrue.

He opened his eyes and had a look around, having forgotten as much as that in under a minute. He sniffed, rubbed the corners of his eyes. The floor was concrete, furred and carpeted. He rose to his knees, smelling coffee, Febreze, cologne, perfume, flat Coca Cola. His tongue held juices of bile and something dry, meatier, akin to jerky.

He was unsure of who all these people were. There was a sea of them, he knew, blurred to shapes in the bright lights overhead and in the dark of where they sat, waiting.

It was his first time in front of a true audience. All of his

182

previous acts had been recorded messily and shared and spread until he got a call and a place and a time at a bar called Blue Jeans.

His skull, a concrete block. His limbs, yarn pulled taut. He did not understand the first phases of demise, in which a body enters that transformative state, going from what was only a minute ago a fully functioning, historical HE to a still collection of items, prone to splintering, melting, vanishing altogether, a fixed, unarmed IT.

Here, clarity: he had challenged a crowded auditorium not to laugh. He spoke in a string of nonsense, non sequiturs, anecdotes, observations. He remembered very little of what he said.

"If you go to a mirror in a dark room at midnight and say BUB-BAGUMP three times, John Travolta's crying face will appear."

"Ghosts are always in a state of torment. They're opening drawers, they're moving things around, they're wailing at 2 a.m. Haven't any of these specters figured it out? This is the ideal squatter's situation: you'll never be caught, and when they get a medium in to investigate, the tenants will leave, and more will move in for the charm of a haunted house. They might be disappointed, because I'll spend my afterlife as the roommate from hell. I'll eat your leftovers. I'll switch channels on the TV—you want to watch *SVU*? Too bad, we're watching *Seinfeld*. I'll leave ectoplasm in the toilet and I won't flush. I'll turn the lights on and off, and on and off, and on and off—because I can, and because I'm not paying for it. And nothing and no one can stop me."

"Have you ever prank-called someone and gotten so involved as the person you're pretending to be that you almost feel guilty when you hang up? Because that was an entire lifetime you concocted, and told to another person, and the guy on the other end thinks, even if it's only for a second, he thinks this character is real. And the minute you hang up, that character is dead. You have snuffed out Mr. Rotch, eighty-five years old, a World War 2 veteran, who stormed the beach at Normandy, who is self-made, who had a dispute years ago with his heir, his only boy, who now wants to make amends, who spent years in search of his long-lost son, Michael Rotch, Jr., better known as Mike—and he needs you to page that name, MIKE ROTCH, loud and clear, in every public place. And once you hang up, all of that, GONE."

He remembered as much as that. It warmed him greatly.

THEY SAT IN RANGER'S truck, ET shotgun and Babe in the back. The radio was quiet now, and the windows were open to the natural percussions of their environment, tweets, two-whits, and clicks. Dawn was as gauzy as dusk and the car smelled of it.

As his passengers trained their eyes for any bobbing head on the road, Ranger remarked at Babe that the last time they had met they were trying to find his house. Now they were trying to find his folks. "Things are just slipping through your fingers, aren't they?" He said it without mockery; more like a joke two men would know, told with an air of *Well, what can you do?* Babe smirked, showing that he was in on it, it was something that happened, losing your folks after losing your house, to anyone and not you alone.

Time moved in crumbs. To Enda, they might have gone a hundred miles. Rosemary told him that, as you grow older, your idea of an hour, a day, a year altered from the way you knew it before. If an hour was forever, it became as a minute. If a year was a century gone, it became as yesterday. He wanted to ask her what Holly thought about all of that, though he had an idea she would continue to live from day to day, as she always had, no matter how old she got.

He then asked ET about it and she told him it was more or less true. "Some people think they can move forward in time," she said. People at Rosemary's had achieved this. They had entered the Empyrean, finding doors where there were none, dissolving, dying and resurrecting, and coming out of it changed. RL was one of them; he had a pin on his jacket that read TURN ON, TUNE IN, DROP OUT. "You're in a whole nother place," he murmured as though waking, like Dorothy at the end of *The Wizard of Oz*. "I can't say. I really can't say." Enda asked if RL had seen him there, too, as a scarecrow or a tin man. They were sitting on the floor and drinking orange juice. "You were," RL said, "but not like that. I can't say." He covered his face with a handkerchief and exhaled hugely. The handkerchief ballooned and contracted into his mouth, where it sank, uninhibited by any teeth, and ballooned again with another breath.

The Empyrean was color and light and blessings and fullness.

The void was its inversion. And on the surface, in words, it baffled Enda at how he could want it more. Where the Empyrean was color and light, the void was blue and dim. Where the Empyrean was blessings and fullness, the void was a pulse that marked time in its slowing, slowing, slowing, until you could not hear it anymore. Where was the upside of the void, as there is often an upside found in other, terrestrial things? By now, Enda knew there was no upside and that was the blessing of the void. You did not have time to peer into the future or anything like it. Like Holly, you lived from day to day, prepared for each one to be your last.

And why was that such a funny thing? Indeed, it made him smile and people wanted to know what the big joke was.

The Pharisee had said in the temple, "Thank God I'm not a sinner."

The publican had said in the temple, "Be merciful to me, a sinner."

Enda had an idea of what he would look like in the coming days. He caught sight of himself in Ranger's rearview mirror, and here were the Son of Man's eyes, red and wet and starry lashed and large and sleepy. He did not look away, for here had come Reason to whisper from a small, scathing corner.

Reason said to him, "AJ has what you want. And you have what he wants."

Enda pressed his cheek to the window, still watching.

Reason asked him, "Isn't that all you want? You haven't thought of anything else since you woke up this morning."

Enda sighed.

Reason went on, "What would you do for just a minute in the void? Truly, would you let him fuck you? Would you let him split you open like a melon? Would you choke on him? Anyone who could give you what you want?"

Enda hissed, "I just want a little quiet."

Reason shook its head and said, "The Empyrean lasts eight hours, at least. The void is thirty minutes."

Enda said again, "I just want quiet."

Reason told him, "Put on earmuffs."

Enda reached in between the driver's and passenger's seats and turned on the radio. He sang along to whatever was playing until ET switched it off, then to anything he could think of. He settled on "99 Bottles of Beer on the Wall" and got to three bottles before Ranger overrode him with something they both knew.

It was a lover and his lass
With a hey, and a ho, and a hey non-i-no
That o'er the green cornfield did pass
In the springtime, the only pretty ring time—

It was not spring but winter—maybe fall. His father had liked to sing it when the first buds appeared on the trees, and when Enda the Younger was small he thought the Elder sang them into being each year, as he sang in each season. "Sigh no more" was for summer, "Baloo, my boy" for fall, "A'Soalin'" for winter. He'd long thought Enda the Elder made up those songs long, long ago, perhaps in the dawn of the ages, taught by Pan and nymphs and angels and daemons, when such creatures were frequent visitors to man. Then he heard Peter, Paul, and Mary at Rosemary's, *An apple, a pear, a plum or a cherry/Any good thing to make us all merry*, and he seethed at the idea of his father having lived in the world, too, at one point, leading him on with the idea that the Elder abided forever.

God bless the master of this house
And the mistress also
And all the little children
That round your table grow

The plan had been to keep to the main road, but Enda heard himself piloting the car this way, take a right here, take a left here, another right here, and ET asked him what he thought he was doing. Ranger commented that the boy had a compass in him somewhere and obliged, signaling, slowing, turning at Enda's commands and he thought such a lot of the older man for it.

There were still two kids in the shoulder and in the grass when the truck came along, one a bald eagle, white capped, the other a crow, glossy black, in costumes made from felt and bedsheets and feathers from Jo-Ann's. They had heard of a truck unloading treasures hereabouts and came to pick through anything that might be left. The bald eagle found a Chinese finger-trap. The crow found a Girl Scout pin. The truck pulled into the shoulder, enough distance from the kids, and Babe leaned out of the window.

"They were throwing stuff all down the road," the bald eagle said, forefinger caught in the trap and wagging like a witch's claw.

"My sister got a rabbit's foot," the crow said. "If it's green that means it's the best luck, and my sister found a green one."

The crow, unable to resist the trap's empty end, let her forefinger slip in and whined when she pulled and found herself stuck. The eagle whipped their joined hands in a little frenzy, up and down, up and down.

"Here—" Babe reached through the window and pinched the finger trap at its middle, and the birds were freed. At once, the crow buried her hands in her armpits. The eagle, intrigued, pinched and watched her finger slide from the trap. It was a little straw thing, made in Taiwan, woven red and gold. The eagle, who was not afraid, tried the trap again, this time with both fingers. When she'd tired of it, she brought her lips over her teeth and gummed it until she was loose.

"They went—" the crow began, then scowled, thinking. "They went—"

"—they went," the eagle stepped in, drawing herself up importantly, meaning to tell stories when, in fact, she told the truth, "—they went to the horrible farm."

Ranger chuckled, but Babe was interested. "What's the horrible farm?" It smacked of the Brig of Dread and the Elysian Fields, and it had Babe thinking there was, really and truly, something fantastic amongst the gobble-dee-goo.

The crow, eager to share what she knew, pointed a feather at the highway's stretch. "It's the horrible farm. They keep kids there and kill them."

"No, they don't. They don't kill anyone," the eagle told her, "they do drugs and things and they sell them. The kids make the drugs. They make crack—"

"—they make crack and they kill the kids—"

"—they have dogs at the gate that are attack dogs—"

"—there's a man there who kills the kids—"

"—the government's going to go there and take the kids away—"

The crow, struck by imagined horrors, "They go looking for kids to feed the dogs—"

Babe, fogged, sorted the truth from the terror, so thick in it he had not noticed the truck jolt back onto the road. The horrible farm was Martin's Valley, founded by Enda Martindale the Elder as a premise for the new and glorious age to come. The kids were his brothers and sisters, bright new faces for a brave new world. They had Secobarbital, Amobarbital, Percocet, Vicodin should the end come, which Enda the Younger had always pictured in operatic proportions, the Vesuvian crack in the sky, the earth convulsing underfoot, the shower of ash and the wailing of those outside who had not prepared for this horrible day. He sat on his hands. More than once, he restrained himself from ordering Ranger to turn the truck around so he could snuff out the tall tales once and for all and set the children straight—

The truth was batshit.

But there were dogs.

THERE WERE DOGS, on the hill and in the grass and bounding for them in a gnarring pack. There were a dozen of them, at least. Had there been a sign, next to those that had said NO TRES-PASSING and OFFENDERS WILL BE SHOT, that warned outsiders to BEWARE OF DOGS? If that were so, AJ hadn't seen it. He and LC listened and watched and did not move. For these initial moments, wherein they felt themselves separated from the rest of the world by a gauzy veil, they were passive observers, explorers in a dream, noting danger drawing close enough to smell.

They could anticipate teeth and carnivorous appetites, and thought they would wake in the nick of time. But it was AJ, knowing nothing else, who felt the sobriety of what was, really and truly, about to happen. Here were dogs. Here were shouts on the hill, two boys and a mechanical cracking that tore at the air, a rifle. Here was a mongrel, a stray like all the others, picked up and trained and rebred to protect its dominion, having nearly snapped at AJ's ankle, prompting him to run.

His mind's eye made a picture of what he heard: LC, yelps that were hers and the beasts', and gobbling, gobbling, gobbling, because she was meat and they were hungry. He made a picture of what he could not hear: LC, now quiet, piled beneath the mongrels that fought and snapped for every available scrap on her bones. They had made quick work of her clothes.

He made another picture: He heard a boy's voice on the hill, above the dogs, close enough that he did not have to shout. It was the boy with the rifle, a keen eye on AJ's crown, tall enough and strong enough to be a man, stern enough and wild enough to know this was his home and AJ was an offender.

And AJ, aware of what he could see, stopped and obeyed the boy with the rifle. His instructions were to kneel and put his hands on his head. To the other, younger boy, the older one told him to run and "—get Dad. Get Dad and don't come back."

A FEW YEARS later, ET showed Babe her mother's house.

"Where was your room?" he asked, and she pointed to the oriel window in front. "Just you and her?"

"Just me and her."

The place was acres of land that faced the shore, and the day was foggy and the sea a line on the horizon that never wavered, giving mother and son the notion they had come to the world's edge. Much of the greenery was overgrown, as there was no one living there at the time, and the ivy writhed and sighed at the suggestion of a breeze.

"I guess the family sold it a long time ago," ET remarked. "An aunt or someone."

"And they didn't tell you?" Babe asked.

"How could they? They couldn't find me."

"They could've looked you up."

"Mother passed after I left the hospital."

"At Rosemary's."

"I don't see how. They wouldn't have known I was there. Or known Rosemary."

"Were you rich?"

ET laughed. "We had a name, and we had property and a small trust that could just about cover the grocery bill. Mother worked, which was right. I think she would've gone stir crazy if she couldn't work. She was a member of the Hysterical Society—"

Babe started.

"—she liked to call it that," ET went on and elaborated, "—the Historical Society. She said it was full of busybody ladies and widows who liked to get together and talk about who was related to who. But she gave walking tours and did some archiving."

They rounded a corner and came back to the front of the house, which loomed with a queer kind of dignity, very nearly like a haunted house. The porch wrapped all around; ET called it a veranda. There were colored installments in the front windows, alternating amber and emerald.

"Where's your dad?" Babe asked.

"He passed when I was little. I don't remember him."

"Can we go in?"

"We shouldn't."

"It's your house."

"Not anymore. Not for a long, long time."

"No one's living in it now."

"Someone owns it."

"Who?"

"Not a clue." ET stepped over a mound of animal turds. "Not a Scooby-Doo." She pointed to the sign staked beside the mailbox, FOR RENT.

"We could rent it. You, me, and Ranger."

"We couldn't afford it."

"I could live in your old room."

"I couldn't live in my old house, that's the real problem."

"Is there a ghost?"

Not ghosts but impressions. They were as clear to ET as the day they happened, much in the way the things that were to come superimposed themselves upon her as she sat on a park bench or ate leftover Chinese with Ranger. There was no avoiding any of it. What had happened had happened. And what would happen would happen. "Be here now," as the gurus liked to say She was as full as she had ever been, knowing that much. Better to keep moving, as the fullness directed her. Better to never be in one place, better to never acclimate, or she might become snared by that which she could not change.

My baby. My boy.

She did not know the day or the date of her boy's demise, though she knew it would be long before her own. She knew when and how she would go herself, at one hundred and three of a stroke, sound asleep in her own bed. People envied that kind of passing because it was the closest you could get to a full assumption, body and soul. To her last breath, folks would approach her, fans of her boy's, inhaling their breathy questions: "You're Babe's mother, aren't you? I'm such a fan of his work." How could she tell them that, while it was well and good that they were fans of his work, she had never really been much of a fan herself? She would want, if anything, to ask what they found so great about him, what made him any different from the George Carlins and the Mitch Hedbergs who came before. Was it because they were here one day and gone the next, the real punchline? Was it because fans of stand-up comedy like to think there is a kernel of wisdom in the gag? *A funny thing happened on my way to Calvary* . . . She'd heard gallows humor before and thought Lenny Bruce did it better. She'd heard observational comedy before and thought Dave Chappelle did it better.

Not that she would ever tell her boy any of that.

A comedian's divinity, if he had any at all, was his ability to tell his audience, "I'm just like you." The Son of Man reminded her people came for Penn and Teller's magic tricks, but they stayed for the laughs.

"Well—" Babe took up a stick from the brush and whacked the hydrangea bushes with it. "When I have my own spot on Comedy Central, I'll buy it."

"I'm not living in it."

"Who says you're living in it? I'll live in it."

"Better get the exterminator over before you move in. There's literally bats in the chimney and spiders in the woodwork. You'll be living in Transylvania."

Babe hummed and sang and twirled the branch. *"I'll go suck blood from a bunny . . . I never go where it's sunny . . . give Dracula a run for his money . . . Transylvania 6-5000."* He tapped the crown of her head with the branch's end. "Made that up on the spot. That's genius. Aren't you proud?"

"We'll get Dr. Demento on the horn."

"Do."

She warned him again that he would have to stay clean if he wanted a long and fulfilling career. The Son of Man told her, elusive, not to worry, not to worry, not to worry.

Through my fault, through my fault, through my most grievous fault.

IF ET WERE a Buddhist, she might have called Mirabel a tulpa. A tulpa was something beyond an imaginary friend, certainly beyond a delusion. It had a life of its own, save for your building of it. There was a theosophist who claimed to have done it herself in her travels to Tibet. The encyclopedia article said her tulpa was a monk that had a close resemblance to Friar Tuck. ET wondered why anyone would want Friar Tuck for an imaginary friend. But then, ET had never wanted a child. It was a "fruit of contemplative life," or so said the encyclopedia.

She knew the Mysteries of the Rosary yielded fruits, too, but she only remembered those of the Joyful Mysteries: Humility, Love, Detachment—she forgot the rest.

Her belly, to her, looked like a peach. LC had liked to rub her palm very lightly over the curve, feeling the fine fur. She had agreed it would be a girl.

Before Rosemary's, ET had been the one who made sure LC had a regular bath, and tried to determine from these unclothed rituals how old the girl really was. Her limbs were twiggy, her stature small, and anyone looking at her in clothes might have thought her to be straight up and down, not yet grown into a man or a woman. They used a mobile shower run by Covenant House on Clare Street, and ET shared a stall with her to make sure LC did not just rinse her head. ET tried to make a game of getting her undressed, Who Can Get Naked the Fastest or a version of Simon Says. The steam would be thick by the time ET got LC under the water, and she was never sure if what she saw was a heat-filled dream, for she recognized these twiggy limbs and boy's hips, but the rest did not match and it always threw her. LC's breasts were long and pendulous, and they tucked easily into the elastic waist of her pants. Her belly made ET think of a shriveled pumpkin. She imagined it had once been a great, round prize-winner many times over, now an almost separate appendage ET had to lift and clean under.

"How old are you?" she'd asked LC. They wrapped themselves in the big, donated towels and she rubbed LC's hair dry. They dressed quickly in the makeshift changing stall.

LC told ET she did not know.

"Sure, you do."

"Well, I don't." LC thought. "I think I'm fourteen."

"I don't think that's true."

"Well, it's what I think."

"Well, when's your birthday?"

"April."

"April of what year? Just count up from then."

"I don't know." LC's face was tight, and so that was that.

LC was the one who showed them all how to scavenge. Her reasoning came from the lingering notions from childhood that everything could be a game, fused with the feral instinct of a being that still finds everything too new and unpredictable to depend on the false promises of supermarkets, credit cards, and Amazon. They were not of the world, having all become untethered from whatever made it run. There was the idea, too, that this was how things would go, once the supermarkets, credit cards, and Amazon had failed, and they were only preparing for that day when everyone would wear layers and find pretty things to trade, because you needed it, because you wanted someone to have it, or because you liked it. What did you do, then, but make a game of what you had left?

ET sighed and remembered something her mother used to say about only being as old as you feel. She'd asked her mother how old she felt, and her mother replied, "Well, I feel like I'm twenty. It's everyone else who insists on my aging." Twenty did not feel so different to ET than fourteen, though it had held a similar, if dissipated, wildness. You no longer lived on the edge of things, you knew how to keep a schedule, you had your priorities in order, you paid your bills on time and remembered to floss. But that didn't describe what else lurked, the slow passage of time, days as eons, the idea that small changes did not mean your life as a whole was not going to be much different from the way it had always been.

At the hospital, there had been a man whom everyone knew as Mr. Gomez. He did not say much beyond two phrases. He said, "Someone must not be living right around here" in the event of a mishap, an overflown toilet, a suicide. He said, "Better straighten up and fly right" in moments of prophecy, a rainy day, an article in *Newsweek*. He was very old and seemed to know everything, despite his limited speech. It made ET look forward to getting old, when everything had already happened and it was almost over and you were free again to talk nonsense and throw food.

ET did not know how old she was and she still did not see the light at the end of the tunnel. You kept going, in spite of all that. You were still curious, you wanted to know how long the tunnel went, because there had to be a way out.

But how awful, to be fourteen forever.

ET moaned. Everything ached, expanded, contracted. She did not know how to tell Ranger what was wrong.

Years later, Babe would tell a joke that would be immortalized by viral video, and a very poor one: "I am evangelistic about weed. The way people are evangelistic about the Lord, I am evangelistic about weed. I want to tell everyone I know about it and what it did for me. And what it can do for you. If you're willing to let it into your lungs."

Years later, as she did now, ET moaned, "Oh my god——"

BABE, THIRTEEN, RECOGNIZED shapes of roads he had seen only in darkness as he ran away from home. Now, coming back to it, he navigated by lines in the horizon, wherein the skyline held a glow from the light pollution in the city like a faraway torch.

Here were the demarcations of the world entire, as he knew it. Here, in this prototype for Paradise, were shrubs and scrubs, spurs in the dirt, snakes in the grass. Here was a place that washed from deepest emerald to brown in the changing seasons, illustrating in his mind the best and the worst of the earth's narrative in God's ongoing, patchwork scriptures. Here were deer. Here was a rabbit, the trot and snort of a boar. Here were short, paddled cacti. Here was needled cedar wood, snags in your clothes, scrapes on your face. Here were boneset and milfoil, an ocean of them amongst the weeds.

In them he knelt to meet the army of dogs, who knew him at once by his smell, his beloved voice, and they bathed him in welcome, yelping, snuffing, nuzzling. At last, at last, the youngest boy who was their favorite, who ran with them, fed them, fed them more than he ought, slept safely with them, the boy who was their favorite was home. They were slow, a little clumsy, drunkenly bouncy; they had just been fed.

They wanted to show him to their feast. They had liked to do that in the past, when they caught a rabbit or overwhelmed a hog in the woods, knowing the boy would not partake, wanting him to join the festivities nonetheless. They loped ahead in the grass, stopping, turning around, looking to him, waiting, running behind to pull him forward. Behold, they said, behold, behold. This is what we have got, and it is bountiful, much more than anything we have had before.

They had clawed through layers to get to the meat, and scraps were all around. There was a bit of t-shirt caught in the grass, a small appendage that had been missed in the gaiety and was snapped up at once by a young pup in the pack. Babe knew who it was, though he did not register her face (there was little left of it) or her name, seeing how far she had gotten before she, too, was overwhelmed by the dogs and brought here, far from the stones marking the children long gone, all the Enda the Youngers, to where the stones were sub-headed MOTHER. He did not know this part of the yard well; it was the first of his demarcations, in fact, the first step away from home, and he did not want to guess at whose mother of his siblings was whose.

The dogs stood attentive, wondering why the boy did not shout for their triumph the way he did before. Deflated, they licked around their snouts, whining.

They had only gotten LC. What of AJ?

A BOY CAME shouting over the hill, and they told him to remove his clothes, too. AJ knew who it was before he could look. His own clothes, laid out in a square a minute before, blew out and around the crater, grounded by the things in the pockets, though made aerodynamic in bursts by the sleeves.

The boy Babe watched the clothes and their pockets. Anyone else might have covered himself. It made AJ want to reassure him, rather than spit at him, that the pills were there and hidden and safe, in the innermost pockets, zipped, no chance of them falling out. It would be, he understood, the easiest thing to do; it would brighten the boy's day, and he would be very grateful.

Babe waved his arms. He wept and called to the older boys on the hill and he knew them. He called them by names, and suddenly they became less beastly. Features now appeared to AJ formed of noses and cheek bones and gestures, makings of Babe in another life, this one a tall brute, the other wiry and flinty eyed. They were Mirando and Jeremy, new incarnations of those long gone. They were favored among the other boys who slept in the bunkhouse. Enda wondered if they now slept in his old warm room in the house proper, just off to the side of the kitchen, the domestic dogs snubbing the beasts in the barnyard.

He called them. They were Mirando and Jeremy. Mirando was the older one, close to eighteen now, and Jeremy was his Irish twin, eleven months his brother's junior. They looked so much like Dad; it went through him like a current. They had his ways, his brawn, his word settled like gauze over them, though Jeremy had been the one to tell Babe their father was batshit.

Jeremy was the one who held the rifle. Mirando had a small handgun. Enda resented never having been let to use the firearms their father kept.

Did they resent him, the favorite, the runaway, coming back to them now ropy and angled and jittery, the idiot who would have been king?

Still, he said, "It's ME, it's ME, it's ME."

Mirando softened and Jeremy quieted, but neither lowered his weapon.

Mirando spoke first, "We're not to let anyone in. You know that."

"But I live here—" Babe heard the audacity even as he said it. He was banished; he was exorcised. In its full weight, he felt the burden of the Elder's temper. The Elder would have to start anew. Babe, the Younger, had chosen to go beyond the family garden and was now outside. It was awful to feel it, at present as it would be forever, as logic, trying to refit itself to any circumstance and splintering, paring down. Other people do not live like this.

But I did. And I'll say it again, "—I live here."

Mirando had the Elder's way of talking that never rose above a certain pitch and, in its magical quality, could be heard as a whisper in a crowd. Babe had seen a few of Clint Eastwood's spaghetti westerns, and the resemblance that made him first want to laugh chilled him just as quickly. Mirando's voice, like their father's, told you to do the sensible thing, which was not to try him. The Elder was always telling the children and his wives not to try him. It was one of his sayings. Mirando told Enda not to try him now, and in that moment, Enda wondered which else of their father's sayings had him fixed. DON'T TRY ME. STRAIGHT IS THE GATE. THE DOOR WILL SHUT. The last eluded him until now, for Enda the Younger never thought of himself as fully and consummately gone from Martin's Valley.

He remembered a story ET told him about a woman in the hospital who was convinced every room she was about to step into was booby-trapped. The restroom was rigged with electricity. The hallway was full of landmines. Every day was a harrowing quest for the TV room, where she would receive instructions from Ellen DeGeneres or whomever happened to be on. Through semaphore and cypher, Ellen would tell her which rooms were safe. The woman did not say much beyond the hospital's many dangers, the bear traps in the dining hall, the cyanide in the showers, but she did like to remark to ET that, "People from up north sound like a lot of oboes and clarinets."

People from Martin's Valley sounded like a lot of hissing in grass.

Mirando was the first to move, toward them, slow, steady, never turning his eye away. Jeremy kept the rifle on them, staying where he was, while his brother took up a jacket, a pair of pants, and began to search the pockets. Mirando had Babe's jacket, not AJ's, not the one that had what Babe wanted most. That jacket still danced, though now the wind had calmed and took with it the lion's share of animation. Clothes skittered along the ground like creatures on their bellies, exhausted, still with some go to them; they did not get far before Mirando took them up, too, t-shirts, short pants with cargo pockets. He discarded the doodads and toys and kept what looked useful, a corkscrew for wine bottles, a repair kit for eyeglasses on a keyring, a vegetable peeler.

"Where is it?" Mirando dropped the jacket and watched Babe, owl-eyed.

Babe, perplexed: "What? Where's what?"

"The box. It was missing from the safe when you took off. Who else could it have been but you?"

"I have it—" He had it, but not on him. He'd left it in his

knapsack, which was at Rosemary's, which he knew would be safe because the people at Rosemary's were a lot of things, but they did not steal, not from each other. "I have it. I have it, and I don't." In spite of, because of everything, he laughed. It was a wheeze, watery, obnoxious.

Mirando said only, "Dad'll kill you." He swallowed suddenly very stiff. He might have been horrified. He might have been admiring. He backed away from Babe, did not turn from him. Upon reaching his brother on the hill, who kept both eyes open and flinted, he spoke into his ear and the two murmured head to head for a minute.

It is the glory of God to conceal a thing—Babe shut his eyes, and for his part, AJ knew what he would do if things came to that.

I will protect you, without question.

From his place on the hill, Jeremy told them that once he and Mirando were through searching, they would let them dress and they could go. Then, the Elder's stiffness left his voice and, without lowering the barrel, he said to Babe, "He'd have blown you away himself if he was the one out here. We've got nobody outside now. Dad dismissed the externs. We're eating what we put up in the summers." Beans and peppers and broth and soup. Babe noted how the diet had whittled at them. "You're better off. When we're done here, just get dressed and go. Don't come back."

Babe asked his brothers why they couldn't leave with him. He remembered AJ and looked at him, wondering how he was faring. To AJ, it must be like entering the middle of a great epic, where the origins have already been given and there is nowhere to go but forward, among floods and foes. This was the part in which the hero and his companion have to outwit the henchmen to the fortress to make their escape.

Babe, Enda the Younger, hadn't any wits. He had to urinate and he was cold and aching for what was in AJ's jacket. The desire had sharpened and then blurred so that he no longer cared about the pills in the pockets. He wanted only to have it in his hands. After that, he would look.

His brother had told him not to move, and he disobeyed. He

leapt for the jacket, still skittering, and AJ did, too.

ET REMEMBERED THE woman at the hospital who thought every room was booby-trapped. She wondered if Ellen was still her trusted advisor from the outside or if she had finally allied with Maury.

Babe had stopped them at a gate with a sign that read, NO TRESPASSING. OFFENDERS WILL BE SHOT. Ranger had repeated "Offenders will be shot" in a Duke drawl, had relented, keeping ET at his side and watching the boy duck between the wires. The boy had then turned, explaining "I used to live here. It's my dad's house." He tried to weigh these words with the happy ending of every runaway story, redemption, repentance, reconciliation, renewed promises all around. He tried to weigh these words so they would not follow him. If they followed him, they would know what he truly wanted.

ET's was a pain that came from outside, happening *to* her, rather than from *within* her. It bounced in and out of focus, so dull it had almost gone before springing back, full force and bright colors. She knelt beside the truck, her forehead to the pavement. Never had she felt so emptied. This was not what it was to bear the spirit of spirits. This was familiar, yet maximized, as things can be when you feel them for the first time, or for the first time in a long time. It sent her home twice in fifth grade, once in sixth before her mother put her foot down and told ET to "just get through it." It was ordinary and low and animalistic. ET did not know what frightened her more.

She bled. It had been months. Her sweatpants were soaked in the back with it.

Things did not have to be reality, they could just be a very, very real possibility. She had overheard a doctor at the hospital describe the illness thusly when a patient's mother had her son committed. Her son understood his body to have been operating remotely for the last year and a half by a machine. The machine was run in the Solomon Islands by an organization he called The Ecclesia. "If I don't do what it programs me to do, someone will come up and stab me in the ear. Do you understand what that kind of situation is? It gives me a headache, like it's breakfast toast." Mirabel was never far. That was what made her real over something as silly as a machine in the Solomon Islands.

There had been a puff of noise from somewhere near, almost like a firecracker, but muffled and coming just once. ET thought this was it. She had set herself up to love and now look what happened. He's gone.

My baby, my boy.

IN ONE OF his few interviews, the second to last one, the Son of Man addressed a question of self-deprecation and whether or not it was appropriate for humor. "It's about knowing the other person, basically. Kind of like a relief, where you think, Thank God, this didn't just happen to me, it happened to that sad bastard, too, and by comparison, maybe I'm a little better off than him because I would never be as stupid about something as he was about this other thing he's talking about. There's a lot going on. I see it like a flowchart, an emotional flowchart. When is it appropriate to laugh with me, when is it appropriate to laugh at me, when is it appropriate to laugh at yourself. And if you can laugh at yourself, you'll be better off for it, you'll add ten years on your life span. I choose to have people laugh at me for a living, and I feel like I'll live a million years. I just feel invincible, you know?"

The PBS series, *Blank on Blank*, who had access to recordings of people like Kurt Cobain and Janis Joplin, took this interview and animated it and sealed the Son of Man's image as semi-cartoon. They caught his tremors, his long limbs, his bandy legs, the gap in his teeth. Because he had a beard at the time of this interview, the cartoon depicted him with a beard, and so that was how everyone thought he looked all the time.

BABE, NO LONGER Enda the Younger, jacket thrown over one shoulder, ran. He was dusted from the crater, making a paste from crown to crotch of AJ's brain matter.

AJ, who gave himself for me, though he did not have to. He

was quicker than me and caught the bullet. I caught the jacket. What will they do with him? Will they bury him with the mothers? Will they douse him in fluid and light him aflame?

LC they would let the dogs finish.

Ranger came at the boy and swaddled him at once in the jacket. Babe felt for the bag and worked the contents through the synthetic lining with his fingers; he counted down to how soon he could swallow the pills with no one's attention. In the cab, in a moment? At Rosemary's, in twenty minutes? Both options were as eternities.

He sat on ET's lap in the back of the cab, Ranger driving west and twenty-five miles above the speed limit. They were going to a hospital, Ranger determined.

ET moaned to accommodate a contraction that began at the top of her belly and ended at her vaginal lips. This was the birth of Mirabel, who was not a baby after all. ET contracted, gathered within until it became a pinprick, then released. And like that, it was gone, and she was full, an accessible fullness she could feel and reach for. It was a love quite unlike any other, without compromise, without consternation, without contrition. She looked at Babe in her lap, who belonged there and belonged now to her.

He shook under the jacket. There were twigs in his hair. He had cowlicks on his crown. He was scratched all over, having run through cedar and brush and briar, over hill over dale. His weight on her thighs was sudden, as though he had fallen there from a great height and she were seeing him for the first time.

And he saw her, too, blinking, saying, "Hi." Now, he understood, I really don't have anywhere to go back to.

Now, she reasoned, I was with child all along, I was right to look for signs, and I will never, ever doubt my keen eye again, though I might never be able to tell anyone.

She repeated him, "Hi."

Ranger slowed the truck, for he was looking back at them in the mirror. The radio, which he hadn't the cognizance to turn off in the hullaballoo, played a campaign promotion for Mike Bloomberg, following a blurb for erectile dysfunction, and Babe remarked that he thought they were the same ad. Ranger's voice was shaky in response, "Well. If it is the same thing, it's an issue I'm glad he's addressing." He, too, seemed untethered, the fullness of a boy and a woman in his car and their solidity, what it was and what it would mean if he allowed them to stay there, if he brought them back to the cottage, because it was just the two of them and he wanted to know what it would be to have his own items and idiosyncrasies, his toothbrush and his habit of talking to the TV when it was on, piled with someone else's.

First, he lost his folks. Then, he lost his house. Now, he lost his clothes.

MEANWHILE, ROSEMARY WOKE and Holly woke. In a slow wash across her sleeping guests, folks turned, jaws unhinged to accommodate yawns, not quite ready for a new day, though in quiet acceptance of it. RL woke and found Babe's knapsack. He knew they were not coming back and reasoned that anything left behind was fair game. He picked through this and that, a jar of peanut butter, a Chinese finger-trap in blue and purple. And he found a box, marble and topped with a sphinx. He opened it, and he had to think for a minute if he was going to keep it for himself.

Holly, closer to fifty than infancy, made her first noise of the day, "HA."

PAM JONES was born in Paterson, New Jersey in 1989 and grew up in Connecticut. She studied Creative Writing at Hampshire College and is the author of *The Biggest Little Bird* (Black Hill Press/1888Center, 2013), *Andermatt County: Two Parables* (The April Gloaming, 2018), and *IVY DAY* (Spaceboy Books, 2019). Her short fiction has appeared in *The Cost of Paper*, *Boned*, and *Heavy Feather Review*. She lives in Austin, Texas with her husband.

www.ingramcontent.com/pod-product-compliance
Lightning Source LLC
Chambersburg PA
CBHW030624190726
48286CB00008B/2388